A
CHRISTMAS
HOUSE
WEDDING

Also available by Victoria James

CHRISTMAS HOUSE SERIES

The Christmas House

BILLIONAIRE FOR CHRISTMAS SERIES

The Billionaire's Christmas Proposal

The Billionaire's Christmas Baby

RED RIVER SERIES

The Rebel's Return

The Doctor's Fake Fiancée

The Best Man's Baby

A Risk Worth Taking

TALL PINES RANCH SERIES

Rescued by the Rancher

The Rancher's Second Chance

STILL HARBOR SERIES

Falling for Her Enemy

Falling for the P.I.

SHADOW CREEK MONTANA SERIES

Snowed In with the Fireman

A Christmas Miracle for the Doctor

The Firefighter's Pretend Fiancee

Baby on the Bad Boy's Doorstep

The Doctor's Redemption

The Baby Bombshell

Christmas with the Sheriff

WISHING RIVER SERIES

Wishing for a Cowboy

Cowboy for Hire

The Trouble with Cowboys

OTHER NOVELS

The Bachelor Contract

The Boyfriend Contract

A CHRISTMAS HOUSE WEDDING

A Novel

VICTORIA JAMES

alcove
press

Published in the United States by Alcove Press, an imprint of The Quick Brown Fox & Company LLC.

Alcove Press and its logo are trademarks of The Quick Brown Fox & Company LLC.

Library of Congress Catalog-in-Publication data available upon request.

ISBN (trade paperback): 978-1-63910-102-3
ISBN (ebook): 978-1-63910-103-0

Cover design by Lynn Andreozzi

Printed in the United States.

www.alcovepress.com

Alcove Press
34 West 27th St., 10th Floor
New York, NY 10001

First Edition: October 2022

10 9 8 7 6 5 4 3 2 1

To Rachael . . . it feels like just yesterday we were picking up our kids after school and drinking coffee during playdates. Who knew that playground chats would turn into a long-lasting and treasured friendship! Thank you for always being the first one to read and grab my newest book . . . your encouragement, support, and friendship are a true blessing.

CHAPTER ONE

Olivia Harris stood outside her Grandma Ruby's beloved Christmas House Bed & Breakfast in Silver Springs and vowed that this year, the holidays would be different.

There would be no remnants of her old self by New Year's.

She gave her eighteen-month-old daughter, Dawn, a kiss on the forehead, the only part of her head exposed to the winter air. Dawn was groggy from her nap, and Olivia loved the precious moments when her toddler was actually willing to be held. She pulled Dawn's red wool hood down a little farther to shelter her from the November wind, not quite ready to go in for the weekly Sunday night family dinner.

She drew a shaky breath of cold, fresh air as she stared at the large, rambling porch, its wreaths and ribbons gently swaying and flapping. This old house used to have the capacity to make her believe that all her dreams could come true.

This house was supposed to have a mystical aura about it, an ability to bring loved ones together. The old Olivia had bought into all that stuff. She'd been a naïve, hopeless romantic, a pushover, and now she was a . . . realist. And she needed to stay here, grounded in reality. No wishes. No daydreams. At the ripe age of twenty-seven, she was too old and jaded for wishes. Vows seemed more appropriate.

She frowned, and her stomach twisted. *Vows.* Right. Maybe that wasn't the right word, since the vows she'd made were null and void.

This time last year, she'd arrived on her grandmother's doorstep with Dawn, exhausted, brokenhearted, and almost divorced. Her relationship with her older sister, Charlotte, had been in shambles, and Olivia had been hiding the fact that her marriage had fallen apart.

But by the end of the holidays, she and Charlotte were as close as ever, if not more so. They had both started over—with Charlotte getting married to the love of her life and moving to Silver Springs and Olivia moving in with their grandmother and getting accustomed to being a single mother.

Olivia had spent this past year living at the Christmas House with Dawn and Grandma Ruby. She had focused on recovering from the emotional abuse in her marriage and had been working on building her self-confidence and a new life for herself. With the help of her grandmother and sister and with lots of interference from her very complicated parents, Olivia had pushed through and made plans for her future.

Olivia shifted Dawn's weight and squared her shoulders before marching up the shoveled flagstone walkway, passing the tall lampposts with their gently swaying wreaths and twinkling lights, anxious to be inside. Even though it was still November, it already felt as though they'd been in the cold for months. While Sunday night dinner with family was a normal occurrence, she and Charlotte already detected that this one would be different. Grandma Ruby had seemed nervous and distracted all week.

As soon as Olivia opened the front door, she was greeted by a rush of warmth and the smell of apple pie and cinnamon and possibly a roast dinner. She didn't think she'd ever stepped into this house without smelling something comforting coming from the kitchen. What a legend her grandmother was in this town. Grandma Ruby was tough as nails and sweet as honey, and this house had been a sanctuary to many in need over the decades her grandmother had lived here.

Charlotte and her husband, Wyatt, appeared just as she was hanging up her coat on the rack beside the door. Dawn was suddenly awake and raring to go, squirming to be free of captivity. "Go, go, go," she yelled. *Go, go, go* was one of her daughter's favorite sentences.

Olivia laughed and put her down, barely getting a chance to take off her coat before Dawn tore down the hallway straight for Wyatt and Charlotte.

True to form, Wyatt expertly hoisted her up and smiled at her and then—exactly what Dawn had been waiting for—tossed her up in the air. Dawn shrieked with glee, her red velvet dress flying with the motion, living her best life. Olivia tensed only slightly at seeing her daughter so high in the air. Wyatt was as trustworthy as they came.

"Hey, how did it go at the studio?" Charlotte asked, standing beside her now even though her eyes were on Wyatt and Dawn.

If emoji heart eyes existed in real life, Olivia knew that's what she'd see on her sister's face as she watched her new husband with Dawn. Charlotte and Wyatt had unknowingly taught her so much about relationships this last year. Watching them fall in love, be in love, and then get married had made Olivia realize her own marriage had never stood a chance. It had been built on childish dreams and hollow conversations. And Wyatt . . . well, he'd set the standard. They had known him when they were all kids in Toronto and each being raised in dysfunctional families. He'd somehow grown up into a responsible, loving single parent. He was chief of police and, while tough and big and intimidating at first glance, the man had a heart of gold. The man Olivia had married hadn't had a heart at all.

As the sisters stood there, smiling at the sound of Dawn's bubbly, unabashedly happy baby-belly laugh, Olivia blinked back tears. It hadn't escaped her that Dawn's fascination with Wyatt might be because she knew he was different from Olivia. He was big. Tall. And he did things that dads were supposed to do—like throwing her up in the air and catching her. Things Dawn's father should be doing. Olivia's stomach twisted, and she forced those thoughts from her head. This wasn't the time or place. Those were things she could worry about later tonight. Alone in bed. When she should be sleeping.

Charlotte nudged her. "Don't worry. He would never drop her. Tell me about the studio. I have the whole morning free tomorrow if you need help."

Olivia's phone pinged, and she reached for it. Normally she wouldn't, but the old, run-down warehouse she'd purchased outside of town for her dance studio was currently being renovated. They had only six weeks left until January, her target opening date, and Olivia needed to be around for any questions. "Hold on, I just need to check this."

Her stomach dropped as she read the text from her contractor:

Sorry, Liv, but a family emergency has come up and I'm not going to be able to finish this job. Good luck.

"Are you okay? You look like you're going to pass out."

Charlotte's voice sounded distant as Olivia tried to process what this meant for her. This was bad. *Really* bad. In a town this small, contractors were hard to find. This close to Christmas? Impossible. It was happening all over again; she was being taken advantage of. Would he have walked off another job if he were afraid of the consequences?

"Liv, what's wrong?" Charlotte said, her voice forceful now.

Olivia took in a deep breath, reminding herself that she was strong. This new version of herself didn't crumple and cry at the first setback. Or tenth. She'd lost count. She plastered on a bright smile and turned to her sister.

She fiddled with the bracelet around her wrist. "Totally fine. A little hiccup in the plans." She lowered her voice and then looked around, making sure no one was around. "Okay, listen, I'm telling this to you only. Don't say anything. My contractor walked out on me. I guess that's to be expected, since it seems all the men in my life walk out on me. Ouch, that sounded bitter. But I guess it's the truth, and now that I live in reality, this is how I speak."

Charlotte frowned and placed her hand on Olivia's arm, ushering her over to the nook by the stairs. "What? When did this happen? And what's this alternate reality you're living in?"

Olivia rolled her eyes. "I *was* living in an alternate reality—you know, the one with white picket fences and men who are actually faithful and monogamous and nice and love their wives and offspring?"

"Liv . . . that's not an alternate reality. There are men out there like that," Charlotte said, her voice dripping with sympathy. Of course it would be dripping with sympathy, because this last year Olivia had become *poor Olivia*. No more.

She was learning not to be the family pushover. And she was determined to be an example for the most important person in the world to her—her daughter. She was the only parent Dawn had, so she had better get it right. It was Dawn who had made Olivia decide to change the course of her entire life last year. Olivia wasn't perfect, but she was trying. She'd grown.

She straightened her shoulders. "I'm just being dramatic. He said there's a family emergency, but I'm not buying it. I think the scope of this was too big for him. I don't even think he knows how to fix up half that old building, or maybe he got a better-paying gig.

"But no worries, it's not a big deal. I'm sure I'll find someone who's available to start tomorrow. And work through the holidays and be done right after New Year's. Of course. That will happen."

"Always whispering like you're conspiring. Some things never change with you girls," said their mother, Wendy, as she wedged herself between them, physically trying to insert herself years too late. Their relationship had evolved over the last year, but Olivia wasn't sure that meant it was better. Olivia and Charlotte were closer than ever, but they still held their parents at a distance. Their upbringing had been unstable and dysfunctional, and neither of their parents seemed as though they'd really changed. At least not enough that either Olivia or Charlotte truly trusted them.

"Hi, Mom," Olivia said, forcing a smile as Charlotte took a step back and hitched her head in the direction of the dining room, where everyone else was gathered.

Olivia pleaded with her eyes for Charlotte not to go. "We're just about to go into the dining room for dinner. Is everyone already here?" she asked.

"Yes, we were all waiting around for you, but now that you and that adorable granddaughter of mine—who couldn't even be bothered to say hello to me—have finally arrived, we can eat."

Charlotte gave their mother a tight smile. "Dawn's really taken with Wyatt."

"*Everyone* likes Wyatt," Olivia interjected quickly, so the tension wouldn't grow even thicker.

"Well, it's truly a thankless job, being a mother and grandmother," her mother said, as they all heard Dawn and Wyatt laughing.

Olivia winced. "Well, she's kind of obsessed with flying through the air at the moment. I'm sure it's just a phase." It was so *not* a phase. The reason Dawn ignored her grandmother was because she rarely spent time with Dawn. Olivia was fine with that, because she didn't really trust her mom anyway, on account of their family history, and if Dawn didn't get too attached, she could never be hurt the way Charlotte and Olivia had been. By either of their parents.

"Oh, Liv, always defending everyone," her mother said with an eye roll.

"I think that's one of Olivia's most endearing traits. There are so many, I can hardly pick one," Aunt Mary said, joining them. Aunt Mary was actually their grandmother's best friend and happened to be Wyatt's actual aunt. But everyone who knew her well ended up calling her Aunt Mary.

Olivia smiled at the older woman. "Aunt Mary, you are so good for my shattered ego."

Aunt Mary winked. "Well, that's what aunts are for. And I take my role as aunt very seriously. Speaking of which, have Scott and Cat arrived yet?" she asked, her gaze swooping over the hallway like that of a trained detective.

"No, he called to say they were running late and to eat without them," her mother said, her arms crossed. Her mother and Aunt Mary didn't see eye to eye on much. Scott Martin was Wyatt's best friend, and Cat was his daughter.

"What a hardworking and devoted father," Aunt Mary said with a theatrical sigh, a hand going to her heart.

"We should go and see if Grandma needs any help," Olivia said, linking her arm through Charlotte's and yanking her down the hallway before Aunt Mary could marry her off to Scott.

"I wanted to chat with Aunt Mary," Charlotte whispered as they approached the dining room.

"Why, because you've gotten on board the Scott bandwagon as well?"

Charlotte's face turned red. "I have no idea what you're talking about. But first—ten bucks says there's going to be a big announcement tonight," she whispered as they joined Wyatt and Dawn in the dining room. Wyatt's daughter, thirteen-year-old daughter Sam, was also there and ran over to give Olivia a quick hug.

Olivia didn't have time to be worried about whatever plan Charlotte was concocting, because the idea of an announcement seemed much more thrilling if she was correctly guessing what it could be. "Okay, I totally thought something was up. So, you think, *the* announcement?" Olivia said, trying not to raise her voice with excitement.

Charlotte bobbed her head up and down. "I'm positive. This is it."

Their speculation was cut short as Grandma Ruby and her boyfriend, Harry, walked into the dining room and spotted them. Olivia's heart swelled at the sight of them. Her grandmother had never looked happier. *Boyfriend* didn't exactly seem like the right term for Harry. He was so much more to her grandmother—to the entire family.

One of the things Olivia loved most about her grandmother was that she always welcomed her as though she hadn't seen her in months. Her hugs and her smiles were genuine and filled with a warmth that almost made her think everything was going to be okay. Or maybe it was because Grandma Ruby had made everything okay for her and Charlotte when they were little, and ever since.

When they had arrived here at the Christmas House as children—on the numerous occasions their mom hadn't been able to deal with them—Grandma Ruby had taken them in and made them feel safe and loved and cherished. The Christmas House was more than a house to her, to all of them. Every corner of the large, old home had a piece of their family history attached to it, as her grandmother had spent years here as a maid and caregiver and single mother before turning it into a bed-and-breakfast. She'd taken an empty home and made it a safe haven for anyone in need, especially at Christmas.

"Dinner is ready! Let's all sit and eat," Grandma Ruby said as Harry placed a large platter of roast in the middle of the long dining room table. As usual, the embroidered white tablecloth set the tone, and the china dishes with their holly pattern made it feel more festive than formal. Soon they were passing around the roast, and Dawn happily went from one person to another and was rewarded with an abundance of attention.

The family had expanded this last year. While the dining room was the same, with its oversized hanging lanterns and antique table and china cabinet, it was the people around it that had changed. Since Olivia and Charlotte had both moved back to Silver Springs, they were regulars at the Sunday night table. As were Wyatt and Sam; they were a wonderful addition to the family, and Sam was blossoming after her father's remarriage. Then there was their mother, who seemed to have enough personality to take up two seats at the table. Their father was an on-again, off-again guest on Sundays, depending on whether or not he and her mother were speaking. Wyatt's Aunt Mary was also a regular, and sometimes Scott and his daughter, Cat, joined them. Last, there was Harry, the man who shared a complicated past with Grandma Ruby.

Dinner was lively as usual, but Olivia was counting down the minutes until it was over. It was hard to hide her worry from everyone about the fact that her contractor had just walked off the job. She needed to spend the night on Google compiling a list of people to call tomorrow. But she did hope that her sister was right about the big announcement coming.

As dinner came to an end, Harry and her grandmother stood, both of them looking as though they were about to burst. Charlotte nudged Olivia, and her coffee sloshed over the rim of her cup.

Aunt Mary let out a little squeal and then nudged Wyatt so hard his cake fell off his fork. "Aunt Mary, is there something you're excited about?"

They all laughed. Wyatt and his aunt had a very close relationship, and he loved teasing her.

"Okay, well, don't keep us waiting, building and building all this drama," Olivia's mother said, making a rolling motion with her hand.

Harry, God bless the man, barely let his irritation show. Instead, he reached out to give her grandmother a kiss on the cheek before turning back to all of them. They were such a beautiful couple. He was all dressed up in a three-piece suit and her grandmother wore a beautiful burgundy velvet dress, and they both looked years younger than their ages.

Harry lifted his glass, clasped her grandmother's hand, and said, "I'm sure all of you know by now how we met, but I'm not sure I ever told you what it meant to me when I met Ruby. There are few moments that can stand the haziness of decades gone by with crystal clarity. The moment I met Ruby is one of those. I noticed her first with the appreciative eyes of a young man, but seconds later, it was my soul and my heart that had been captured. I knew that Ruby was the woman with whom my soul belonged.

"Every year on Christmas Eve, after everyone had gone to bed, I'd go into my study, pour myself a Scotch, and toast to Ruby and hope that she was living a good life. And now, over fifty years later, we have found our way back to each other. We are finally living the life we were meant to live. We wanted you to be the first to know, to share in our happiness; we're getting married. On Christmas Eve!"

Olivia's mouth dropped open, and she was laughing through her tears—sobs—because who knew Harry was such a romantic? *The woman his soul belonged with.* Wow. She caught a glimpse of Wyatt looking at Charlotte and knew it was the same for them. Wyatt held that kind of love for her sister too. The room erupted in cheers and laughter as everyone congratulated the newly engaged couple.

"Harry, you're a gem!" Aunt Mary yelled, before blowing her nose loudly. She bolted out of her chair so quickly to hug the couple that Wyatt had to catch it before it toppled to the ground.

"Grandma, Harry, I'm so happy for you," Olivia said, reaching out to hug them both when it was her turn.

"Thank you, dear. We'd hoped everyone would be excited for us," Grandma Ruby said. Her eyes were sparkling, and her smile was the widest Olivia had ever seen.

"Well, Mom, I don't know how you always manage to have a happy ending," Olivia's mother said. Olivia frowned, making eye contact with Charlotte, who opened her mouth. But Harry beat her to it.

"This is hardly an ending, Wendy. This is our beginning. But I agree with the sentiment that Ruby is a strong woman who perseveres and deserves all the happiness in the world."

Olivia shared a secret smile with her sister. It was nice to see Harry step in and defend their grandmother. Not that Grandma Ruby was one to shy away from conflict, but she'd had to for so many years. Olivia thought Harry had a dashing, old-world, heroic nature to him. She and Charlotte were also pretty sure their mother was jealous.

But thinking about their mom and dad would only ruin this event. "Grandma, I'd love to help you plan the wedding."

"Me too," Charlotte piped in.

"Okay, but we don't want anything over-the-top. That is very sweet of you girls. I can hardly believe this is happening," Grandma Ruby said, looking down at the enormous ruby ring on her finger.

"Well, I don't think it'll be hard to forget with a rock that big and flashy," Olivia's mother said with a slight snort.

"It's as beautiful and elegant as Ruby. And your mother could never outshine a ring," Harry said, smiling down at Ruby.

Olivia almost sighed audibly. Harry was the real deal. He was also great at alleviating the pressure of having to always come up with some kind of retort to her mother's snide comments. He just swooped in like some gallant black-and-white-movie-era hero. He didn't even look the least bit ruffled by her mother's comments.

"This is the best news," Charlotte said, as the crowd dispersed slightly.

"It is. I love him, and I love them together," Olivia agreed.

Wyatt also nodded. "I've never seen Ruby happier."

"She looks just as happy as the two of you," Olivia said, her gaze darting back and forth between Charlotte and Wyatt. It was true. There was rarely a time Olivia saw them when they weren't touching in some way. Not with overt PDAs, but rather that touch that was almost instinctual, the kind that came from simply being deeply connected with someone. Or maybe it came from the years Charlotte and Wyatt had been apart before reconnecting. Whatever it was, their love was palpable. And genuine. And like nothing Olivia had ever experienced herself.

Maybe if she'd seen her grandmother and Harry together, or Wyatt and Charlotte, before she'd married Will, some alarm bells might have gone off. Will had never looked at her the way Harry looked at Ruby and Wyatt looked at Charlotte. There had never been that intrinsic need to touch a hand or rest an arm on a shoulder. Or say wonderfully romantic things, like how a giant gemstone couldn't outshine the woman by your side. Good grief, who were these men?

The need to escape the room overwhelmed Olivia without warning. It wasn't that she begrudged her grandmother any of this happiness, but she knew the questions were going to start. If she could escape before her mother launched into another tirade about what a jerk Olivia's ex was, that would be a victory.

Also, sometimes it was simply exhausting pretending to be okay. On the surface, she was getting her life back. She had saved a lot of rainy-day money by living with her grandmother this last year. And her daughter was thriving with all the love and family she was surrounded by.

So . . . what was the problem?

The problem was, this wasn't the way her life was supposed to have gone. And despite knowing, after a year of therapy, that she had been emotionally abused by her ex, she was still hurting.

Somewhere deep inside her, she still held on to all those old insecurities, and they had a tendency to come out when she least expected it. Sometimes she heard Will's voice. When she was nervous. When she looked in the mirror. When she tried something new. She heard it and then shoved it aside, but by then her mood had already shifted. This was all normal, she supposed. Part of her recovery. It wouldn't go away overnight.

"Are you still going to give us a tour of the warehouse?" Wyatt asked.

"Now?" Olivia asked.

Charlotte nodded. "Yeah, let's go. Maybe Wyatt can offer . . . some advice," she said with a pointed stare.

"You're right. Okay, why don't I go put down Dawn for the night."

"Great. We'll help clean up and tell them our plans. Let's meet at the front door," Charlotte said.

Half an hour later they were speed-walking down the long porch when their mother yelled out after them. "We were so close," Charlotte whispered as they turned around.

She was hanging on to the doorframe. "I forgot to mention—Olivia, you must bring a date to the wedding."

Olivia's stomach twisted. "I didn't hear Grandma say that."

"Well, it's obvious. Good night. I hope you all have a great time, wherever it is you're going," she said, tilting her chin up.

"I'll be back in an hour," Olivia said, feeling like a child again.

But her mother had already gone back inside.

"I have the perfect guy in mind," Charlotte said, glancing up at Wyatt.

He shook his head.

Olivia sighed and let out a theatrical sigh, hoping it would dissuade Charlotte from continuing. "I'm not the least bit interested in dating anyone. For one night or for multiple nights. I want nothing to do with any man in this town or any other town. Nothing you can say will change my mind. I'm done with the entire gender. No offense, Wyatt," she added with a sheepish grin.

His lips twitched. "None taken."

Charlotte crossed her arms, her gaze going beyond Olivia's for a moment. "I just think that maybe getting back out there might be a positive step forward."

"Oh, like how you were out there in the dating world?" Olivia said with a smug smile. It was true, though. Charlotte was a notorious introvert, and while she had her reasons for not trusting people, she had been a loner. Far more of a loner than Olivia had ever been.

Charlotte tilted her chin. "We all know I'm the one who hated people. That was my thing. Not you. You're the one everyone loves."

Olivia rolled her eyes. "Was. Was. I can be an introvert too now."

"Okay, sure. Fine. But what if I told you I have the perfect man for you?" Charlotte said as she nudged Wyatt. How this poor man so calmly tolerated their sibling arguments, Olivia had no idea. He must really love her sister.

Wyatt cleared his throat and gave a quick shake of his head.

Charlotte frowned up at him. "Wy, I thought we already talked about this?"

"Not a good time," he said stiffly.

Olivia's muscles tensed. She knew exactly where this was going. She would stop it right now and save them all minutes of arguing in the cold. "Let's follow Wyatt's advice."

"Wait. Just hear me out—Scott is a great guy. He's Wyatt's best friend. Wyatt wouldn't be best friends with a jerk. What have you got against him?"

Scott. Tall. Dark. Handsome. So cliché, yet so accurate. Scott was a little too everything she no longer wanted. At one time, he would have been perfect. Not anymore. He was a little too good-looking for this new version of Olivia. She had plans to live the rest of her life in cat-printed flannel pajamas; she couldn't do that in front of a man like him. Men that good-looking couldn't be trusted. Just like Will. Too good-looking. Men like that also had certain standards she had no intention of meeting anymore. The only standards she was meeting were the ones she set for herself. "He's not my type."

Charlotte scoffed. "Oh, come on. He is so your type, Liv. He's a walking Ken doll."

Olivia stiffened at the reference. She had been a notorious fan of Barbie and Ken and would play for hours. She'd imagine this perfect family and all these kids . . . and it was so pathetic. She hated Ken and Barbie and the entire world of perfect-looking figurines now. "I'm not a child, Char. I know the way the real world works. Men like Scott are an absolute nightmare. They think they're God's gift to women. They care more about how their hair looks than current events. They want their women to look like models. And he's exactly like Will, dating half the town. There is no way in hell I will ever go on a date with Scott. Ever."

So maybe it was a little harsh, but she had to make her point, because the new Olivia made killer points like that. Judging by her sister's suddenly white face and round-as-a-wreath eyes, she had won. She glanced over at Wyatt, who looked like he was torn between laughing out loud and wanting to hide, and she felt satisfied that this ridiculous topic had been dealt with once and for all. See? She could be assertive.

"Well, I don't think it's been half the town exactly. Maybe a quarter of the single female population. And I have been called a lot of things, but never a nightmare."

So much heat shot through Olivia's body when she heard that deep, unmistakable voice that she was pretty sure she was capable of melting all the snow around them. *Scott.* If she turned around, she knew she would see Scott's gorgeous face staring at her.

So instead, she decided to stand perfectly still and glare at Charlotte.

CHAPTER TWO

"They're all gone. There seems to be a little showdown on the porch, but it's not my problem, and I'm sure I'll hear all about it tomorrow morning," Ruby said with a relieved laugh as she shut the door. Wendy and Mary had left through the kitchen door after helping with the dishes, and the younger generation were huddled on the front porch, deep in conversation.

Harry took her hand, and they walked back into the parlor. She could hardly believe this was her life now. For so long she'd been on her own, first raising Wendy as a single mother and then taking over and helping with Charlotte and Olivia when Wendy had been unable. It was almost scary to have hope in the future like this, or to allow herself to tie that hope to Harry.

She had built her life around relying on no man. The burn left by Harry's brother had been too scarring for her to ever make herself want to give her heart away again. Now, though, as an adult, she knew there had been warning signs with his brother, things she *should have seen, clues she should have picked up on. But the ripple effects of loving the wrong man were so wide, so consuming, that she'd shut herself off from love entirely. Until Harry had walked into her heart again last Christmas.*

"Why do I get the feeling that you're worrying?" Harry said, sitting beside her on the couch, still holding her hand.

She looked down at his larger hand holding hers, her engagement ring a symbol of this new phase in both their lives. She wanted to keep everything she was feeling bottled up, to process it herself, to hold on to the worry and solve it herself. But she knew in her heart that a real relationship required more. It meant being vulnerable and trusting that Harry would understand. She sighed and looked up at him, into those blue eyes she'd dreamt about for years.

"You're right, actually. I'm not sure if that's a good sign or a bad one," she said with a laugh.

He smiled, deep creases crinkling the corners of his eyes. They were the lines of a life lived fully. She had asked him about so many of those memories, and he'd shared willingly. "Of course it's a good sign. It means we know each other. We always have."

His thumb slowly moved back and forth along her hand, the gesture comforting and electrifying all at once. The electrifying part was a whole other problem she wasn't ready to deal with now. Maybe she'd save that conversation for her best friend, Mary.

"There's so much to worry about, Harry. I'm happy that everyone here was so excited for us, but what about your family? It's different for my family, because I didn't have a spouse. How will your children feel when they know you're remarrying? Yes, they're all adults and have families of their own, but they might resent me."

He placed a hand on her knee, gently squeezing. "Ruby, ultimately, this is my life to live. I had a good relationship with their mother; they were raised in a loving home. I was faithful, devoted, and five years have gone by since she passed. This isn't a rebound relationship or a rash decision. I also know not to take a day for granted. We could have decades together or months; I'll take whatever I can get. Even if they're reluctant at first, they will come around."

"But you have told them about me, right?"

His jaw clenched. "Not exactly. They know I've been seeing someone."

Her stomach dropped. "Harry . . . we can't just spring this on them. You go from seeing someone to announcing that you're getting married in six weeks? And what about my connection to them? Do they know they have a bunch of cousins and an aunt they've never met? Do they know I'm the reason your brother isn't here anymore?"

* * *

It wasn't that Scott was overly heartbroken at Olivia's assessment of him. Some of the things she had said were flattering—in an unflattering kind of way. But the part about the women got under his skin a little. Though he didn't know Olivia personally, he did know, through this odd sort of Christmas House family grapevine he was now a part of thanks to Wyatt and Aunt Mary, that Olivia had been married to a royal ass who had cheated on her. So being compared to him did insult his character. As did her odd analysis of what he thought about women and how they should look.

He had been married before, and though he was far from perfect, he and his late wife, Hillary, had had the perfect relationship.

Until the end. Until his career had almost finished him, until she'd broken his heart, until he'd almost lost everything.

Hillary could have said a lot about him, but not that he was a cheat. Far from it. He'd been devoted. But they'd had other problems—ones he hadn't realized until after she died. Maybe ones he never would have been aware of if life hadn't catapulted him into a different career. But she had never looked at him the same way after he'd told her he was turning in his badge.

It was stuff he didn't talk about with anyone. Not Wyatt, not his daughter Cat, no one. But there was a layer of shame he carried with him underneath the smile and laughter. To be in a real relationship, you needed to be honest. Being honest meant talking about your past. He was never going to do that again. So dating here and there kept him happy. It was a good distraction from the tireless and lonely job of raising a teenager.

Besides, maybe love like that came along only once in a life-time. It was Wyatt and Charlotte who'd inadvertently made him think that. Those two had known each other when they were preteens and never really found anyone else. Then lo and behold, Charlotte had come to town, and they'd fallen in love as though they were always meant to be together. Their relationship sup-ported his theory.

Also, this family situation he'd been pulled into—namely, Wyatt's family, first with Aunt Mary and then Ruby and the rest of them—would make dating Olivia impossible. Not that he wanted to anyway. Despite all that, now he felt like a jerk. Because Olivia's face was as red as her winter coat and she was blinking rapidly. Dammit. He tried to remember that she was coming off a rough relationship, and even though she'd insulted him, he still felt bad.

He avoided looking at Wyatt and Charlotte, but he felt the weight of their stares nonetheless. He'd have a few words with Wy later for getting him into this mess. Because the biggest thing— way beyond his bruised ego—was that Olivia, based on the limited history he knew from Wyatt, would always be off-limits to him. His past was too close to Olivia's father's. And Wyatt had to know that would be a deal-breaker for Olivia if she ever found out, so he had no idea what the hell he was thinking if he was in on it.

Olivia slowly turned around, and damn if that twinge of awareness didn't jolt him. She was a beautiful woman, there was no denying it. She had those famous blue eyes all the Harris women shared, and on her, with her dark hair and flawless porcelain skin, they were almost haunting. There was a familiarity in them, a pain in them, that he understood. It was the kind that got into the hollows, the shadows, and lingered there. And that was why she was off-limits. The fact that he could see all of this in her already, despite barely knowing her, was way too unsettling. She would be personal; she would drag him into something emotional, and he didn't want that ever again.

Olivia was wringing her hands. "I'm so sorry, Scott. That sounded so much worse than it was supposed to. I was just trying to get Char and Wyatt off my back about dating. It's nothing personal."

Scott shot his friend—who looked the appropriate level of humiliated—a wry glance. "Of course not. And now I think we've successfully dealt with Wy and Charlotte and their awful attempts at matchmaking."

Olivia gave him a relieved smile. "Ha. That's true. *So* awful."

Wyatt frowned. "We have great skills. Not our problem if you can't recognize them. We were actually just heading out to look at the warehouse Olivia is renovating for her studio. Want to come along, Scott?"

Boy, his friend just wouldn't quit. He hesitated, watching Olivia shoot her sister a glare. "Uh, that's okay. I should go in and say hi. I told Ruby I'd be late, but I'd hate to be a complete no-show."

"Then why don't you come with us and then come back here? You know Grandma Ruby will leave a plate for you," Charlotte persisted.

He eyed Charlotte and Wyatt and wondered at which point exactly his friend had switched allegiances to have his wife as an accomplice instead of Scott.

It was right, he supposed. Who was he kidding? It was downright enviable. And he was happy for Wyatt—deeply happy for him. Wyatt had had a rough childhood, and there were times when Scott hadn't known how he'd kept going, how he'd managed to be there for Sam. But he had, and then Charlotte had come into his life like destiny last Christmas.

Olivia gestured in his direction. "Scott is obviously busy. Maybe he even has a date. It's fine, Scott."

He frowned, squaring his shoulders. "No date. I was coming here for dinner. Aunt Mary said there was some kind of big announcement. I guess I missed it. I'll join you."

He ignored Wyatt's choked laugh and the way Charlotte's face lit up. Those two couldn't even attempt to hide their matchmaking schemes. When he glanced over at Olivia, though, she wasn't smiling at all.

"Really, it's okay."

Something in him stilled. Maybe it was instinct, the way her chin tilted up slightly, or the flash of something that made him uncomfortable in her eyes. He'd seen that look before.

As a former detective, he was well trained in subtleties. As the single parent of a teenager, he had to quickly decipher even the subtlest shifts in mood. He knew enough of Olivia's history to know she didn't trust him. She was entitled to her opinion, of course, but it bothered him. He didn't want to be associated with the man who'd hurt her. "Well, Cat has been talking about your studio nonstop, so I don't want to miss the opportunity to see it up close."

Olivia glanced over her shoulder at her sister. "Okay. If you're sure. If you're not, that's okay," she repeated.

"Nah, I'd like to see what's happening at that old place anyway. But what was the announcement I missed?"

Her face transformed as a gorgeous smile lit her face, and for a second he caught a glimpse of who she might have been before the events of the last year had unfolded. She was even lovelier than usual. "Grandma Ruby and Harry are getting married."

A jolt of happiness hit him in the chest. "Ah, that's great news. I'll stop by on my way home then and congratulate them. Wyatt, I think Cat and Sam are planning on going to your house."

"Sure, I'll drop them off on the way."

"Perfect," he said. They all walked to their cars, and Olivia went with Wyatt and Charlotte. Scott declined the offer of riding with them. The last thing he needed was more awkward matchmaking attempts. Besides, having his own vehicle would give him an easy way out if he needed to escape early.

When they reached the old warehouse on the edge of town, he was already having doubts that they'd be able to get this place up and running in six weeks. The roof hadn't been fixed yet—and that should have been done right away, considering one big snowfall or freezing rain event could cause a leak and damage whatever interior work had already been completed.

"Well? What do you guys think?" Olivia asked as they started walking across the parking lot toward the warehouse.

He wasn't going to be the one to shut down that enthusiasm.

"Liv, you know I think this place is great. Let's go see the progress," Charlotte said, linking her arm through her sister's.

Scott held back a few steps so he and Wyatt could walk together and he could tell his friend to stop meddling in his personal life. "What the hell, Wy?"

"Yeah, it looks rough for a place that's supposed to be opening in six weeks."

Scott scoffed. "You know I'm talking about throwing me under the bus back at Ruby's."

"Oh. Are you referring to when Liv said there was no way in hell she'd date you because you remind her of her douche of an ex?"

Scott resisted the urge to shove Wyatt into one of the snowbanks. "Yeah, except I don't think she said that exactly," he snapped.

"Just trying to help by paraphrasing. It reminds me of that time you told me we were old and pathetic and handed me a cheese basket."

Scott could have laughed, except it wasn't funny. "I gave you a cheese basket because Aunt Mary forced me into the cheese store, and I had to buy something because I felt bad, since I was the only customer. And since Aunt Mary is technically your aunt, you should owe me."

Wyatt looked nonplussed but kept walking with an expression of underlying bliss that Scott was beginning to loathe. "Whatever happened with Meghan anyway?"

"You know what happened—nothing."

Wyatt nodded with newfound wisdom. "Because you ended things."

Scott held on to his temper. "Not really."

Wyatt lowered his voice like he was some kind of wise, deep therapist. "Yeah you did. You're always the one to end things."

"I can't force something that isn't there. I had the real thing once, Wy. I don't need it again in order to be happy. I'm throwing in the towel. Don't want anything real. Also, real relationships need time—I have zero time. I have way too many projects right now at work, and no one wants to work with the holidays coming. Plus you know the dance schedule this time of year with all those extra rehearsals."

Wyatt glanced over to where Olivia and Charlotte were standing. "Yeah, fine, it's busy, I get it. That's why we carpool. I find it suspect, though, that all of a sudden, now that we're trying to set you up with Liv, you're throwing in the towel. Has it ever occurred to you that the reason you have been serial dating is because you know full well that it will lead to nothing? That maybe the reason you're so resistant to Liv is because you actually feel like there might be a spark there?"

Scott shoved his hands in his pockets and scowled at Wyatt for a moment before turning his attention to the old warehouse.

"I'm not sure when you became the expert on relationships and hidden feelings, but as your best friend, I feel it's my obligation to tell you it's obnoxious."

Wyatt laughed. "I've learned a few things this year. I've also gotten to know Olivia, and, well, I think Charlotte is onto something."

Scott wasn't about to tell him that maybe Charlotte was as delusional as her husband was. "Anyway, let's get back to important conversation. Who's the contractor for this place?"

Wyatt grimaced and finally turned his focus on the building and away from Scott. "Casey's, I think. Totally slacking by the looks of things. I don't want to scare Liv, but I certainly hope the inside is further along than the outside."

Scott was thinking the same thing as they approached the front door, where Olivia and Charlotte were standing. When Olivia saw them coming, she quickly turned and fumbled with her keys. Great. Now, thanks to Wyatt, she was avoiding him and things would be awkward.

"You're such an idiot," Scott said in a low voice.

"Idiot or genius. We'll see in a few weeks," Wyatt answered smugly.

Olivia straightened up, her palm on the door handle, and gave them all a tight smile. "I know this looks rough, but um, I think it'll be okay. A lot can happen in six weeks. There's been a little bit of a setback, but everything is totally under control."

At that exact moment the old sign, bearing the silhouette of a creepy jack-in-the-box, came crashing down.

They were all standing under the covered entrance. "Omigosh," Olivia said breathlessly.

If they'd been standing outside, one of them would have been seriously injured.

"Liv, you've got to call Casey's," Wyatt said, placing his hand on Olivia's shoulder.

Dread filled Scott's gut when Olivia's face turned whiter than the snow. "He . . . I didn't want to say anything and ruin the festive mood tonight . . . but he quit."

No one said anything, and Scott stood perfectly still.

And then Wyatt slowly turned to him.

He already knew. He already knew that, despite being completely booked this holiday season, this was going to fall on him. He already knew it before Wyatt opened his big mouth.

"Wow, what an ass that guy is for ditching this project and leaving you like this. If only there was someone we knew and trusted. A licensed contractor. Someone who wouldn't leave a single mom in the lurch right before the holidays. Someone—"

"All right, Wy," Scott snapped, putting himself out of his misery. He quickly forced himself to sound amenable, but he took a moment to scowl at his friend before schooling his features and turning to Olivia. Charlotte had her arm wrapped around her sister's shoulders.

"Olivia, I can totally help you out with this. I'll just rearrange a few things in my schedule. Why don't we meet here at eight tomorrow morning?"

He waited for Olivia to speak. To thank him for doing this, even though it was completely last-minute and not at all the time of year to be taking on even more work.

Instead she lifted her bright blue eyes to him, hand on the door again, and swung it open before saying, "No thanks."

CHAPTER THREE

At eight o'clock the next morning, Ruby and Mary sat down at their favorite table in the large, multipaned window of Greens on Main. They had a long history at this restaurant and had spent many an hour deliberating big decisions over big cups of coffee and even bigger pieces of cake. But now that the new owners had turned it into a healthier restaurant, they each had their new favorites. The candy-cane lattes, sweetened only with honey and using almond milk as the dairy replacement, were their current favorite.

They were both ready to rehash last night's events. "Mary, he hasn't told them about me," Ruby whispered in the crowded restaurant.

Mary rolled her eyes. "Just like a man, putting off a conversation like that."

Ruby winced. "It's not like Harry at all, which is what worries me so much. They have no idea they even have cousins. They don't *know a thing about us. And now I'm going to his house this Sunday for dinner with all of them. So I'm going to be introduced, he's going to reveal our history, reveal the family they don't know about, and then tell them we're getting married in six weeks."*

"We should be drinking at a bar instead of sipping on lattes with all that on your plate," Mary said with a wry smile.

Ruby sat back in her seat as their coffees and croissants were delivered to the table. "That's not a bad idea, really. But seriously, I'm so nervous I couldn't sleep a wink last night. And then there's Olivia—something is going on, but she won't tell me. I think it has to do with the studio. Who would have thought, when I bought her dance lessons as a child, she'd be going on to start her own studio? I'm so proud of everything she's overcome this year, but I worry she's taking on too much."

"First things first. Have you told Harry how you feel?"

Ruby put her croissant down. "I told him I'm really upset with him, and I know he feels badly. He even sent flowers at the crack of dawn. I think the reason he hasn't told them is because he's worried they won't be happy. So, if he puts it off long enough, he won't have to deal with their wrath for so long."

Mary plucked the end off her croissant and popped it in her mouth. "It's a good thing he's so handsome and that he really does adore you. I think you need to be clear that he cannot do this kind of thing again. Let him know this is causing you a lot of stress. Be as honest as possible with him."

Ruby nodded. "I know. I will. It's so odd . . . dealing with a relationship. I mean, his brother and I were barely together. And besides, we were kids in a different era. There was no figuring out our different personalities or anything like that. What he did . . .

when he broke his promise to me and left me alone to deal with everything, it's like it left this deep hole of mistrust. Rationally, I know that Harry hasn't told them because he's scared and worried about their reactions. I also know that just because they might be upset, that doesn't mean he'll take back the ring and change his mind. But a part of me does worry that I'll be left standing alone again. That I'm not worth fighting for when things get difficult."

Mary leaned forward. "You need to tell him that, Ruby. He would never think that in a million years. But that's what's on your heart. Those are part of your battle scars, and he needs to know. He's a good man; he has a heart of gold. He would never do that. But you need to hear it from him."

Ruby took a deep breath, letting her friend's words sink in. Mary was a good friend, a smart person. They had been beside each other for years, and Mary had never judged her. "There is this part of me that can't quite seem to let go and let life happen to me again. I've been alone for so long, and then Harry appeared on Christmas Eve, like a dream. And I got swept up in all of it, in him, in possibilities. And now . . . I don't know. I feel like it shouldn't be this hard to trust."

Mary reached out to place her hand on top of Ruby's. "Trust is one of the hardest things. Especially when you've been burned. But you can't miss out on life just because one man hurt you. Harry has never been like his brother. You need to trust that. As for Olivia, she'll figure it out. She's tough. She reminds me a lot of someone else I know."

Ruby nodded, but she was unable to shake the unease in her chest, for both herself and her granddaughter. She was about to give Harry everything, just as she had once given it all to his brother. But *she couldn't tell him this; she couldn't tell him she didn't trust him as deeply as she should.*

It would break his heart.

* * *

At a few minutes before nine Monday morning, Olivia and Dawn stood in the middle of the lobby of her warehouse. Her back stiffened, and a jolt of nerves hit her as she spotted Scott's truck pulling into the parking lot. Dawn yanked on her hand and pointed to the staircase. "Mama, go."

Olivia forced a smile for Dawn, despite her mounting anxiety. That was one of the takeaways from her childhood—acknowledge your children. She had way too many memories of her mother's drunk, blank stare when Olivia would ask her something. That memory was one that had plagued her during her pregnancy and had made Will's rejection of Dawn even more painful. Olivia felt as though she'd failed Dawn with Will. So she was going to make it up to her. And at least Dawn had a loving extended family. "Dawn, Mama brought you a snack. I'm going to put you in your stroller and you can eat, okay?"

Dawn shook her head, her light-brown curls bopping with the motion, her blue eyes alarmed at the prospect of being strapped down and missing the exciting climb up the stairs. Olivia nodded, trying not to laugh. Dawn was too cute to stay mad at, even when one of her flailing legs almost jabbed Olivia in the face as she plunked her daughter into the stroller. She had no choice. "Mama, go" started from the moment Dawn got out of her crib until the moment she went back in at night, and there was no way Olivia would be able to have a conversation with Scott if she had to run after Dawn—especially in a construction zone.

Scott. She handed Dawn a baby cookie while watching him walk across the parking lot. Good grief. Even his walk was that of a man who oozed confidence. It wasn't a swagger per se, and there wasn't anything about him that was really disingenuous, which might make his attractiveness even more dangerous—it was just natural. He was just being himself.

And she'd humiliated herself last night.

First with him overhearing what was supposed to have been a private conversation. And then he'd gone ahead and let it go with charm and humor. But then that creepy sign had almost killed all of them, and she'd outright refused his help. She had no idea what she'd been thinking. Well, she did: pride. She was so tired of being the woman who couldn't get anything right. The fact that she had to ask her brother-in-law's best friend for a bailout was mortifying. But her final disgrace was when they'd entered the building only to find there wasn't even any power, and she'd known she was in way over her head.

At least at that point she'd been humble and appreciative and kind. Scott had gallantly agreed to meet her here as though she hadn't rejected his offer mere moments earlier.

She'd tossed and turned for an hour before falling asleep, only to have Dawn wake up saying she needed to go. Olivia had no idea where this adorable child needed to go all the time, but when she'd finally gotten her back into bed, she hadn't been able to fall asleep for another hour. She stifled a yawn as Scott swung open the glass front door.

He grinned as though she and Dawn were his best friends. "Good morning. Hi there, Dawn." He crouched down in front of the stroller to greet Dawn, who was currently mutilating the cookie. But she did offer him a genuine smile, which had him chuckling before he stood and gave Olivia his full attention.

Her mouth went dry. "Morning, Scott. Um, thanks again for meeting me. And for . . . dropping everything. Feel free as we walk through the building to decide you really can't take this on. No hard feelings, I promise."

Something flickered across his features. "Why would I do that? I told you I can help you out, so I will."

She drew in a shaky breath and tore her gaze from his. "Okay, thanks. I guess I'll show you around."

She pushed the stroller in the direction of the first studio. She didn't know why things suddenly felt awkward. She had met Scott many times over the last year—at her grandmother's, at Wyatt and Charlotte's house, at the ballet studio when she went to watch Sam and he was there with his daughter. But now, all of a sudden, she was aware of him in a way other than just as Wyatt's best friend.

And who knew how much Wyatt had told him about her ex? That was embarrassing to even think of. So was the idea that he was taking this job out of pity. She stopped in the doorway while he walked through. He didn't say much as he looked around. He touched one of the windows and took a picture, crouched down and pressed his hand into one corner of the hardwood, and then stood. "Okay. Let's keep going."

They did that for the next hour, traveling from one room to another, including the washrooms and change rooms.

When they finally finished, they stood together in the lobby. Dawn had fallen asleep after her cookie, so Olivia had been able to handle most of the questions he'd had for her with a clear mind. Her hands tightly gripped the stroller handle as she braced herself for the bad news. He continued to type notes into his phone.

"Okay, uh, if you don't mind, I'd like to get started right now," he finally said, tucking his phone into the back pocket of his jeans. "I've made some notes, but I want to stay here and make some calls and see what I can do."

Olivia cleared her throat. "How bad is it?"

He ran a hand over his jaw. "For real?"

Oh no. He thought she couldn't handle reality. "Of course, for real."

His lips twitched. "It's not that bad. Give me today. I'll know more by tonight. I need to know how many trades I can get in here. It's a bit dicey being this close to the holidays. But I have favors to call in. I've been a contractor for a long time, so I have a lot of connections. Don't worry. Also, do you have a key for me?"

She nodded, relieved by what he was telling her, and handed him one of the spares she'd had made. She was careful not to let her fingers brush against his hand for some reason that seemed foolish and wise all at the same time. "Sure. Thank you. I . . . there's something else I should tell you. I didn't ask you to do this in the first place because you're friends with Wyatt and I didn't want things to get complicated. You know, business and personal. I . . . just didn't want you to think I didn't ask you because of all that stuff I said last night."

He flicked the tip of his baseball cap up a little, and she noticed the sparkle in his eyes. "Oh, you mean when you said I was too handsome?"

She shut her eyes briefly. "Right. All of that."

"No worries. My looks don't usually get in the way of my job performance."

She stood still, holding her breath, not sure how to respond. Until he grinned.

"I'm joking, Olivia."

She was dying of humiliation. She needed to get out of here. "Right. Of course. Ha. Okay, so I'll head out then and leave you to it," she said, walking to the doors as fast as she could without looking obvious.

He followed her and held open the door. A blast of wintry air hit them, and she tucked Dawn's stroller cover down as far as it would go. "It'll be okay, Olivia."

She nodded, uncomfortable showing him how much that reassurance meant. "Thanks," she said, and pushed the stroller with added gusto to get it over the few inches of fresh snow that had accumulated on top of the older snowfall. She heard the door close behind her as she walked toward her SUV and breathed a sigh of relief. She didn't know why being around Scott made her jittery and silly. It had to be last night. She was going to have to thank Charlotte later for that. But she needed to be confident that he knew what he was doing. Then maybe getting this place open for January would actually happen. She glanced at the old warehouse, a knot forming in her stomach. This had seemed like such a good idea a few months ago. She had always loved dance and the idea of having a career for herself. Especially since she'd given all that up for Will, who'd only thrown it all back in her face anyway.

She opened the back door and started carefully unbuckling Dawn. She needed to stay focused, and the appointment she had coming up next would help her do that.

An hour later, after leaving Dawn with her grandmother at home, Olivia sat down with a hot mug of coffee and looked out the large window at Greens on Main.

Snow was tumbling down at a rate that foreshadowed slick driving conditions later on, but that didn't bother her; it was too enchanting a picture. Main Street Silver Springs at Christmas was straight out of a Hallmark Christmas movie. Speaking of which, she and Charlotte still had their binge-watching night planned for next week.

It was funny, or maybe comforting, to think that last year during their annual binge-watching of Hallmark movies, she had been a very different person. Kleenex and wine and popcorn had been involved—and even though the latter two would still be involved this year, she was hoping to replace the Kleenex with laughter.

But now, Olivia was ready to move on from Hallmark movies. In fact, crime had become her latest fascination, and she was planning on binge-watching *Prison Break*. Sure, the series was a little old, but she felt like she was ready for something new and daring.

The woman sitting at this table alone had pulled herself together. She tore her gaze from the streetscape to look down at the planner and pens—a gift from her color-coding, planner-aficionado sister—and marveled at the difference a year could make. It wasn't that she had it all together yet, but this time last year she had given up on herself. She had almost hated herself. And now . . . she was starting her own studio and about to have a business meeting. Who was she? She caught her reflection in the glass and sat a little straighter.

She had slumped her shoulders for years when she'd been married to Will. She had never had self-esteem issues before. She still heard his voice, though, when her guard was down and she looked in the mirror—mean things, toxic things, things that broke her heart when she imagined her daughter one day thinking those things about herself. That was one of the reasons she'd gotten therapy—to help redirect her thoughts. Because Will's voice and her own voice would mix, and she realized she believed the things he said about her. And then she thought the whole world was thinking them. She didn't even know what she thought about herself anymore, and that was what she'd worked on, along with learning to care less about what the world thought of her. She was doing just fine. She was a good person. She was trying her hardest as a single mom and granddaughter, daughter, sister. And now an entrepreneur.

"Olivia! I hope I didn't keep you waiting?"

Olivia looked up to see Harper from the dance studio in town making her way over to her. Harper had been an unexpected surprise, and they had hit it off immediately. Olivia had first thought to open a dance studio for children and teens but then realized there wasn't a market big enough for it in the small town and surrounding area. And she didn't want to directly compete with another woman's small business either, so her plan involved working with Harper, and now she was very excited about where she was headed. "Not at all. I'm enjoying this view and coffee. Did you order?"

Harper nodded, taking off her coat and draping it on the back of her chair before sitting. Olivia recognized a familiar pang as her gaze swept over Harper's lithe and perfect ballet form; the pang was envy, and she immediately pushed it away. Body image was one of the struggles she had faced after Will shredded her to pieces over her pregnancy weight gain. He'd been a jerk and super critical before that, but then she'd been able to maintain a lighter weight. Once she'd put on weight during her pregnancy, he'd completely destroyed her self-esteem. She'd already been at a low point because she'd distanced herself from her family and her marriage was on the rocks.

After she left him, her goal had been to get back into shape rather than achieve a certain weight or dress size. She had always danced and had always been fit. Her intention had been to get into dancing form, to increase her strength, flexibility, and cardiovascular fitness. She had achieved that. But the last twenty pounds had stuck around. And she was okay with that . . . most days. So sitting across from Harper shouldn't be a big deal. Except she knew that Harper and Scott had dated . . . and . . . well, none of that meant anything. She redirected her thoughts as she'd learned to do and remembered she was strong, she was healthy, and she was worthy of good things. And Scott was Wyatt's best friend and her contractor. Nothing more.

"I did, thanks. I'm so excited for you. The countdown is on. How's the studio coming?"

Olivia wrapped her hands around her mug and crossed one leg over the other. "Thanks. It's . . . moving along. I had a situation with the contractor, so, um, Scott Martin stepped in and is taking over now."

The waitress came over and placed a mug of steaming coffee and a sandwich in front of Harper. After Harper thanked the server, she looked at Olivia. "He's a great guy. I'm sure he'll get the job done on time for you. We got to know each other when Cat started attending my studio. Things didn't really work out, but we're friends."

Olivia nodded. She really didn't want to talk about Scott right now—even if she'd thought about him a little too often since last night. "He seems like he knows what he's doing. Anyway, I have those signs we were talking about," she said, pulling out a file folder to hand to Harper and shifting the conversation away from Scott.

Harper flipped through the signs. "These are great."

"Thanks again for agreeing to put these up in your lobby," Olivia said, taking a sip of coffee.

"Are you kidding? Of course. I mean, I totally agree that it's best for both of us to work together. I think our businesses really complement each other. And I know you could have taken your business in a different direction."

Olivia leaned forward. "This is way better. I think there are a lot of women who might be looking for a low-pressure studio. So far, my goal is to have beginner barre twice a week, advanced barre twice a week, a flexibility and stretching class once a week, a full-body weights class, and a mommy-and-me class three mornings a week, and then toddler hop."

"That's perfect. I've already started spreading the word to some moms that I think would be interested. So far the response has been great."

A shiver of excitement went through Olivia. "I can hardly believe this. The website should be live on Monday morning at nine. Then I'll have a good idea of class sizes . . . or if there will be any classes at all," she said with a nervous laugh.

"Trust me, you'll have sign-ups. I'll hang up the signs, and I'll also do an announcement in each class and add you in the weekly newsletter."

"I can't thank you enough."

Harper waved a hand. "Don't even. We've been through this. It's good for both of us. So do you have enough teachers lined up too?"

Olivia gave her a smile. "Thanks to you and some of the part-time instructors from your studio. I'll pick up a few classes too. Especially the ones that don't need certification. I mean, I didn't want to hire anyone else and go into debt and have to pay them if there are no students. If I can fill each class, I could handle teaching them all for a little while. If I had to. I made sure the times are ones where I can get help with Dawn. Of course, I can bring her with me for the mommy-and-me classes, I think. It won't be easy, but I'm hoping that since the classes are either toddlers or moms with littles, they'll be understanding."

"I think that's perfect. You'll totally be able to handle that. Not that I would actually know, but I mean, it makes sense. I'm here too, if you're in a bind."

Olivia took a deep breath. "Thanks. I want it to be a no-pressure, no-perfection-required type of place. I don't want women coming in worried about how they look or if their baby is cranky or if they have zero skills or flexibility. I want it to be a really nurturing environment."

"You're totally onto something here. All we need is for word to get out, and then you're all set. How is the reno going?"

"Great, now that Scott has taken over. I feel bad because I've just dumped a bunch of extra work onto his already filled plate, along with an almost impossible deadline."

"He's the best. He really is. Hardworking, honest . . . handsome," she said with a laugh that ended on a wistful note.

Olivia picked up her mug of coffee and took a sip, grimacing because it was now cold. Well, it was a good distraction from having to answer right away. The normal response would have been to agree with everything, but she wasn't sure how things had ended between Harper and Scott and she didn't want to pry. "He is. Yes to all of the above."

The server came over and gave Olivia a much-appreciated top-up of her coffee. "I know this might sound totally out there, but Scott and I ended things really well, and . . . if you're interested in him, there will be absolutely no hard feelings."

Olivia choked on her coffee. "What? Interested. Oh, I'm not interested."

Harper put down her sandwich and leaned forward like they were about to have a heart-to-heart. Olivia resisted the urge to back away. "I just assumed, since I asked him to renovate one of the studios in my building and he told me there was no way he'd be able to get to it until the spring. So the fact that he's fixing up an entire building for you, after he already said no to me . . . I just assumed that you were dating."

Olivia tried to process that information rationally and also not look guilty. "There is nothing going on between us at all. He's helping me because he's best friends with Wyatt, who's married to my sister. Really, Scott and I are basically family now. There's nothing else," she said, glancing out the window.

"Oh, no, don't feel bad. I'm sure it's what you said and he wants to help you out. If there's a family connection there too, then that explains it. I just kind of assumed," she said with a shrug.

Olivia toyed with the rim of her coffee mug. It was weird to think that someone else thought Scott would be interested in her. She knew Wyatt and Charlotte were pushing them together, but she'd just assumed that was because they were trying to help. But she had sort of pegged herself as not the type of woman Scott would be interested in. And not in a self-pitying kind of way, but merely as fact. And she was okay with that. She didn't want to date anyone at all, let alone someone like Scott.

She couldn't help but think again about Will and all those things he'd said about her. Maybe her self-image had been fragile going into the marriage . . . or maybe he was just really convincing with his criticism. She didn't want to spend the last few years of her twenties suffering in Spanx on a daily basis to look better for some guy. And that was not the image she wanted to project to the women and children at her studio. So no, she thought again as she made eye contact with Harper, she was not dating him. "That's totally fine. I'm not ready for any kind of relationship. I'm just grateful that he could step in and keep the renovation on track."

CHAPTER FOUR

"Mom, stop being such a downer and let's just go take a peek," Wendy said, all but shoving Ruby through the door.

Mary nodded. "I have to agree with Wendy on this one, Ruby. It'll be fun to just browse through the dresses. There's no pressure to buy anything."

"I'll try not to be offended that you sounded reluctant to agree with me, Mary," Wendy said as they entered the small boutique on Main Street.

The last thing Ruby felt like doing was buying a wedding dress. Or outfit. She felt ridiculous. And the other problem was that everyone in Silver Springs knew each other, which meant that Sandy, the owner, would know exactly what they were looking for. Not that it was a secret that she was getting married. She just felt . . . silly. Especially since Harry's family didn't even know he was getting married.

"Hello, ladies!" Sandy called out. They all greeted her before Wendy made a beeline for the formal dresses in the back of the store.

Ruby tried not to let on that the dress in the window had caught her attention. It was a deep burgundy with intricate beading, long sleeves, and a modest V neckline, and it looked ankle length. It was too much. Too formal. Too fancy for a wedding at home at her age. But she did give it one last glance before turning her attention to Sandy.

"Can I help you find anything special? I've brought tons of dresses in for Christmas and New Year's," she said, gesturing to the front of the store.

Mary had already abandoned Ruby and was riffling through the dresses at the back with Wendy. Great. Those two together would be a tough tag team when it came to defeating any reluctance she felt. Ruby forced herself to appear casual. At least there was no one else in the store. She'd opened her mouth to tell Sandy they were just browsing when Wendy beat her to it.

"Mom's looking for a wedding dress! What do you suggest, Sandy?"

Sandy's face lit up brighter than the Christmas lights around the shop window. "Ruby, how exciting! I just knew that handsome man I've seen you around town with was serious. Okay, let me show you what I think would be stunning on you," she said, marching to the back of the store like she was a soldier.

"I'm not sure I really want an evening gown," Ruby said, hurrying to follow her and trying not be startled by the fact that Sandy already knew about her and Harry. Luckily, the door chimes rang and Sandy's attention was diverted.

"Sandy, we're fine to look on our own. I'll be sure to call out if we need help," Ruby said, relieved when Sandy agreed and went to help the new customer.

A Christmas House Wedding

"Come on, Mom, just have some fun," Wendy said, sifting through the assortment of gowns.

"I didn't even say I was coming to look at dresses today. There's a lot going on with Christmas and the girls. Poor Olivia is so stressed out," Ruby said, desperate to distract them.

Mary turned around. "I thought Scott was handling things?"

Ruby knew that Mary just adored Scott. "Of course he is, but that doesn't mean he'll be able to get the studio up and running on time."

Mary gave her a wise smile. "Yes he will. Scott is a very determined, hardworking, and reliable man."

"I know he is, but he's not a miracle worker."

"I don't know how my daughters do it, but they always manage to find hot men ready to drop everything for them!" Wendy said.

Ruby's mouth dropped open at her daughter's insensitivity to what Olivia and Charlotte had been through. "Wendy, Olivia is still recovering from that awful husband of hers. Yes, he was awful, regardless of what he looked like. And Charlotte was basically a hermit until she came back here last year. Besides, Scott is working for Olivia; there's nothing else there."

Mary's eyebrows lifted. "But there could be. And he's a good man. The best. Next to my Wyatt, of course. But such a close second! He's handsome. A good father. A great father. He might be a little jaded, but that's just because of his past."

Wendy stopped flipping through the racks, and Ruby held her breath. "What past?" Wendy asked, finally acting like a concerned parent rather than a teenager.

Mary's face grew red. "Oh . . . I didn't mean like a bad past. I was just . . . I was just referring to the fact that his wife died. That's

47

all. Nothing else there . . ." she said, quickly turning to the racks of clothes as her voice trailed off.

Ruby made a mental note to ask Mary what that was all about. Of course, she knew Mary must be referring to something else, and if it was relevant to Olivia's well-being, then she needed to know about it.

"Well, that's good. I mean tragic, of course. But maybe Olivia needs to let loose a little. She's getting far too serious. She's practically acting like Charlotte. Next thing you know, she'll be alphabetizing the pantry," Wendy said, holding up a glittery fire-engine-red dress. "This is perfect for you, Mom. It'll match that rock Harry gave you."

Mary's muffled laugh offered her no comfort.

Ruby clasped her hands together in an effort to contain her irritation. "It's not my style, Wendy. I was actually thinking of a suit."

Both women froze and then turned around to face Ruby. "What, are you going to a board meeting on Christmas Eve? A suit? You've waited like a century to marry this man, and you're going to show up in a suit?"

"Again, I'm sorry, Ruby, but I'm going to have to agree with Wendy," Mary said, wincing.

Wendy shot Mary a look.

"First of all, we haven't known each other a century, and secondly, lots of people wear suits at weddings. I'm not talking about a business suit. It can have beading or whatever," Ruby said, scrambling to make her idea sound better. Was it a bad idea? Was there something wrong with trying to keep things simple?

"But it's your first wedding, Ruby, and it's on Christmas Eve, at the Christmas House, to the love of your life. Come on," Mary said, a hand over her heart.

Ruby groaned. *"Well . . . when you put it like that."*

Wendy rolled her eyes. *"How is that better than what I said?"*

Ruby sighed. *She didn't know if she wanted to do this today or if she wanted to come back here by herself later.* *"I just don't want to feel silly,"* *she said, finally breaking the silence.*

"Why would you feel silly?" *Mary asked.*

Ruby held her breath for a moment. Maybe she should just do it. Mary was right. Harry was the love of her life. He'd come back after being rejected so many times. He'd loved her all these years. How could she show up as though it were just any other formal event? This was her wedding. *"Okay, maybe you're right. There is a dress . . ."* She turned, looking over her shoulder and expecting to see that burgundy dress in the window.

But Sandy was wrapping it up in a big box, a younger woman handing her a credit card at the counter.

Ruby's mouth dropped open. She'd waited. Once again. She'd waited out of fear and insecurity, and now it was gone. How could she have not learned her lesson by now?

"Which dress?" *Wendy demanded, her gaze going following Ruby's.*

Ruby shook her head. *"No dress here . . . I just mean there is a dress, I'm sure, that we can find. I'll even try on that red one, Wendy,"* *she said, forcing a laugh.*

But all she could think about as Wendy and Mary handed her dress after dress in the changing room was that this was a sign. That dress had been purchased right out from under her nose for a reason. How many times would she have to learn the same lesson?

* * *

"This place is going to be really cool, Dad," Cat said.

Scott slid his phone in his back pocket and glanced over at his daughter, who was sitting on a bench in the partially finished studio of Olivia's building. It was Thursday night, and he'd spent every day here. He'd asked Cat if she wanted to hang out while he finished a few things, and she'd agreed. They'd gotten fast food on the way, and she was inhaling it while getting her homework done in the empty space. He was happy for her company and pleased that she didn't mind hanging out. It made him feel less guilty than thinking of her at home alone. The week had flown by, and he was feeling a little better about the progress he was seeing. He'd called in a bunch of favors, and his contacts had come through for him.

"I'm glad you think so. I'm hoping I can pull this off in time for Olivia to keep her original opening date."

He took a step back and surveyed the studio. The mirrors that had been installed on the walls were now up to his safety standards. The windows still needed to be replaced, as did the lighting. The floor needed to be sanded and refinished. All in all, the previous contractor had left Olivia in the lurch, and Scott was spending a lot of time fixing poor workmanship.

After their walk-through, he'd spent the week fixing as much as he could while he waited for different trades to come in. It had proven to be an exercise in patience because, this close to the holidays, everyone was already down to the wire. The rest of it would fall on him, but he was also juggling a packed schedule.

But there was no way he'd leave Olivia hanging. Especially since the more he got to know her, the more he sensed this was so much more for her than just a business. There was also the fact that he liked her. It felt like she'd been trying to avoid him, though, and most of the week he'd been too busy to wonder or worry about it.

He paused, hearing a loud thud downstairs. "Did you hear that?"

Cat nodded, putting down her container of fries. "Sounded like something fell."

"Stay here," he said, jogging across the room to the door.

Cat followed him. "Dad, this is Silver Springs. I'm sure a bird flew into a window or something. Not everything is a crime scene. It's not like the ax murderer of Silver Springs is out hunting people down in warehouses."

He took the steps quickly, deciding he didn't want to engage in teenage sarcasm and know-it-all-ism as Cat's laughter trailed after him down the stairwell. But as he approached the lobby, his muscles tensed because of the odd noises coming from the vestibule. "Cat, just wait for me here," he said, purposely using his harsh "dad voice" because that was the only way she actually listened to him.

He ignored the theatrical sigh as she leaned against the wall.

"I'll be waiting right here as soon as you send the poor bird back into the wild," she called out.

He didn't find a bird.

He found Olivia struggling with a box about twice her height. The sound was her trying to get it into the building, but the box was caught in the first doorway. "Hey, need a hand?" he said, opening the door slightly so that she didn't topple backward.

She gave him a startled glance. "Omigosh, that would be great. But if you're busy, it's totally fine. I can manage. I was just about to get both these doors at the same time."

He didn't want to argue, but there was no way she would have made it. Well, not without some serious effort. "It's a two-person job. Why don't you hold this door open and I'll grab the box?"

"Sure, thanks," she said, ducking under his arm and then switching places with him. Standing this close to her, he could smell lilacs, and he noticed that her eyes were the exact shade of blue in her sweater. And that . . .

None of it mattered. He refocused on the box and getting a good grip.

"Where do you want it?" he asked, once he'd dragged the box through the entryway. It was too big to pick up.

She pointed to the first room off the entrance. "My new office. That's the desk."

"No problem." He placed it in the middle of the room and stood there.

She gave him a smile. "Thanks. You just made my job fifty percent easier," she said with a laugh, walking into the room.

"Oh, look, it's the ax murderer of Silver Springs! Just a little Thursday night inside joke. Hi, Olivia," Cat said, appearing in the doorway and shooting him her smarty-pants, gloating look.

He ran his hands through his hair, about to explain, but Olivia answered Cat.

Olivia's face lit up. "Hi, Cat. I hope you didn't get dragged into staying here after school because your dad is bailing me out."

Cat shook her head. "Not at all. I was promised junk food. And I was getting my homework over with anyway. Tons of homework and dance."

Olivia unbuttoned her coat. "Of course. I know Sam has been talking about it a lot. I can't wait to watch. It wouldn't be Christmas without it. Don't let me keep you from whatever you were doing. I don't want you staying here any later than you have to. I just thought, since Dawn is down for the night, I'd get over here and get this thing assembled. But by the looks of things, I might be here for a few hours."

He didn't like the sound of that. Not that it was his place to tell her what was safe or not, but still. It was already pitch-black outside. "Actually, that reminds me; I wanted to talk to you about lighting and security out here. I know Silver Springs is safe, but this place is pretty isolated. There are no streetlights. It would be an easy place to target."

Olivia's face turned white. "I, um . . . that's a really good point."

"My dad is super paranoid about these things, Olivia. Don't let him freak you out. Just now he thought someone was breaking in, and it turned out to be you," Cat said, leaning against the doorjamb with the infinite wisdom and confidence of a kid who had no idea how the real world worked. And he was happy about that. That was the way it should be. Until she was an adult and would have to face the realization that there were seriously twisted people out there and that a person could never take their safety for granted, regardless of the town they lived in. She wouldn't get it. Not many would. Wyatt did, though. But even then, the two of them rarely spoke about what he'd been through.

"Thanks for that assessment, Cat. But seriously, Olivia. I have a guy who does security cameras and lighting and monitoring. Great prices. Reliable. I could get a quote," he said.

"Sure, that sounds good," she said, her expression serious.

"Do you want help assembling that?" Cat asked as Olivia crouched down by the box.

"Oh, Cat, that is so sweet of you. But I'm sure this is going to be super boring, and judging by how flat this box is, I'm assuming it's like five thousand parts."

"That's okay. My homework is done, and my dad's not doing anything interesting," she said, walking into the room and sitting cross-legged beside the box.

"Then, sure. I'd love the company," Olivia said.

"Okay, then, I'll leave you to it," Scott said, walking across the small room. "I'll head upstairs. I should be done in about an hour." He locked the front doors and headed up the stairwell, placing his call to his friend in security. The more he thought about it, the more he didn't like the idea of this place being so isolated.

Almost an hour later, Scott paused in the lobby to check a text that had just come through. Relieved that his buddy had said he'd be by tomorrow, he texted back and forth with him, listening—without really intending to—to the conversation from the office.

"I don't know what it is about instructions that make me feel like I'm looking at something written in a different language."

"I know what you mean. But the more you practice this stuff, the easier it gets. My dad made sure I know how to do all this stuff. Honestly, it was so boring to listen to—especially his lectures on how to safely use power tools—but it was kind of useful information."

Scott almost laughed at Cat's description of him. He hadn't realized he lectured, but whatever.

"Well, I'm thankful to your dad, because you're like a pro," Olivia answered.

He finished his text and went to meet them. The large white desk was in the middle of the room. It was plain and simple but looked good.

"Thanks. This was actually fun," Cat was saying. "I like seeing it all done. This is going to be a great place. I poked around when I came in with my dad."

"Looks great," he said, standing in the doorway.

They both turned around. "Thanks. I couldn't have done it without Cat. She knows what she's doing."

He grinned. "She is. I don't know where she gets her skills from."

Cat rolled her eyes and patted him on the shoulder. "You totally heard us."

He laughed. "Maybe. Unintentionally. I'm ready to go. I brought your backpack down," he said.

"Thanks."

"Well, thanks again," Olivia said, unpacking one of the boxes that had been stacked in the corner.

He shoved his hands in his pockets, choosing his wording carefully. "Do you need a few more minutes? We can wait and walk out with you."

She looked up, surprise flashing across her eyes. "What? Oh, no, of course not. I don't want to keep you. I'll see you tomorrow."

Damn. "It's not a big deal to help you unpack a few boxes," he said, walking into the room and lifting one of the ones in the corner. He placed it on the desk.

"Scott, really. Go home," she said, pulling a ream of paper out of the box.

He rubbed the back of his neck. "I'm not leaving you here by yourself."

She paused, her shoulders stiffening. Cat had come to stand in the doorway and was watching them like a TikTok video. "Why not? I'm not your responsibility. I can come and go as I please."

This was what he was afraid of. This wasn't coming off the right way. But he knew too many things and had seen too many things to just leave her here. He didn't care if she hated him; at least she'd be safe. But he would hate it if he was somehow reminding her of her ex. He didn't know their history; he just knew the guy was a jerk.

He tried again. "I know that you can come and go as you please. Of course. I'm not trying to tell you what to do, but there are no lights out here. None. No security."

She looked down at her box, and he hated that he was standing here telling her this. It wasn't fair, and he knew it. But fair and safe were two separate things. "I know that. If I want to stay, then I can stay."

She met his gaze, and he saw the defiance there. They were arguing from two completely different places. He was now a controlling jerk in her eyes. "Fine. Then stay. Go ahead and stay until midnight if you like. But maybe give a thought to how it will feel at midnight when you're locking up this big, old empty building and then walking out into a deserted parking lot when it's pitch-black."

He spotted the tremor in her hand when she reached into the box for another ream of paper. "Thanks. I know what I'm doing."

He shoved his hands in his pockets. He didn't know if the tremor was from what he was saying or the fact that they were arguing. Hell, he didn't know what she'd been through, and he was just trying to watch out for her. He didn't want to trigger any bad memories. "Okay then," he said, turning to leave.

Cat was standing there, keenly observing everything. "Night, Liv," she said, swinging her backpack over her shoulder.

Olivia smiled at her, but it was strained. "Night, sweetie. Thanks so much for your help."

"No problem. Oh, and don't worry about my dad; he comes across as really pushy and bullying, but he's just super paranoid about safety because of—"

"Thanks, Cat," he choked before she blurted out the little she knew about his past.

She rolled her eyes and patted him on the shoulder. "No worries. Anyway, he's just paranoid because Wyatt is his best friend and he's also just super paranoid. It's one of the reasons they're best friends. The other is to drive me and Sam crazy."

He was surprised to see Olivia's features relax into a smile. "Ha. I'm, um, actually, getting tired. So maybe I'll walk out with you," she said, grabbing her jacket and purse.

He stood there, silently taking all this in. This wasn't what he wanted. There was no victory here. She should have been able to stay as late as she wanted without being afraid. He shouldn't have had to point all this out. And now she was embarrassed. And it was his fault. He held the door open for her. "Thank you," she said stiffly as she passed through.

"No problem," he said, following her out and waiting while she locked up.

Cat was already at the truck. "Dad, can you open the door? I'm going to die of frostbite soon," she yelled.

Clearly the impending frostbite had not affected the level of sarcasm she was capable of. He unlocked the truck remotely, and he and Olivia walked down the steps together. "Well, uh, good night," he said when she reached her SUV.

"Good night, Scott," she said, before opening her door and sliding into the driver's seat.

He walked back over to his truck, feeling responsible for stealing all the light and enthusiasm she'd been filled with just moments before. He hopped into his truck and turned the ignition on.

"Well, that was awkward," Cat said, leaning forward to crank up the heat.

His eyes were on the road, on Olivia's taillights in front of him, and he didn't even know what the hell to say anymore.

"I mean, Dad, you totally came across as bossy. Just because you boss me around doesn't mean you can boss the entire female population around."

He gripped the steering wheel tightly. "That wasn't my intention. Of course I don't think that. And I don't boss you around. I'm a parent."

"No, no, I get it. Listen, next time I see her, I'll put in a good word for you."

He coughed. "Please don't. It doesn't matter. We're just friends."

"Right."

He shot her a look. Sure enough, she was smirking. "What's that supposed to mean?"

"Olivia's so nice. Pretty. A bit girly compared to Mom, but maybe you just needed a change. I'm not like Mom either. I'm more of an Olivia type, much to your disappointment," she said.

He almost drove off the road. "What the hell are you even talking about right now? Where is this even coming from? You just threw everything at me, Cat. What are we talking about first? You and me? Or me and Olivia?"

"I get to choose?"

Hell. "Yes."

"Okay then, Olivia."

He took a deep breath. He was losing badly tonight. "First of all, I barely know Olivia. Also, she's not a type. You can't just go around saying people are types. I wouldn't say you're a type or Mom was a type. It's not that simple. I don't know if she's like Mom or not like Mom. And besides, no two people are alike anyway."

"Well, that's not true. Mom was all into sports and stuff. And she was a cop. You would have never told her she couldn't walk across a parking lot by herself."

He didn't think he could grip the steering wheel any tighter without risking pulling it straight off. "I did not tell her she couldn't walk across a parking lot by herself. I wasn't giving her orders. Olivia doesn't answer to me. Mom was different because she knew how to defend herself. She was trained. She was armed, for crying out loud, Cat."

"Sure."

"What's that supposed to mean?"

She crossed her arms. "Maybe it means that you'll never find someone else if you keep comparing everyone to her."

He swallowed past the lump in his throat. "That's not what I'm doing. And I hope to hell you're not implying that I'm somehow disappointed that you and Mom are very different. I'm proud of you and love you for who you are. You're smart and talented and hardworking, Cat. And those are all characteristics your mom had—just different interests. I don't care that you're not interested in hockey or basketball. I love you. No matter what. I just love you."

He glanced over at her when he didn't hear a reply. Her head was turned and she was staring out the window. Hell, sometimes he didn't know if he was doing a good job with this whole parenting thing. One minute he felt like he and Cat were totally in sync, and then the next, like now, he had no idea what she was thinking. This whole thing had come out of left field tonight. He always told Cat how proud he was of her. He'd had no idea she was insecure about what he thought. Funny, because most of the time she was criticizing him.

Just when he was about to launch into another speech about how proud he was, Cat reached across the seat and clasped his hand. Just like she used to do when she was little. He took a second to glance down at her smaller hand in his, and a pang of nostalgia caught him by surprise. He didn't like to think back to those early days when it was just the two of them. He'd barely been getting by. Wyatt had come back for support. His parents had been there to help. But nothing had made him be the father he needed to be until Cat had cried out for him.

He would do anything for her. He would do anything to keep her safe. To keep her happy. She had reached out to him and found him when he was lost. He would never be unreachable to her again. "I love you, Dad."

And just like that, all was right with his world again. He squeezed her hand. "Love you more, kid."

"Gosh, you're competitive," she said with a laugh, before turning on the radio.

He laughed along with her as "Holly Jolly Christmas" came on the radio. He watched in silence as Olivia took the turnoff to Ruby's, and an odd sense of loss hit him as her taillights disappeared. He had no idea what she was thinking about him now. But clearly, if his daughter knew so little about what he thought of her, he could only imagine what Olivia thought.

Yeah, Cat might know he'd been a cop at one time, but she didn't know anything else. And Olivia probably didn't know he'd been a cop at all. It wasn't stuff he shared. The last woman he'd shared those details with had been disappointed in him.

Maybe it was for the best that he'd pissed Olivia off tonight. She was off-limits for him, for all the reasons he already knew. Now he'd just made things easier for both of them.

CHAPTER FIVE

Ruby opened the front door, surprised to see her son-in-law, Mac, standing there with a poinsettia. She couldn't help but remember the last time he'd arrived holding a poinsettia and all hell had broken loose. Before that, no one had seen him since he'd walked out on his family without warning almost twenty years earlier. He had moved to Silver Springs last year to try to rebuild his relationship with all of them, but so far things had been rocky. "Evening, Ruby. I was hoping you had a few minutes?"

She opened the door wider, stepping aside so he could enter. "Of course. Why don't I put on a pot of coffee, or is it too late for that?"

He smiled as he entered, handing her the poinsettia. "It's never too late for a cup of your coffee. Here, this is for you. I would have called first, but I was worried I might not be welcome."

Ruby started down the hall as he closed the door behind him. "You know that you're always welcome, now that everyone knows you're back in town. And thank you for this beautiful poinsettia. Red is my favorite."

"I remembered," he said, following her into the kitchen.

"Have a seat, Mac." She placed the plant on the counter and got out her freshly ground coffee beans.

"I guess Olivia and the baby aren't home?" he asked, taking a seat at the island. The disappointment in his voice was obvious.

She turned on the coffeemaker and turned to look at him while it brewed. "No, Olivia is at the studio still. Dawn is already asleep for the night. How have you been? Taking care of yourself?"

He nodded, his eyes filled with worry. "I'm fine. Thanks for . . . asking, for caring. I, uh, when I came back, I would have hoped that by this time I would have made greater inroads with Charlotte and Olivia. I guess I'm just a little disappointed and worried, honestly. It feels like there are still so many walls up with them. Wendy is the only one who's given me a real chance."

Ruby took a deep breath, feeling the weight of his regrets, of his broken family. "Mac, you know I'll always be honest with you, even if it's not what you want to hear."

He gave her a smile, the lines around his mouth and eyes showing his years, even though she could still picture him as that young man who'd asked her blessing to marry Wendy. Those two had been so naïve and immature and not at all cut out to deal with the world ahead of them. It pained her to think that way, but the truth had become more and more obvious the further into their marriage they'd gotten. Unfortunately, their girls had paid the price.

"That's why I'm here, Ruby. I've hidden far too long. I just want to fix what I broke."

They stood in silence as she carefully considered her words. She wanted to help him, but she would also never stop feeling the need to protect her granddaughters. Charlotte was on her way to a happy, solid life, but Olivia was still fragile. The coffeemaker beeped, and Ruby took that opportunity to rehearse her words as she poured them each a cup. She handed Mac his, knowing he took it black.

"I don't think it's as easy as fixing a broken object. The family you and Wendy created is gone, and you both played your roles in that destruction. You were out of their lives for so long, Mac. You can't expect to come back after being absent, without any communication, for almost two decades and think that within a year you can reclaim that. You may never reclaim that bond you had with those girls. Women, now, of course."

"You were never one to pull punches, Ruby," he said, taking a sip of his coffee.

Ruby wrapped her hands around her mug and leaned against the counter. "I say it all without judgment, Mac. It's just truth. And I'm saying it with the hope that you'll keep trying. I know you have a good heart. I know Wendy does too. But that doesn't mean you're trustworthy either. It's not black and white. Just because the bond you had before might be irreparable doesn't mean you can't build a new one. Get to know them as they are now."

He ran a hand through his hair. "I'm trying, but it feels like they never have the time."

"They're both busy, right? I mean, Charlotte just got married, moved her entire life and business to Silver Springs. She wants to spend time with her husband, and he has a grueling schedule, and then they have Samantha too. Olivia has a baby, is a single mom, and is trying to get over a really abusive marriage. They're giving you

what time they have. Honestly, maybe a part of them feels that you never had the time to make them a priority, and now . . . you come back into their lives expecting them to make all this time for you."

His head stayed turned down for a long time, and she worried that she'd pushed him too hard. But he finally raised his gaze to hers. "You have a clear way of looking at things. You're right, I guess, as much as it's not what I wanted to hear. Who am I to demand their time? I wasn't there for either of them. I'm glad Charlotte is with Wyatt and Sam, and I can tell they're happy. I can tell he's a good man, that he's responsible and strong and is able to be there for both of them. And I'm honestly unable to forgive myself for what happened to Olivia. I can't help but think it's my fault she ended up with a man like that."

Ruby pursed her lips. They were entering dangerous territory now, and she didn't want to betray Olivia and the few things her granddaughter had confided in her. "What can I say to that, Mac? I don't know. We won't ever know. But she's strong. She's starting over. Maybe you should try telling her how you feel? The guilt? The worry? Tell her what you hope for by being back here. She won't know what's on your heart unless you tell her."

He nodded, his eyes focused on the inside of his cup. "You're right. I will. And I'll keep trying. I keep waiting for an invitation to Charlotte and Wyatt's house, but that hasn't exactly happened either. But I think Charlotte might never forgive me. She was closest to me. She was there for me . . . more than I was there for her."

Ruby's throat constricted painfully at the regret in his voice, at her own memories of that dark time. "Then you need to tell her. You can't expect her to know that. Sometimes just being honest and real is what's needed."

He nodded. "Okay. I'll try."

She cleared her throat, almost not wanting to know the answer to her next question. "I haven't seen Wendy in a few days. How are things with the two of you?"

He gave her a sheepish grin. "I think she's mad at me right now. But we're going out for dinner tomorrow night."

Some things didn't change. "Well, at least you keep trying," she said, swallowing a laugh.

He glanced at his watch. "It's a bit late for Olivia to still be at that studio, isn't it? I drove by it the other day, because I was curious and she hadn't invited me, but uh, it's in the middle of nowhere."

Ruby ignored the jolt of worry. "I agree. But Scott is there."

Mac frowned. "Scott?"

She nodded. "I think you've met him before. He's Wyatt's best friend. Mary's basically adopted him as her nephew as well as his daughter, Cat."

He nodded slowly. "Right. Okay, that makes me feel a bit better. He wasn't the original contractor, was he?"

Ruby shook her head. "No, that scoundrel walked off the job and left her in the lurch. Scott stepped in and saved the day."

Mac ran his hands down his face. "God, I screwed things up. I could have helped her out too. I'm her dad. I could be doing so much there. I don't know if she even thought about asking me at all. The fact that she didn't think to ask is the worst part of all."

Ruby gave him a long look. "Don't give up. Trust is earned, Mac. It's a gift. And after what Olivia has been through, it's probably the last thing she'll ever give."

* * *

The next morning, Olivia smiled at Dawn as she finished putting her hair in pigtails. "You're so cute," she whispered, giving her daughter a smattering of kisses on her cheeks.

Dawn giggled and held on to her. Olivia had just finished getting her dressed in a red sweater with Rudolph on the front and matching red velour leggings. "You know, Dawn, I wish they had this outfit in a grown-up size. You look so cozy. Way better than jeans. Okay, let's go see GG and have some breakfast."

She and Dawn walked down the hallway together, and she held on to Dawn's hand tightly as they descended the grand staircase. She was in desperate need of coffee this morning. She had tossed and turned all night, bothered by what had happened between her and Scott. She didn't know what to think. She had immediately jumped to conclusions, because there had been a part of that whole situation that reminded her of Will. Not in Scott's voice or his mannerisms, but what he'd said had made her think of Will when he would tell her what to do. No, not tell her what to do. Yell at her to do it. Not out of concern, because it always had to do with appearances.

She knew Scott wasn't like that. It had been genuine concern. And he'd had valid points. It was reassuring to know there would be a security system, lights, and cameras installed, for her and for the customers who attended the studio and the people who worked there.

But she hadn't told him that. Instead, she'd been cold and standoffish, and he hadn't deserved that. He'd stayed late, he was pulling long hours for her—even Cat had helped. But there was something else; she genuinely liked him. He appealed to her in a way that no one ever had, and that scared her. It didn't matter anyway, though. He wasn't interested and she wasn't interested. They both had their own kids and it was clear that Cat was his priority, as she should be. Just like Dawn was her priority. There was no time for anything or anyone else.

"Good morning, Grandma," Olivia said as they walked into the kitchen.

The smell of freshly brewed coffee and banana bread filled the kitchen. Dawn broke free and ran up to her great-grand-mother for a hug. "Good morning, my darling girls," Grandma Ruby said as she enveloped Dawn in a big hug.

Staying here this last year had been so healing. Olivia had felt so isolated in the city all by herself with Dawn. Sure, she'd been hiding from her family, from Charlotte. But Grandma Ruby was special. She was a cup of hot chocolate with whipped cream in a blizzard. Olivia was closer to Grandma Ruby than she'd ever been to either of her parents.

"Can I pour you a cup of coffee?" she asked her grandmother.

"That would be wonderful. I have some scrambled eggs, just the way Dawn likes them. Would you like some too?" Ruby said, spooning the eggs onto a melamine dish with Rudolph in the middle.

Dawn ran over to her high chair, and Olivia lifted her and buckled her in, stopping to give her a kiss on the head. "No thanks, Grandma. I'll just stick with coffee this morning."

While Olivia poured the coffees, her grandmother gave Dawn her food. They both knew Dawn would be feeding herself. Soon the three of them were around the kitchen table, and Olivia soaked in the moment, realizing how special this was, the three generations they represented.

A Christmas House Wedding

These days here, this year here. Her grandmother's old kitchen was decorated everywhere you looked, from wreaths in the windows to garland over the doorways. The view from the windows was trees and pristine white snow. It hadn't changed since she was a girl. There was comfort in that, in knowing some things didn't change. She took in the beautiful sight of her grandmother smiling at Dawn. And her daughter unabashedly smiled back, before grabbing her sippy cup and swinging her head back and drinking from it.

"Grandma, I don't know if I've told you this, but everything you've done for me, for Dawn, this last year—I don't know how I would have gotten through everything if it weren't for you. You have always been there for me, and I hope you realize just how much I appreciate everything."

Her grandmother's eyes misted over. "There is nothing I wouldn't do for you girls. For Dawn. As much as you think I've helped you—you and Charlotte and Dawn have helped me too. Now, before we get all teary-eyed and sidetracked, you must tell me what's happening with Scott."

Olivia sat a little straighter. "You mean what's happening with the renovation?"

Her grandmother's eyes sparkled over the rim of her coffee cup as she took a sip. "Yes, yes, of course that's what I meant."

Olivia picked up her mug and added a splash of cream, avoiding her grandmother's gaze. Scott. The memory of last night played across her mind. Ugh. She was going to have to see him soon, and she was worried that things might be awkward now. "Things are fine. He's very hardworking and has sort of taken over everything. Even security, apparently."

Her grandmother raised an eyebrow. "Oh?"

Oh, why had she let that slip? She had thought she was just going to play it cool. "It's nothing. I just mean—it's nothing I had thought of. But he raised some good points about there being no lighting or cameras and that the building is quite isolated."

Her grandmother placed her mug down, the sparkle leaving her eyes. "That's very true. I'm glad he thought of that. Think how many late nights you might have there. Or an employee of yours."

Olivia traced the print of holly on the front of her cup. "You're right . . . he's right. I, um, I think I might have made a fool of myself last night, Grandma."

"Impossible."

Olivia almost laughed at her grandmother's staunch loyalty. "No, no, quite possible. Probable, in fact—"

"Olivia, don't talk about yourself like that."

Olivia snapped her gaze up to her grandmother's. "I was just joking."

Her grandmother leaned across the table to take her hand. "I hope so. But you have to be careful that you're not actually putting yourself down. Our scars don't just disappear overnight. Or even in a year. Some things may even be a lifelong process. Be very careful you haven't let Will define who you are."

Olivia stared down at her grandmother's hand on hers. Grandma Ruby's hands were smooth, her veins more pronounced now with age, and Olivia knew just how hard she had worked to survive as a single mother. They had lived such different lives, yet there was something about Grandma Ruby that always made her feel connected, understood, and never judged. Her grandmother's words registered deeply, so much so that she couldn't jump to a quick defense. She forced herself to meet her grandmother's gaze and face more of that thoughtful wisdom, even if it was painful. "What do you mean by that?"

Her grandmother squeezed her hand, a comforting gesture, before she delivered the truth. "I mean that we come into this world perfect, Olivia. It isn't until the outside world starts telling us what's wrong with us that we lose faith in who we are and who we were meant to be. Will's words, Will's treatment of you, has had lasting effects. You may not even be aware of it. You were my dreamer, my happily-ever-after princess. He destroyed that. He made you believe you weren't good enough. He stole your joy, your faith."

Olivia's throat constricted painfully. "I let him."

Her grandmother's eyes glittered. "He took advantage of you, of your innocence. Do not take the blame. Do not. And do not bring him into your other relationships."

Olivia blinked back the tears that threatened to spill over. "I'm working on it. I promise. And there aren't any other relationships."

Her grandmother's lips twitched and her eyes sparkled again. "Right. So what were we saying about Scott?"

Olivia almost laughed. "Scott, the contractor . . . yes, I was at the warehouse with him and Cat, and they were ready to leave, and I wanted to stay and finish unpacking. He didn't want me to stay by myself."

"A wise man."

Dawn threw her sippy cup on the ground and tipped over her plate. Olivia sighed and picked everything up. "Mo," Dawn said.

"More eggs?" Olivia asked, grateful for the interruption, even if it meant wiping up egg remnants.

Dawn nodded.

Olivia walked over to the pan for more eggs and refilled Dawn's cup. Once she had everything placed on the tray and wiped the floor, she sat back down across from her grandmother. "And . . . well, I got my back up. I was irritated that he was telling me I shouldn't stay there. I know he was just looking out for me, I get that, but it reminded me of Will. It wasn't fair to Scott, but I couldn't help it. It triggered a memory, and I couldn't separate what he was saying from Will ordering me to do things like I was stupid. Now I have to see him in less than an hour, and I'm so embarrassed."

Grandma Ruby didn't say anything for a moment, her eyebrows knit together. "I don't think Scott is judging you. I'm sure he probably feels bad for coming across like that. You know, something I've realized with time is that we all approach things based on the experiences we've had. He was probably forceful in his opinion because of things he's seen or things that have happened to him."

Olivia took a sip of coffee, warmed by it and her grandmother's words. But there was no denying she still felt silly. She felt exposed. Like her behavior had told Scott that she'd been through a lot. Or maybe he just thought she wasn't appreciative of everything he was doing. Heck, she didn't even know what she thought anymore. She didn't know what was right. Who was right? Was she the old Olivia or the new Olivia? She stared into her mug, avoiding her grandmother's intense gaze a little while longer.

"I guess you're right. Though I'm not sure there's something in his background that warrants all the security stuff and talk."

Her grandmother bit her lip for a moment and then looked away. "Well, I guess we don't really know what someone's been through. And he is a single father to a teenage daughter. I think it's natural for him to worry."

Olivia kept her gaze trained on her grandmother. Grandma Ruby knew something. Olivia wasn't exactly surprised. Her grandmother and Aunt Mary seemed to know everything about everyone. But then she reminded herself that it was none of her business. Because she wasn't interested in Scott, and he wasn't interested in her. They were friends. He was helping her out of a bad situation. Just because their family and friends thought they would make a great couple didn't make it true.

"You're right as usual, Grandma. But enough of that. How are you and Harry doing? Charlotte and I are meeting up to do some wedding planning."

Her grandmother smiled, but it lacked the usual ease. "Oh, we're fine. Just lots of decisions to be made. We've both led such different lives."

Olivia nodded and walked over to Dawn, who was trying to figure out how to get out of the high chair. She unbuckled her daughter while she spoke. "Sure. I guess there are a lot of plans to make. But we love Harry so much. We're so happy for you."

Her grandmother stood and took Dawn from her. "I know. Thank you, dear. Now why don't you hurry and get out to

73

the studio. If you could be back by three today, that would be wonderful."

Olivia picked up her empty mug and placed it in the dishwasher. "Of course. I don't know how I would have managed without you. But as soon as the warehouse is safer, I'll be bringing Dawn with me and free you up."

Grandma Ruby reached out and gave her a kiss. "I love this time with Dawn. Don't even think twice about it. It's my pleasure. Besides, Mary is coming over this morning, and she just adores spending time with Dawn. I keep trying to talk her out of putting any pressure on Wyatt and Charlotte to have kids. But you know Mary. She's like a bulldozer."

Wyatt and Charlotte. Huh. She hadn't really given it that much thought. But then again, it would make sense. She knew that Charlotte and Wyatt both had their own scars, and her sister hadn't even hinted at kids. She pushed those thoughts aside and gave Dawn a quick kiss. "Well, good luck to Mary, but I don't think Wyatt and Char are the type to take advice."

Grandma Ruby laughed, following her to the door. Dawn ran ahead, making a beeline for her activity area in the front parlor. "You're right about that. Have a good day, dear. Remember what I said about Scott."

Olivia nodded, shrugging into her coat and then swinging her purse over her shoulder. She stopped to glance in the mirror and then quickly looked away. She didn't want to think about the way she looked today.

"So beautiful, Olivia. Inside and out." Her grandmother patted her shoulder and opened the door.

She had walked through it, about to head out to the driveway, when she paused. "Grandma, I just want you to know that I'm happy on my own."

"I'm glad. There is nothing wrong with being on your own. Rushing into new relationships is never a good idea."

Olivia nodded. "Right. Exactly."

Her grandmother tapped her finger against her chin, not looking the least bit cold without a coat on. "But then again, you wouldn't be rushing. Your marriage was over for a long time before you admitted it to us last year."

Olivia's mouth dropped open. "Well, true . . . but I've also been giving a lot of thought to cats."

Grandma Ruby's eyes grew wide, and she glanced over at Dawn, who was happily playing on the ground with a set of wooden puzzles. "Clearly, it's time for an intervention. Funny story, dear: last year, when your lonely and hermit-like older sister came here, I was worried she was going to become my cat-lady grandchild. That's not your fate, Olivia. Live your life while you're still young. You are beautiful. Go and talk to Mary's handsome nephew."

"Gram, you are so good for my self-esteem," Olivia said, forcing a laugh as she huddled further into her coat. She didn't even bother remarking that Scott wasn't technically Mary's nephew. And she wasn't about to tell her that Scott was too good-looking for someone like her. That would open up a can of worms, and she was working on quieting those unhealthy thoughts.

"It's all true. Just like the part about Scott being one handsome man. Bye now, dear."

With that, her grandmother shut the bright-red door in her face.

Olivia almost laughed out loud, but then she remembered that she was on her way to see Scott. And it was going to be awkward.

CHAPTER SIX

"Are you mad at me?"

Ruby pressed a Christmas tree–shaped cookie cutter into the rolled dough and avoided eye contact with Mary. They were in the kitchen making a few dozen sugar cookies while Dawn sat happily on the ground with crayons, piles of paper, and blocks. Olivia had left an hour ago, and their conversation was still fresh on her mind. It wasn't that she wanted to push Olivia into a new relationship, but she was worried by how reserved her granddaughter seemed now. Of the two girls, Olivia had always had stars in her eyes and a hope for the future that Charlotte never had. Ruby couldn't remember the last time she'd seen that expression in Olivia's eyes, though. Sure, people grew up, but Olivia had been so hurt by the men in her life that Ruby worried she had given up. She didn't want that for her; she didn't want Olivia to be closed off from love like Ruby had been for so long.

"What are you talking about? Why would I be mad at you?"

Mary winced as she pulled her sugar cookie up and decapitated Santa Claus. She tried joining his head with his body on the cookie sheet. "Because of the dress ambush. Honestly, we were all just so excited. I'm so happy for you, Ruby. I got caught up in the romance of it all," she said with a wistful sigh.

Ruby carefully separated the dough from the pressed shapes. "Oh, please, I'm not mad. Honestly, I don't know what I am. I don't know how I should feel, how I should dress, none of it. I'm worried about Olivia. I wanted her to be further along by now—her confidence isn't back. Between you and me, I think she thinks she isn't attractive enough for a man like Scott."

Mary placed a hand over her heart. "That poor girl. You know, I really wish I could get a hold of that Will and tell him what I think of him. He was lucky to be married to Olivia."

"I know. I agree. He's an awful man. I don't even know the half of it—she never did tell us all the details. I don't know how bad it got. I can't even imagine what she's been through. And I'm worried about the fact that we still haven't told Harry's kids we're getting married. And then there's the fact that Harry's kids still haven't met Wendy or any of my family. I don't know what Charlotte and Olivia are planning for the wedding, and I can't even let myself get worried about that."

Mary peeked inside her coffee cup. "Maybe we should add some Baileys to this, Ruby. That is a lot of stuff you're dealing with."

Ruby let out a laugh and then glanced at the time on the oven clock. "It's still too early for that. Also, there was a dress I saw, and by the time I got up the nerve to say something, someone else had already bought it."

Mary gasped. "Well, why didn't you tell Sandy?"

Ruby grabbed the leftover dough and rolled it out, taking her frustrations out on the rolling pin. "I don't know. I'm just not sure about anything, it seems."

"You and Harry need to tell his kids. You have to get this over with. Then I think maybe you'll be able to be excited about the dress. Are you nervous about telling them?"

Ruby stared at her engagement ring sitting off to the side of the counter. She'd taken it off for baking. Yes, old wounds were surfacing. Old doubts. Just the thought of telling Harry's kids they were getting married made her want to break out in a cold sweat. There were things that made Olivia think of the past, and it was the same for Ruby.

She and Harry had a complicated past, and she didn't know that he'd told his children any of it. But the last time she'd tried explaining anything to Harry's family . . . well, it had been devastating. Traumatic.

How many years ago had it been? And yet it still gave her pause, made her limbs feel heavy and made her want to sit down. But things were different now. She wasn't eighteen anymore.

She wasn't pregnant and homeless.

She was a strong, independent woman, and she knew who she was.

And maybe she wasn't that different from Olivia after all.

* * *

Olivia took a deep breath, pushed aside the doubt that had trailed her from her grandmother's, and pulled open the interior door to the warehouse. She had already spotted Scott in the small studio.

"Good morning," she called out, trying to sound casual while balancing the tray of coffee in one hand and her purse in the other.

Scott turned around, surprise lighting his features. He had probably thought she was still angry with him. She tried to ignore how good he looked this morning. He hadn't shaved . . . and that was kind of attractive. Okay, maybe a lot attractive, because he wore stubble well. It kind of suited the worn-in and faded baseball cap that sat low on his forehead. It also went well with the fitted T-shirt and lived-in jeans. So, basically, the man wore everything well. And he'd probably only had to roll out of bed, shower, and get dressed to look that good. "Hey. I didn't know you were going to be here."

She sort of thrust the tray of coffee in his direction. "A peace offering."

His brow furrowed as he approached her and accepted the tray. "Thanks. But for what?"

She pulled her coffee out when he handed her the cardboard tray after taking his coffee. "I feel like I snapped at you last night."

His lips twitched before he took a sip of coffee. "Oh, you mean when I bossed you around? Cat's description, not mine."

"You didn't. I get it. You were looking out for me. I mean, like you'd look out for anyone alone in a warehouse in the middle of nowhere . . . speaking of which, any progress with the security company?"

"Wait a sec. You didn't need to apologize or bring a peace offering. Really," he said, tilting his head, his pale-blue eyes serious.

She swallowed hard. "Sure. Thank you. I just don't want things to be tense between us."

He shook his head. "Not at all. And about security, yes, my buddy is coming by today, and by tonight this place should be hooked up and safe and lit."

"Wow, that was fast," she said, taking a sip of coffee.

"He owed me a few favors. I will also be working on your numbers tonight, if you want to stop by my place tomorrow night? I know it's the weekend, so if you have plans, that's okay."

She paused. Plans? At his house? "Um, sure."

"Cat will be there, of course. It's a business meeting," he clarified.

Right. Of course it was. Not that she was interested in Scott—because she wasn't. And someone like him wouldn't be interested in her. While he obviously wasn't Will, there was also no denying the kind of man he was—too appealing for his own good. Definitely for *her* own good. "Okay. Is seven okay? I usually put Dawn down around six thirty. Then I don't have to worry about my grandmother getting her to bed."

"Sure, that works great. Wow, six thirty. I remember those days," he said with a warm smile and a casual sincerity that told her he'd been an involved father. Something Will had never been, not even for a day.

She held his gaze, sensing there was more there. But he didn't elaborate. "Yeah, I guess thirteen-year-olds don't go to bed that early?"

He laughed, his aqua eyes twinkling, and her stomach fluttered like she was . . . like she was someone she hadn't been in a long time. "Not for a long time. Anyway, I should get back to work here. Your office is good to go, by the way. Floor is all fixed, outlets all working."

She took a step back from him and eyed her office. Her own office. For her own business. She swallowed hard. This was so far out of her comfort zone. It was real, and the fate of this business depended on her. There was no husband to fall back on, no deep pockets, just . . . her. "Then I guess I should finish unpacking and setting that up. Maybe having a functioning office will make this seem more real."

"This is a pretty big undertaking."

She nodded, her eyes on that empty office as she let his words sink in. He said it in a way that didn't make her think he doubted her abilities. There was almost a tinge of admiration in his voice, and that knowledge warmed her, made her shoulders relax a little. "Yeah, it's um, not something I could have imagined myself doing last year."

"A lot can change in a year," he said, his voice holding notes of understanding.

She glanced up at him, suddenly aware of his height, his strength, and not sure she liked that awareness or this easy conversation between them. "Yeah. Right. And, um, I look forward to going over those numbers tomorrow and seeing where I'm at with this reno. I will pencil in our meeting for seven thirty tomorrow night," she said, feeling the need to act professional and shake off the jittery feeling of being around him.

Scott paused. "Seven, right?"

Heat flooded her face as she realized her mistake. So much for looking professional. "Omigosh. Yes. I don't know what I was thinking. Yes, seven."

"You're an idiot. You screw everything up. And you're an embarrassment to me. Lose some fucking weight before this baby is born, because you're making me look bad." Will had been yelling at her because she'd gotten the time wrong for one of the dinners they were supposed to be going to for one of his endless work functions. She'd been so sick with nausea that she hadn't been thinking clearly, and they had been half an hour late. He'd stopped her in the parking lot, grabbing her arm forcefully. She had almost lost her balance and that had scared her, the idea of falling while she was pregnant. Then she'd thrown up in the bushes while he went inside and played the suave businessman.

"Olivia? You okay?"

She blinked, her heart racing when she realized where she'd gone and how quickly that humiliation had engulfed her again. She swallowed hard and tried to catch her breath before looking up at Scott. "Yeah, yeah, sorry. Um, Dawn doesn't always sleep through the night. Last night she woke up a few times. I'm just tired and . . . you know how it is. Anyway, um, Scott . . . thank you. Thank you for stepping in and saving me with this reno. I haven't actually said how much I appreciate what you're doing. I can only imagine what you've had to do on your end to make time for this. I hope you don't think because of last night that I'm not appreciative."

His jaw clenched for a moment, and the way he was watching her made her believe he didn't buy her excuse. But then the storminess cleared away and was replaced by a softness she hadn't expected. "You've said thank-you. And you're not a charity case. I'm being paid. And . . . for the record, if you want to disagree with me or tell me to go to hell about something, do it. I don't have a fragile ego. You don't owe me anything, okay?"

A tremor ran through her that she hoped wasn't detectable. But hearing him say that, hearing the thickness in his voice, the compassion, made her almost want to believe he could be something more. But he couldn't. Because she could never give up this independence she'd fought so hard for. She could never put her happiness or Dawn's in someone else's hands again.

She hadn't gone into her marriage with no self-esteem. But she'd come out of it floundering, broken, and unsure of who she was. She would never let anyone have that kind of power over her again.

*   *   *

"Hello? Are you even listening to a word I'm saying?"

Scott gave himself a shake and glanced over at Wyatt. They were sitting at dance rehearsal, drinking coffees, at seven in the morning. While his eyes had been on Cat, his mind had been on Olivia. He was hoping she might stay for dinner tonight, but he honestly didn't know what to expect. "Uh, yeah. Sorry, I was up late working on Olivia's estimates."

Wyatt took a sip of coffee. "Oh yeah? How's that going?"

Scott shifted on the uncomfortable bench and wished that just one Saturday he could sleep in. "It's going."

"That's it? It's going? That's all you have to say?"

"Where's Charlotte?" he asked, trying to get his friend off topic. Charlotte was always at the Saturday morning rehearsal. He didn't want to discuss Olivia with Wyatt, and usually when he asked about Charlotte, his friend would go off on some long-winded tale of how amazing his wife was. If it weren't so irritating, it would be endearing.

"Not feeling well. Nothing serious; I think she's just over-tired. She has a lot on her plate with work and wedding planning."

"Oh, well, I hope she feels better soon," Scott said, sipping his coffee.

"So back to Liv. I hear she's coming over tonight?"

Charlotte. He should have known. "Just to go over my final numbers."

"Dinner?"

"I don't know. If we've eaten, then no; if we haven't, then yes."

"Hmph."

The image of Olivia standing there yesterday flashed across his memory, and he wondered if he should ask Wyatt about her marriage. He sensed it was more than just a bad divorce. It was in the way she carried herself, the way she seemed so unsure. "Okay, Wyatt, what's the deal? Before I screw this up. What are you all hiding about Olivia?"

Wyatt stared straight ahead, his jaw clenched. "Why do you want to know?"

"Because . . . because I don't want to do something that's going to hurt her."

Wyatt turned to him slowly. "What are you talking about?"

Scott gave up. "What the hell, Wy. I'm interested. Okay? There, I said it. I just need to know what I'm dealing with first, because I sense there is a lot more going on than a woman get-ting over a divorce."

"Her ex was an asshole. That's the gist of it. For more info, you'll have to ask her. Just . . . don't be a jerk."

Scott tried to keep his temper in check. "This is such great information, Wyatt. Very enlightening. I'm so glad I asked you."

Wyatt made a sound. "Fine. Look, I don't know details. He was abusive. I don't think physically, but he did a number on her. She was a wreck when she came back to town last year. Charlotte can't talk about him without swearing and threatening bodily harm."

Scott stiffened. That didn't sound like Charlotte. Now it made sense. Olivia's reaction to his telling her she shouldn't stay by herself. And yesterday, that distant look in her eyes, the flustered answer when she'd gotten the time wrong. His gut churned just thinking about it. "Is he out of the picture?"

"Uh, yeah. Doesn't see Dawn at all."

"Jerk."

"The worst. She's come a long way, though. I think this studio is good for building her self-confidence back up. She's smart and hardworking. I remember her back in Toronto, when we all lived there. She's four years younger than Charlotte, so she kind of trailed behind us when we'd walk to school together, but sometimes I see that same expression in her eyes. She was the dreamer, the kid with her head in the clouds. Knowing what I know about their upbringing, I think a lot of it was a coping mechanism. We all had them. But I'm happy she's getting her life back on track. So don't screw things up."

Scott shifted in his seat, his eyes on Cat through the glass. "And, uh, their dad is back in town, right?"

Wyatt groaned. "Yeah. He's another one. Don't get me started. He walked out on them. He was a cop. PTSD, but he didn't deal with it until it was too late. And then when he did, he still didn't go back to them. He stayed away for almost twenty years."

Scott stiffened at the news about her father. He was processing the insight Wyatt had just given him. Normally this type of thing might have made him back off, but not this time. Maybe because Olivia appealed to him in a way that no one had in a very long time. In some ways, she appealed to him like no one ever had. And he didn't know why exactly—a hint of something here and there that he connected with.

As the dancers leapt across stage, the lively music blasting around them, Wyatt's warning sat there like a dark cloud. Scott thought about Olivia's father and his own past. His years as a detective were something he didn't talk about. Even now, with Wyatt. But it was there, it was part of who he was. Same for the reason he'd left. And his leaving had been something Hillary had never understood or ever forgiven him for. It was something Olivia might never be able to deal with, because of her past. He didn't know how to reconcile that. How to tell her the truth about his past without scaring her off.

CHAPTER SEVEN

Ruby smiled at Sarah, Harry's eldest daughter, as she passed out the last cup of coffee. She had been trying to concentrate on conversation and learning about each of his children instead of on her nerves, and so far, the evening had gone perfectly.

They were all seated at the dining room table of Harry's house, having just finished a lovely dinner. His three adult children, Sarah, Matthew, and Anne, were here. Sarah's and Matthew's spouses and children had joined them, and they were all welcoming and friendly. If anyone was surprised about her, they hadn't let on. Harry had told her that he'd given them a little info about her but not everything. She was hoping he would get it over with soon.

The moment she'd entered the house tonight, she had felt out of place. She had been here before and was familiar with it and all the family photos, but tonight was different. She wasn't just a person on the outside anymore. But she also wasn't here to replace Harry's wife. She'd made sure to sit beside Harry and not at the other end of the table, where his wife used to sit. She needed to be clear that she was not here to take away from the family he had already built.

"Dad, did you make this pie?" Anne asked, her blue eyes sparkling.

Harry let out a deep chuckle. "I can't take the credit for it. Ruby is a wonderful baker."

Ruby blushed as all eyes turned to her. They were friendly eyes, though, so she forced her shoulders to relax. "Thank you, Harry. It's an old favorite pecan pie recipe, Anne. I hope you enjoyed it."

"I did. It's fantastic—which is why I was sure my dad didn't make it," she said, as laughter erupted around the table. Ruby watched them all with a smile. Harry and his wife had done a fantastic job with their kids. Everyone seemed happy and at ease with each other.

Harry's smile tightened, and Ruby braced herself, already knowing what was happening. "I, uh, I wanted to share some news with all of you. But you'll have to bear with me, because there are lots of parts to this story, and it's not a simple one. There is a lot of family history that you aren't aware of. There were things on my side of the family that your mother and I thought best not to tell you about, so some of this may be a bit of a shock. But I also want you to know that the family history part, keeping you from it, was a decision your mother and I made and Ruby had no part of."

Everyone's faces had turned white, and their gazes went back and forth between Ruby and Harry. Ruby could barely take a breath, and it took everything in her to keep a poised expression.

"So Ruby is a part of your family history?" Matthew asked.

Harry nodded. "She is. You all know that I had a brother . . . and that he died . . . well, he was supposed to get engaged the night *he decided to end his life. Ruby was the woman he was supposed to marry."*

Gasps filled the room, and Ruby wished she could cover her face with the tablecloth. Or that Wendy were here to steal the show. She hated being in the spotlight like this. Harry hadn't even gotten to the hard part yet, and she was already squirming.

She smoothed her sweaty palms down the front of her skirt, trying not to let that night back into her mind. But the memory of sitting at Harry's parents' dining room table, ashamed and embarrassed, kept her in a haze of insecurity. These were different times; she had to remember that. The scandal she had created wouldn't be a scandal now. But maybe it wouldn't be about her. Maybe the scandal was that Harry had hidden this for so many years.

Just when she thought Harry was going to continue, he reached down and grasped her hand in his. He looked down at her, the tenderness, the compassion in his eyes the same as on that night when he had defended her in front of his parents.

He'd always been noble. He'd always believed the best in her. He'd been her defender since the beginning. He was the most noble man she knew, and as soon as tonight was over, she was going to tell him so. She was going to tell him she really was ready to move forward. She was ready for the vows. She was ready to be a part of him finally, body and soul.

* * *

Olivia took in the Cape Cod–style home with admiration. It looked like a newer home, but the design was classic. With its wide front porch and pristine white trim, a striking contrast to the deep-blue wood siding, it stood out against the landscape.

Tall pines and white birch trees filled the property and almost made the house feel secluded, even though they were still in town. Twinkling Christmas lights lined the rooftop and porch, and roped cedar draped over the front door. It was a house that would have made her slow down as she drove by, so she could admire the decorating and wonder about the people who lived inside. Growing up, she had done that. Somehow she'd come to the conclusion that people who decorated like this for Christmas must be happy people. Her parents had never done anything like it. Their apartment had always been chaotic and messy, and so she had naïvely thought that a house like this must mean happiness.

As if things could actually be that simple. And her flawed and immature logic had been proven; she had decorated her and Will's traditional two-story home to the nines. Wreaths on all the windows, twinkling lights, red bows, pots bursting with fresh cedar arrangements, and boxwood garland around the front doors. And she'd learned the hard way that there was no amount of fresh-cedar scent, or lights, or bows, that could make up for a lack of love.

She wondered if Scott had built this house with his wife or if he had moved here after she died. A pang of sympathy hit her in the chest. He was a devoted father and had been on his own raising Cat for a long time. Despite that heartache, he managed to be there for his daughter. Even this house, with the meticulously shoveled driveway and abundant decorations, showed how much he cared. It didn't look like the house of the reckless playboy she'd so desperately wanted to peg him as. Maybe she had done it as a security measure to protect herself from falling for someone who could hurt her.

Taking a deep breath, she grabbed her purse and got out of her car. Time to stop delaying and get to work. This was just a business meeting and nothing else. She needed to stop overanalyzing everything and just get back to normal living. She stomped her feet on the front rug, feeling slightly guilty to be smashing her boots on Santa's face, and then rang the doorbell.

Scott opened the door a moment later, looking as good as the smell wafting out of the house. His dark hair was slightly messy, and a dark shadow lined his strong jaw. But it was those eyes, filled with that warmth, that made her want to believe he was one of the good guys. She was learning things . . . from the men that were nothing like her husband. They were things she should have known, things she should have seen. How could she have missed the fact that Will's eyes had never shone with warmth?

"Come on in, it's freezing out there," Scott said, holding the door a little wider for her.

Olivia stepped into the foyer and almost immediately felt at ease. The lamp on the dark hallway table was on, casting a comforting glow across the space. Wide-planked hardwood floors seemed to extend to the entire main floor, which she could see from the entrance. The large family room, with its peaked ceiling and cozy fireplace, was inviting, complete with an overstuffed leather sectional and a rustic dark coffee table and end tables. Throw blankets and red-and-green Christmas-themed pillows dotted the dark leather. And the house was pristine. Straight out of a Pottery Barn catalog.

"Scott, your home is lovely," she said as she took off her coat.

He accepted it and hung it on the coatrack. "Thank you. I built it three years ago. Cat has always been into decorating, so she helped with that. Come on in. I hope you haven't eaten; we're having spaghetti and meatballs—Cat's request."

"Oh, I hadn't expected to stay for dinner. Really, that's not necessary," she said, following him into the kitchen.

She stopped in the doorway and took in the scene with avid interest. Scott was already over by the enormous gas stove, stirring a tall pot of what she assumed was spaghetti. There was another pot with sauce bubbling away. A glass of red wine sat on the counter near the stove along with three large pasta bowls. The kitchen had white cabinets and stone counters, and the hardwood had been carried into this room as well. A dark table with four chairs nestled in a nook surrounded by massive windows, and she could see trees swaying gently outside, giving the impression of being in a tree house. The massive island housed a sink, next to which sat a cutting board stacked with fresh basil and Parmesan. There was another nook on the far end of the kitchen with a built-in desk made of the same cabinetry, just in a darker color, and a pinboard filled with an assortment of papers and pictures.

"I didn't get around to making dinner earlier, so we're having a late one; I was hoping you'd be able to stay. No pressure, though, if you have other plans," he said, turning to her.

She fought for words as he looked at her. He was a man who was impossible to ignore. His dark-gray Henley fit his broad shoulders and pulled at his chest and then hung loosely over his flat stomach. His worn-in jeans fit like they were made for his athletic frame. But more than all that was how . . . at home . . . he seemed, in any situation. She had made so many assumptions—and she had been embarrassingly wrong about him. He was strong in a very nonthreatening way.

"I . . . no, I have no other plans, but I don't want to impose."

He grabbed a bottle of wine and held it up. "No imposition. Cat would love it if you stayed too. Can I pour you a glass of wine?"

She nodded, walking a little farther into the kitchen when she realized she was still standing in the entrance. "Sure, I'd love one. Um, it smells amazing in here. Did you do all the cooking?"

He nodded, pouring the wine. "I did. It's a hobby. My mother was Italian, and cooking was very important to her—so was teaching me. I learned to cook from a young age. She made me help her in the kitchen, and I learned along the way. I loved her cooking and I loved eating, so it became something I really enjoyed doing."

He placed the glass of wine on the island.

"Thank you. I didn't know you were Italian. I wouldn't have guessed. Are your parents still alive?"

He shook his head. "No, they both passed within a year of each other. Two years ago, actually. It was a car accident. They couldn't have kids for the longest time, and when I came along, I was a surprise in their forties. They were good people."

"I'm sorry to hear that they're both gone." She reached for her glass of wine, his words and what he'd been through sinking in. She knew he was the same age as Wyatt, so not much over thirty. He'd lived life. He'd lost both parents and a spouse and was raising a teenager. He owned his own business, a house, and had somehow remained a positive, good person. Maybe it was his upbringing. That's what she wanted for Dawn, and she panicked sometimes, thinking she'd already messed everything up for her. But she had to believe that although their situation wasn't ideal, she could still give Dawn enough love and stability that she wouldn't have to endure the kind of childhood she and Charlotte had.

He glanced over at her. "Thanks. They were good people. They left me with a lot of great memories and a strong sense of family."

She let her eyes roam the kitchen, her gaze landing on the gingerbread house on the far end of the counter. "Did Cat make the gingerbread house?"

He followed her gaze. "We both did. It's a tradition we started when she was a toddler. Those gingerbread houses were a bit wild but still fun."

"I bet. I can't imagine Dawn with a tube of icing."

He grinned as he stirred the pot on the stove. "Yeah, proceed with caution. I did learn along the way that traditions hold a lot more meaning than I gave them credit for. But kids pay attention; they notice when something is missing. I guess maybe they give stability or security—they say that not everything has to change. The year after Cat's mom died, I didn't want to do any of the Christmas stuff, and I didn't think Cat would want that either. But when the holidays were over . . . she told me how sad it made her. And that gutted me. I had unknowingly brought her more pain. So now we do it all. The gingerbread house, the lights, along with my childhood traditions."

Somehow knowing all that made her feel not so alone. What had happened to her was different, but it was still pain. So that wasn't what separated them. They'd both been through things. Maybe it was the fact that she felt as though she had inflicted her own pain on herself. It was her fault that she hadn't seen Will for who he was. It was her fault for being so desperate for the life she'd imagined as a little girl. It had been naïve to think she could have it all. But Scott hadn't done anything to deserve the heartache he'd faced. And yet he'd found a way to be a positive parent to his daughter, all on his own. "That's great parenting advice. I'll have to remember that."

"I'm not sure I'm qualified to give parenting advice, but maybe it will help. And Dawn has some big traditions built in there because of Ruby."

"You're right. Sometimes I think I get so caught up in what she doesn't have that I forget all that she does have."

"She has a lot. And you're doing a great job," he said, opening a cupboard door.

She sipped her wine as she watched him pour olive oil and vinegar over a salad and toss it in a bowl like he was on a cooking show. His reassurance was handed out so easily, and it warmed her more than the wine. "I feel bad for just standing here. Can I help you with anything?"

He shook his head. "Not at all. Just enjoy your wine. Or you can go call Cat to dinner. I'd yell, but I might scare you off," he said with a lopsided smile.

Her heart leapt a few times, clearly not as guarded as her mind and clearly affected by the smile and dimple, which was utterly charming. Like the man. Needing to get a little space from her unexpected reaction to him, she nodded. "Sure, I'll go call her."

He pointed out the door. "First door at the top of the stairs. She's studying. Or should be studying. She has a history test Monday. Dinner will be ready in about ten minutes. I've learned to give her a ten-minute lead time."

Olivia smiled. "Sure."

She stepped out of the kitchen and in the direction of the stairs, relieved to have the heat leave her face. Pausing at the top of the stairs, she knocked on the door, and when Cat invited her in, she opened it.

Her room was pretty as a picture, pale-pink walls and white furniture. A large window seat filled with plush pillows and twinkling fairy lights took up almost an entire wall. It was framed by built-in bookcases bursting with books and picture frames and memorabilia.

"Oh, Cat, I love your room."

Cat beamed, looking up from the pile of books on her desk. "Thanks. When we moved here, Dad promised me a window seat. I've always wanted one."

"It's gorgeous. I've always wanted one too. And what a gorgeous view on a snowy night," Olivia said, walking forward to admire the snow-covered trees that sparkled like in a storybook.

"I know. I was thinking my room might be getting a little too juvenile, but I guess, since I'm not in high school yet, I can keep it," she said with a shrug.

Olivia sat down on the window seat. "Oh, I'd hold on to this for as long as you can. You'll grow up fast enough, and you can't ever go back to being a kid. Besides, I don't even think it's juvenile. It's very feminine."

Cat smiled, a dimple appearing exactly like her father's. "It's very girly, but I like it."

"As long as it's you, then who cares, right?"

Cat nodded. "You're right. That's what Dad said too. My mom was a total sports addict like my dad. She would always joke that she didn't know where I got the girly gene. I was the one obsessed with ballet when I was a toddler and my mom had to learn how to do the buns and all that. She and my dad would play everything together—they were a part of all those adult leagues for soccer, basketball, hockey, baseball. They desperately tried to get me interested, but I wasn't," she said with a laugh.

Olivia smiled. "Well, your dad seems very proud of you, even if dance wasn't something he was into. And I'm sure your mom would be so proud of everything you've accomplished in dance. You're obviously a hard worker," she said gently.

Cat glanced over at her bookshelf, hopped off the bed, and handed Olivia a framed picture. "This is a picture of the three of us at a baseball game."

Olivia accepted it, her heart squeezing at the picture of the three of them smiling. They all had Toronto Blue Jays baseball caps on and matching T-shirts. It was hard to breathe as she took in the captured moment of their family history. Scott looked younger, not just physically but in his eyes, in his smile. Cat was probably five or six and smiling ear to ear. And her mom, she was so pretty, so happy as she held on to Cat. It was heartbreaking, and Olivia fought the tears that stung her eyes. It wasn't fair. It wasn't fair that these lovely people had had to endure a loss like that, to have such a strong family shattered.

"This is a beautiful picture, Cat. Your mom was beautiful too. You look so much like her."

Cat nodded. "I think so. I have all the pictures from when she was young, and sometimes I look at them to compare."

"That's a good idea. I see a bit of your dad there too, peeking out in the dimple," Olivia said with a smile as she handed back the picture.

Scott appeared in the doorway, a dish towel thrown over one shoulder. "Sorry to interrupt, but dinner's ready."

Olivia stood. "Sorry, I totally got sidetracked."

"My fault, Dad. I was just showing Olivia some of our family pictures. Remember the time we went to that Jays game? That was the best day ever," she said with a wistful sigh before leaving the room.

Olivia watched something flicker across Scott's face as Cat skipped by him. "Dinner smells amazing," she said.

He turned back to her. "I hope you like it."

They made their way back to the kitchen, and Olivia marveled at how clean and tidy the house was. When they arrived in the kitchen, Cat was already sitting at the table, and they joined her. Scott had placed their wineglasses at their places, they each had a heaping bowl of spaghetti and meatballs, and a large salad sat in the center of the table. He'd sprinkled fresh basil and Parmesan on the top of the pasta, and it was a presentation worthy of a cooking show. Cat said grace and, at the end, added that she hoped her mother was watching over them.

Olivia caught something in Scott's gaze as he turned to Cat, who didn't seem to notice as she shoved a large forkful of spaghetti in her mouth.

"Scott, this is delicious," Olivia said, once she'd tasted the rich sauce.

"Thanks. I'm glad you like it. It's a family classic."

"Do you cook, Olivia?" Cat asked, swirling spaghetti onto her fork like a pro.

Olivia took a sip of wine and tried to avoid a firm answer. She had cooked. She had cooked really well. But it had never been good enough. Some nights she'd spent hours making dinner and homemade desserts, only to have Will tell there was something wrong with each dish. And then she'd stopped loving it. And she'd stopped thinking she was even good at it. She forced a smile for Cat. "I do, but not like this. Definitely not Italian."

"My mom was a great cook. She and Dad would cook all the time."

Scott sat back in his chair and grabbed his wineglass. "Not really, Cat. Your mom actually hated cooking. Even Nonna tried to teach her, but she said she'd rather just help clean up instead of cook."

Cat's face turned red. "So you're saying Mom sucked at cooking?"

Scott ran a hand over his jaw. "No, I'm saying she didn't like cooking. Maybe you're just remembering wrong. That's okay. It's not a big deal."

Cat kept her face turned down as she ate, and Olivia felt a pang of sadness for the girl. She was starting to get the impression that Cat felt threatened by her. While Olivia understood why, she was curious if she behaved like this to all of Scott's dates. Not that this was a date. But clearly Cat thought there was something going on between them.

Olivia was determined to break up the tension and maybe help Cat not feel so insecure or alone. "My Grandma Ruby is the great cook in our family. I guess every family has to have at least one. I'm afraid that gene didn't get passed down to me," she said with an awkward laugh.

"Ruby is in a league of her own. Though it's funny, because my mother thought Italian food was unbeatable. She'd try different foods and would always say it was good, but Italian was better," he said with a laugh, glancing over at Cat, whose eyes were still cast down.

"She was right. Nonna was the best cook."

Olivia glanced at Scott. His brow was furrowed and his jaw was clenched. "We have really good memories. And you can make gnocchi from scratch. I have my mom's old tin filled with all the recipes," he said, his voice thick.

Cat gave a shrug, picked up her plate, and walked it over to the counter. "Yeah. Memories. We have lots of great memories about great people. People that can't ever be replaced."

She marched out of the room, and Olivia blinked back tears, her chest heavy as she watched Cat. Scott said something under his breath and then turned to her. His eyes were wet and his jaw was set. "I'm sorry. Those are old wounds, and it's getting directed at you. Unfairly."

Olivia toyed with her napkin and forced herself to maintain eye contact. "I think she's feeling threatened by my being here all of a sudden. Maybe she's misinterpreting all of this, you and

I. We're just working together on this project, but Cat clearly thinks there's more."

"Olivia . . . maybe she's picking up on something, and maybe she's right. Maybe there is something more here. At least there could be, if you wanted that."

She broke out in a cold sweat. This was not what she'd expected. He was supposed to deny everything. He was supposed to say they could only be friends. He was also not supposed to look so . . . alluring.

She shouldn't want to reach out and touch his hand, to see what his skin felt like. She cleared her throat and stood, needing to get out of there. Now.

"I, um, I've had a really crappy two years. Four years, maybe. I'm only now just getting my life back together with this business and figuring out how to be a single mom and now planning a wedding too. I just . . . casual stuff isn't in the cards for me, and neither is anything long-term. Even though you do a really great job of presenting like man of the year and not a pig or anything . . . omigosh, I keep rambling. I'm going to stop talking now," she said as she loaded her plate in the dishwasher and prayed that she could somehow take back every stupid thing she'd just said.

Scott walked over to her, coming to her side of the dishwasher so it wasn't separating them. "I'm not sure where exactly to begin with all that. Pretty loaded."

She nodded repeatedly, because she didn't trust herself to speak.

His lips twitched. "I'm glad I haven't been grouped into the pig category, first off."

She almost groaned out loud at her stupidity but managed to stay composed before walking to the front door. "It really was meant as a compliment. And I really need to get going. Maybe you could just email me all the quotes and final estimate? That would be best. Oh, and I'm sorry for just taking off, but it's for the best. Just like that compliment. It was just a compliment."

"That's how I took it."

He held out her jacket for her, and she found herself a tad flustered at the gesture. "Good. And the whole casual stuff was really just referencing all the women I've heard about you dating in the last year or so."

Somehow, with that statement, all the humor left. The hint of a dimple, the twitching of his lips, and the lightness in his eyes just vanished. She held her breath, waiting for the fallout. Would he be insulting now that she'd inadvertently offended him? He rubbed the back of his neck, and when his eyes met hers again, she wondered how she ever could have thought he'd be mean to her.

His eyes were filled with something that belonged to only him—a pain that only he knew and lived and that had made him who he was. Her remarks hadn't punctured a thin veneer. He knew who he was and wasn't threatened by her opinion.

"When you said you've had a crappy few years, I get it. Different situation, but I get it. I know certain relationships aren't easy to move on from. I never meant to add pressure. And yes, I've dated a lot this last year. It was my attempt at moving on with life while I'm still young. As for Cat, I didn't expect this reaction from her, but I think it's because, in all the dates I've been on . . . no one has ever come home with me. No woman has ever sat down and had dinner with the two of us since her mom. I should have realized that and prepped her for it. This wasn't a date, but she thought it was. I'm sorry you were caught in the middle of this."

Olivia opened her mouth, but the words she wanted to stay were stuck inside. Like her heart was telling her to hold on and hold back because it could be too dangerous and they had both already been through so much. But there was something about him, a gentleness in a strong package, that made her want to trust him. And yet she just couldn't.

"She's a great kid. And I hate to think I've brought her any kind of sadness tonight. I . . . it's probably for the best that you and I had this chat so we know where we stand. Thanks, Scott. Dinner was delicious. I guess I'll see you at the studio tomorrow."

She stepped out into the dark night, the distinct feeling that she had ruined something that could have been great following her to the car. She was aware of him still standing there and realized he was waiting for her to get into her car. When her headlights were on and she was driving away, she glanced back to see the front door closing.

She breathed an audible sigh of relief. It was quickly replaced by the realization that not once had she felt self-conscious or not good enough. She had been consumed by Scott and Cat and the world they had built together.

But more than anything, she believed she was the one missing out. On Scott and the wonderful little family he'd created. She had walked out like a coward when he could have used a friend.

*   *   *

Scott watched Olivia drive away, inwardly cursing himself. Clearly, he'd pushed too hard. He knew from Wyatt that Olivia's divorce had been messy, that her ex was a douche. But Scott had misinterpreted the warmth in her eyes for something more . . . or something she wasn't ready for. But he'd loved having her over here, and it hadn't felt strange to have a woman here with them. For a long time, he couldn't have even entertained the idea of having another woman in the house with them, but tonight it had felt right.

Olivia had a warmth to her that made him want to believe that family could be a possibility for him again. Tonight, when Cat had been speaking about her mom, about her grandparents, it had gutted him. It was just the two of them and had been for too long. And maybe that was part of the reason Cat was playing games tonight. Regardless, he needed to sit down with her. He knew it wasn't Olivia she had an issue with but simply having any woman here.

He took the stairs two at a time and knocked on the door.

"Busy. Studying, remember?"

He fought the urge to come back with a reminder that he was the one who'd originally told her to study. But whatever. One of the best pieces of parenting advice he'd received was to learn to pick his battles. This wasn't one of them.

"Yeah, I won't be long."

"Fine."

He opened the door and forced a smile as he walked over and sat on the edge of her bed. He moved aside a textbook, glancing at the cover. "This looks interesting."

She rolled her eyes. "Sure, if you have no life."

He shrugged. "Well, then it's perfect for me."

She shifted her eyes back down to her notes. "I didn't say it. You did."

He chuckled. "Cat, what's up? What was going on tonight?"

She sighed heavily and leaned back against the headboard, staring up at the ceiling. "Honestly, Dad, I don't know. I don't know what I was thinking. It was messed up. Like, I know you can get married again. You're like not *that* old to have to be alone for the rest of your life. I know everything you're doing for me, and I was good with you going on dates. But there's something about Olivia. I liked her from the minute I met her at Ruby's. Tonight it was different . . . when she knocked on my door, I remembered Mom knocking on my door. And at first I was angry that it wasn't Mom, even though I knew it wouldn't be. But then I was mad at myself that I wasn't exactly angry that it was Olivia standing there."

Scott rubbed at his shoulder, the ache in his chest painful as he listened to Cat's vulnerability. "I think I understand that, Cat."

She blinked rapidly, still staring at the ceiling. "I was mad at myself for being happy to see her. And she has this way about her . . . not that she reminds me of Mom . . . but like, she's a mom who feels like a mom. And I was angry about that because I don't want another mom, and I don't want to like her as much as I do."

He took a deep breath, praying for the right words. "Everything you just said is normal. And actually really insightful. This is hard. Losing a parent is hard. So when we try and build a new life without them, it's going to feel weird. For me too."

"Is that why you built this house?"

Hell. She was way too intuitive. "Not exactly. But there got to be a point where it became hard to move on with a new life when we were living in a place that was so much a part of our old life. I wanted a fresh start for us. I wanted us to build new memories. Not to forget the old ones, but not to have to relive old ones day in and day out and have them compete with the new memories we're trying to make.

"Not everyone is like that. But for me, for us, I thought it was the right way. I was drowning back at the old place, you know? You and I are building this new life together, and I wanted where we live to reflect that. Not to erase the family we were or to erase Mom, but to give us a better shot at moving on. I will love your mom for the rest of my life. Nothing, no one, will ever change that."

"I miss her so much," Cat choked out.

He swallowed against the lump in his throat. "I do too."

"But also, you should date Olivia."

He let out a laugh. "Thanks. So glad you approve. I just don't think she's interested or ready right now."

Cat scowled and scrambled to sit upright. "What? Who wouldn't be interested in you?"

He grinned. "Was that an actual compliment?"

Her face turned red. "Maybe. But seriously, Dad. I think this is my fault, and she probably thinks I'm a brat and doesn't want to have to deal with me."

"You're not a brat, and you're not the reason. She had a difficult divorce, and she's probably afraid of getting hurt again. I can't blame her."

Cat tapped her finger against her chin, the gleam in her eye making him nervous. "I think I should talk to her. She's great. I really like Olivia."

"Uh, please don't talk to her about this. It's kind of a delicate issue. If she's ready, she's ready. If she's not, then I'll move on." The minute he said he'd just move on, though, that didn't feel right either.

"Don't worry, Dad. I still think this is my fault. I'll find a way to make it right with her. Maybe we can invite her for dinner with her baby. She's adorable. Oh! I know, why don't we ask her to go skating at the outdoor rink. Do babies skate?"

He was growing increasingly worried about Cat not taking no for an answer. Who knows what she was planning on telling Olivia? "Uh, I'm not sure she skates. And that's nice of you to want to invite Dawn, but maybe we'll just take a break from planning," he said, standing, hoping this was the end of this conversation.

"Dad, I can totally see you backing away from the bed. Don't worry, I got this."

He stood there, jamming his fists into the front pocket of his jeans as he remembered the last time Cat had told him, "I got this." The time she proceeded to set their dinner on fire.

Yeah, this wouldn't be good.

CHAPTER EIGHT

It was amazing to Ruby that even though over four decades had passed since the night she'd sat with Sister Juliette in Richard and Harry's home, scared and humiliated and announcing her pregnancy, she could still feel the emotions coursing through her body. As though no time had passed.

As though she hadn't raised a child on her own, as though she hadn't run her own business, hadn't come to terms with everything and realized she shouldn't be ashamed. Richard and Harry's parents had loved her. They had always been kind. Until they hadn't. Until they'd turned on her and tossed her out like garbage, just like her own parents had.

Sitting here, in the silence of the freshly shared secret, Ruby braced herself for censure. Maybe they would blame her for Richard's death too. Maybe they would think she wasn't good enough for their father. Sarah was the first to speak, her eyes filled with tears, as she stood and walked over to Ruby. And the condemnation Ruby had braced herself for never came. Instead, Sarah hugged her and whispered how sorry she was, how painful that must have been. And then there was Anne, who did the same. And then Matthew.

"Thank you so much for understanding," Ruby said as the three of them surrounded her and Harry. "But there is more to the story. I was pregnant when Richard died. I had a girl. She's alive. Her name is Wendy."

"She would be our first cousin?" Matthew asked.

Harry nodded. "Yes. And Wendy has two daughters and one grandchild."

Sarah smiled. "This is amazing. Family we didn't even know we had. And they all live in Silver Springs?"

Ruby nodded. This wasn't over. She was anxious for Harry to finish and tell them the rest. "They do. They would love to meet you. I have been running a bed-and-breakfast there and would love to have you all over on Christmas Eve. It's an annual tradition, and anyone who doesn't have a place to go or food to eat on Christmas Eve is welcome to attend. There is usually some kind of excitement, and I'm hoping that maybe you will be the Christmas excitement this year."

After a round of warm promises to attend, Harry interrupted. "There's something else I wanted to tell you."

He reached for Ruby's hand, and she clung to its solid warmth, thinking that when this was all over, she was going to tell him how much it meant to her that he was always willing to be her champion. She was sorry she'd doubted it before, that she'd held back because of fear. The first time, all those years ago, and again these last few weeks.

Harry's hand in hers went from warm and solid to clammy and cold a moment later. She looked up at him, frowning when she saw he'd broken out in a sweat. He wasn't looking at her anymore. He had stopped speaking. "Harry?" she prompted.

But instead of answering, he leaned forward, gasping out loud, as Matthew caught him.

As they all circled around him, Sarah called 911.

Ruby held on to his hand, somehow thinking that if she held on, he wouldn't leave her. She was praying that he would make it, out loud; she was praying in front of all of them. Like Sister Juliette had prayed when the woman who'd taken Ruby in was dying.

Her heart pounded as though it were breaking, as though it were reliving the loss. It couldn't be too late; their love story couldn't be over like this. She prayed that he wouldn't be taken from her again, that she hadn't ruined her second chance with him because of fear.

*   *   *

"Thanks so much for meeting me here instead of Greens on Main to discuss plans for the wedding," Olivia said as Charlotte walked into the lobby of the studio.

Charlotte gasped, looking around. "Liv, this looks like an entirely new place. I can't believe the progress."

Olivia was comforted by her sister's genuine response. "Thanks. I know, this was one of the first spaces we needed to fix up. Scott has been here night and day. One of the studios is all finished too, which is such a relief."

"Well, it's great. This looks like such a welcoming space. And I bet there's a ton of natural light through those glass double doors. What are your plans for this?" She motioned to what would be the lobby.

"I'm going to have some viewing benches facing this room. It will probably be the toddler classroom, because it's too small for a full studio. And those parents will definitely want to look in. Then at the front entrance, I'm thinking some more seating and maybe cubbies and hooks. Then over here is the office. I'm not sure there will be anyone sitting there besides me when we start, but I think this is the perfect spot."

Charlotte nodded as Olivia spoke. "That all sounds amazing. You must feel so much better now that Scott is here and getting this back on track."

Olivia tried to look casual, even though Saturday night immediately popped into her head. She hadn't mentioned anything to Charlotte, and she hoped Scott wasn't going to tell Wyatt either. Her behavior had been embarrassing, and so far, she'd managed to avoid Scott all day.

"He's great. Okay, I've got my planner and a notepad behind the desk. Why don't I meet you at the bench?"

"Perfect. I have my planner too and all my color-coding markers," Charlotte said with a laugh.

"Okay, well, maybe we get down all the details we already know?"

Charlotte ripped off a piece of paper. "Already done. Grandma is insisting on immediate family and closes friends only. But even then, with the size of Harry's family, I think we're sitting at around fifty people, so I don't know how we'll pull that off."

"Cocktail reception. It has to be. That way it doesn't become too formal either. Oh, and then it can be a candlelight wedding."

Charlotte inhaled sharply. "Yes, candlelight wedding. Okay, what else? How about a local caterer?"

Olivia nodded. "Perfect. Grandma said finger foods and desserts."

They continued planning and jotting down notes and dividing up who was doing what for the next hour. Feeling better that they had finally gotten a handle on everything, they started packing up their things.

"So Wyatt and I were wondering if you wanted to come by for dinner this weekend?"

Olivia paused, eyeing Charlotte carefully. Charlotte never formally invited her over. "Oh, sure. Is it just me?"

Charlotte squirmed in her seat. "I think Scott might be there."

Olivia leaned forward. "I knew it."

Charlotte rolled her eyes. "It's nothing like that. Just some friends getting together for dinner. Don't make it a big deal."

Olivia sat back in her seat. "Char . . ."

"Come on, Liv, it's not like you have plans or anything."

She folded her arms across her chest. "Maybe I do."

"I just saw your planner, and you don't."

"Ugh. I haven't finished my Christmas shopping yet. I've barely started."

"Well, everything in town closes at like six anyway."

Olivia shot her a look. "You're all done with your shopping, aren't you?"

Charlotte winced. "For a month, but that's totally not normal, and I acknowledge that. Back to you. Come over."

Olivia sighed dramatically. "Well, maybe Grandma has plans and won't be able to watch Dawn."

"Then bring her. Scott loves babies."

"I knew it! It's a total setup." She picked at some imaginary lint on her sweater before eyeing Charlotte again. "Has he said yes?"

Charlotte smiled. "Yup, and he seemed quite enthused."

Olivia ignored the jolt that ran through her. "He was probably just excited he didn't have to cook dinner."

"Nope. Wrong again. Here's how I know he's genuinely happy that you're coming—I told him Wyatt is doing the cooking, and he still sounded happy. No one is excited when Wyatt cooks."

Olivia almost laughed. Her poor brother-in-law's reputation in the kitchen was legendary. "Is Cat coming?"

"Probably. She and Sam are inseparable."

That could be a problem. The image of Cat, desperately talking about her mom, still stung. Olivia really liked Cat and hated that the girl was so threatened by her. "I'm not sure it's a good idea, Char."

Charlotte frowned. "What? Why not? What now?'

Olivia groaned and sat back in her chair, avoiding Charlotte's hawkish gaze. Instead, she focused on the view of her empty office. Why couldn't things be simple anymore? Why weren't the cedar roping and twinkling white lights and wreaths and jingle bells enough to make everyone happy? When had life gotten this complicated?

"I think Cat feels threatened by me. She misinterpreted my relationship with Scott, and she made it clear she doesn't want him involved with anyone."

"Oh, Liv. Are you sure?"

Olivia nodded. "Not that anything was going to happen. But still. I don't want to make her feel awkward or stress her out. She's only thirteen."

Charlotte bit her lower lip. "Well, I think if Scott thought it was a problem, he wouldn't have accepted. This might be difficult for Cat, for sure, but it doesn't mean that Scott can't ever have a relationship again."

"Charlotte, we barely know each other. There is no relationship. You are totally reading into something that isn't there."

Her sister smiled sweetly. "Then there isn't a reason for you not to come. You won't have to worry about Cat if you and Scott are just friends."

Olivia tipped her coffee cup, wishing there were more inside. She was just going to have to be clear with her sister. "Char, I'm not interested in anyone. And if I were, it wouldn't be Scott. I thought we already went over this. I need someone less good-looking."

"Says no one ever. What is wrong with you?"

"Uh, how about someone who has been told over and over again that they're a fat pig?"

Olivia stopped breathing and put her head in her hands. She couldn't believe she'd blurted that out. She wanted to crawl under the table and not come out until the new year. It was one thing for Charlotte to know that Will had been emotionally abusive, but to actually repeat one of his insults out loud was humiliating.

"I'm going to kill him."

Her sister's thinly whispered threat forced her to remove her hands from her face. Charlotte was sitting there, her face red as the stuffed Santa suit in the corner, her eyes glittering with tears and rage.

"You're not going to kill anyone. We're divorced. It's over."

Charlotte shook her head, tears spilling from her eyes. "It's not over. It's not. Because if it were, my beautiful, amazing little sister wouldn't be sitting here telling me that she can't go out with a gorgeous man. It means that Will's words are still impacting your life. And that breaks my heart and makes me want to break things of his."

"I had no idea you had such a violent nature," Olivia joked through her own tears.

"It's not funny, Liv. No. So this is what we're going to do: you're coming to our house on Saturday night, and we're going to have a great time and you're going to claim the life you deserve. You're not going to let Will have control over your life now. You gave him control once, and now you've taken it back. Right?"

Olivia found it hard to breathe, the emotion clogging her throat making it almost impossible to speak. "You're kind of a bully, Char."

"Just never let me in a room alone with that man."

Both of their phones pinged at the exact same time. Olivia's stomach dropped, and they both stood at the same time, phones in hand, as they read the family group text.

Harry was in the hospital.

CHAPTER NINE

Ruby didn't know how long she'd been sleeping when she felt a hand on her shoulder. She awoke with a start, and her eyes immediately sought out Harry's closed ones. The beeping of the hospital machines had been a constant in her dreams. She looked up to see Anne standing there, her face pale but her smile warm.

"Your family is here, Ruby. We all spoke and made introductions outside. They can't come in, but they would love to see you."

Ruby tried to take a deep breath against the heaviness in her chest. Of course they were here. She'd known when she had texted them from the ER waiting room that they wouldn't leave her here alone, even though she'd insisted she was fine and was with Harry's family.

Ruby nodded and stood. "Thank you, Anne. Here, you sit with your father now. Can I get you a coffee?"

Anne took over her seat beside the bed. "No thank you, Ruby. If I drink any more coffee, I don't think I'll ever sleep again."

Ruby nodded and squeezed her shoulder. "Good point. I'll go visit with my family."

She opened the door that led to the waiting room and was immediately enveloped by hugs and whispers from all her girls—Wendy, Charlotte, and Olivia.

"Mom, I knew this was a bad idea. I could tell for weeks that Harry wasn't looking good. It was all this pressure about the wedding. Does he even have the cash to afford a ring like that?"

Before Ruby could even laugh at that ridiculous statement, Charlotte stepped in, ready as always. "Mom, you did not know Harry wasn't well. No one did. And I hardly think that buying that ring and marrying Grandma was the cause of his heart attack."

Wendy rolled her eyes. "Always such a cynic, Charlotte. What happened to you?"

Olivia put her arm around Ruby's shoulders and led her over to the chairs. "Okay, Grandma, tell us how he is. How bad is it?"

Ruby sat down wearily. "He didn't actually have a heart attack. But they did find a heart defect that had gone undetected all these years. So the bad news is that he will have to undergo heart surgery within the year, but the good news is that the prognosis is good. And his doctor said he was in good health and is fit for a man his age."

"Well, how could he be in good health if he's here?" Wendy asked.

Charlotte opened her mouth, but Ruby shook her head. She did not want Charlotte getting upset on her behalf.

"Mom, honestly. You don't know anything about Harry's health. I don't think the doctor would have said that if it wasn't true," Olivia said.

Ruby was intrigued that it was Olivia who had stepped in to say something. That was usually Charlotte's role. But speaking of not looking well, Charlotte was rather pale. "Thank you, Olivia. Charlotte dear, are you sure you're all right? You're not coming down with something, are you?"

Charlotte's face turned red. "What? Really? I feel fine. Just a little tired, that's all."

"Mom, Harry is the one in the hospital. Charlotte is fine. She always looks like that when she's stressed. So tell me, what did his family say about you getting married?"

Ruby inhaled sharply when she made eye contact with Anne, who was walking toward them. Her mouth dropped open, and the pain that swept through her face told Ruby that everything she'd feared was happening all over again.

"What? Married?" Anne repeated.

Ruby nodded, standing slowly, very aware of everyone's eyes on her now. She had to show her girls she wasn't the same young woman who had been so ashamed. "Yes, we were going to tell all of you tonight."

"Wait, who's getting married?" Matthew asked, approaching with Sarah.

Ruby dared not look toward Wendy, who was probably ready to fall off her chair at this drama. "Your father and I were going to tell you tonight. He, well . . . he proposed, and I accepted. I know we haven't known each other long and all of this is a huge surprise. Take some time to let it sink in. I just want you to know that I love your father very much. But I also know that you all are his priority. I know how much he loves his family and how much he loved your mother. I don't ever want to try and replace her or disrespect

119

her memory or the love they shared. I just want to be with Harry for as long as we both have left." She stopped speaking when her voice wobbled and she was pretty sure she'd wrung her hands into a wrinkled mess.

Anne's eyes were on the ground, but Sarah and Matthew came rushing forward with hugs and congratulations.

"We just want Dad to be happy, and he seems so happy with you, Ruby," Sarah said, giving her a kiss on the cheek.

"Welcome to the family, Ruby," Matthew added, shaking her hand.

Anne looked up, offering her a smile that wasn't reflected in her eyes. "Yes, welcome."

*   *   *

"Olivia, I need a ride to Toronto tonight."

Olivia put her hairbrush down on the bathroom counter and forced herself to remain calm as her mother appeared in the doorway with her demand. "Mom, you know I'm going to Charlotte and Wyatt's for dinner. You agreed to look after Dawn. She's already asleep."

"That's easy. We'll just put her in the car seat, and she'll doze off again. Just blow them off. You see them all the time. Besides, Wyatt is cooking. I'll spare you the Tums you'll be taking later."

Olivia forced herself to remain calm. This was classic behavior. The old Olivia might have actually caved and stressed herself out by driving to Toronto with Dawn and then rushing back and arriving late at Charlotte and Wyatt's in an attempt to keep everyone happy. Everyone but herself.

"That's mean. I'm not going to blow them off, and I'm not going for the food, I'm going for the company. I never get out. You volunteered to do this before I even asked you."

Her mother sighed theatrically. "Of course, because I really wanted to. It's just that one of my dearest friends is in town, and I really wanted to see her."

"Then take a bus," Olivia said, reeling. She would have to bring Dawn with her. It was fine, of course, but who the heck wanted to wake a baby once they were finally asleep? And then there was the fact that her mother never babysat. What had really happened here was that her mother had gotten a better offer.

Her mother rolled her eyes and walked into the bathroom. "You know, you're going to a lot of effort for a night with your sister and Wyatt."

Olivia swallowed the urge to tell her to mind her own business. "It's been a while since I went out and got dressed up and did my hair."

Her mom nodded, her face softening. "That's true. You deserve it. Especially now that you lost some of the baby weight."

Anger, then shame shot through Olivia. She clutched the edge of the counter and squeezed her eyes shut. She had worked hard to get to the good place where she didn't hate the woman looking back at her in the mirror. Where she could stand in front of a bunch of women in dance leggings and not obsess over her appearance. Where she could get ready for an evening out and be confident.

She slowly turned to face her mother. "So if I *hadn't* lost some weight, I wouldn't deserve this?"

Her mother pursed her lips. "Don't twist everything I'm saying so I'm the bad guy."

Olivia's heart raced, blood pulsing, her skin prickling with heat. "I'm not. I'm just asking you to clarify what you meant by that."

Her mother threw up her hands. "Yes, yes, if you hadn't lost weight, then a man like Scott wouldn't be interested in you. And he's going to be there, and that's why you're dressing up. That's what I'm saying. Those are facts. That's the real world. You always had your head in the clouds, always playing with Barbies and pretend families."

A year ago, that comment would have made Olivia shut her mouth and retreat. She'd have felt exposed and ashamed of her daydreams and her childhood behavior. The shame and the hiding had branched out to all areas of her life—in how she'd hidden Will's abuse from Charlotte and Grandma Ruby, in how she'd stayed away from friends and family after she'd gained weight. She had never had the confidence to just be who she was, whatever that was at any moment in time. If something went wrong, it was her fault, or else her reaction was her fault. But not anymore.

She stared at her mother, who was standing there without a clue, without a smidgeon of self-doubt or awareness. "Did you ever wonder why? Why those stupid dolls were so important to me?"

Her mother frowned. "Are you about to blame me for your obsession with dolls?"

Olivia was shaking with suppressed rage and resisted the urge to pull her hair out. "Yes. Yes, I am about to blame you, because I have never blamed you for anything, because every time I watch someone in our family try and tell you what's wrong with your behavior, you just play the victim. So I've been too afraid of hurting your feelings, even though I've had to witness you hurting everyone else's feelings. I played with those dolls to escape all the yelling in our house, to escape watching you drink yourself into a dead sleep, then to escape the fact that we didn't have a dad who wanted us anymore, and then a mother who tossed us out to our grandmother's because you would rather drink then take care of us. And then, when it was all over, when you finally decided to get your shit together, you walked back in as though nothing had happened."

Her mother held up her hand, not looking the least bit contrite. "Wow. Talk about throwing back all my tragedies in my face, Olivia. I have lived through hard times, and I would expect that if you really loved me, you would show some compassion."

Olivia blinked, the rage in her body gradually giving way to incredulity. They weren't having the same argument. Somehow it was all about her mother again. Slowly, her hand shaking, she shut the door to the bathroom.

"Well, that's gratitude for you," her mother said with a huff.

Olivia leaned against the door and slowly sank down to the floor. It was useless. Charlotte was right: there was no point. The only way to get along with her mother was to not engage in arguments and just simply nod in agreement. But that didn't seem right either. She had accepted all the crap people threw her way. She'd done the blank nod, the *please stop talking so I don't have to dream about poking my eyeballs out* stare. She couldn't spend the rest of her life doing that.

And how the heck was she now supposed to walk over to Wyatt and Charlotte's house and pretend everything was fine? And worse, how was she supposed to see Scott again?

She picked up her phone and stared at the screen, wondering if she should just text Charlotte and tell her the truth and then ask her to come up with an excuse for her.

No. She couldn't do that. It would mean she'd spend the night here wallowing in self-pity while her mother went to the city without a care in the world. She needed to get her mind off the family drama. She would just have to bring Dawn with her.

An hour later, she was finally standing on Wyatt and Charlotte's doorstep, a sleeping Dawn tucked on her shoulder. She'd parked the stroller on the corner of the porch and grabbed the diaper bag. Their house was lit up almost as brightly as Grandma Ruby's, and Olivia felt a pang of loneliness as she stood there alone with Dawn. This wasn't how the night was supposed to go. She was still carrying the hurt from her mom bailing on watching Dawn, but she knew she had to push it aside or she wouldn't be good company.

The front door swung open, and Charlotte was standing there. "Omigosh, why are you standing on the porch and not ringing the doorbell? Okay, what happened? Here, give me Dawn. You look wiped."

Great. She already looked tired, and the evening hadn't even started. She took her coat off, her eyes going to the Christmas decorations. The Christmas tree was in front of the bay window. She'd seen it from the street, those twinkling white lights beckoning her. Since her sister had moved in, the house had taken on a softer edge, and Wyatt had willingly given up control of the decor.

"Mom bailed. Some friend in Toronto is more important than looking after Dawn. Even though she'd already committed. Whatever," Olivia said, hanging her coat in the closet.

"Ugh. Why am I not surprised? Well, don't worry, we're happy Dawn is here."

Olivia smiled. "Thanks, Char. I left her in her pajamas. I didn't have the heart to wake her and get her all dressed up."

"Of course not. She's family. And frankly, I'd rather be in a Christmas-tree-patterned velour onesie right now than jeans," Charlotte said, after they'd taken care not to wake Dawn while removing her coat and hat.

Olivia laughed softly. "I know, right?"

"Come in. The girls are in Sam's room, and Wyatt and Scott are in the kitchen. Poor Wyatt; he already burned the pizza he was making, and now Scott is lecturing him. I think we may have to order out at this point."

Olivia smiled, the burnt smell in the house now making sense. She swallowed her nerves as she followed Charlotte into the kitchen. Scott and Wyatt were standing behind the island, two beers on the counter and a charred pizza in front of them.

They both smiled at her and Dawn as though they hadn't seen her in weeks. The warmth flowing from them was enough to soothe her hurt from her mom's change of plans.

"Hey, my favorite sister-in-law and niece," Wyatt said, walking over to greet them.

"Hey, Wyatt, she's a sleepy little guest tonight," Olivia said.

"Want a break from holding her?" he asked, already reaching for Dawn.

"That would actually be great. She's getting so big," Olivia said, handing her off. Wyatt expertly took her without jostling her or waking her.

"He's just offering so he doesn't have to make dinner," Scott said with a low laugh.

Wyatt sat down at the set table with Dawn. "As if. I can cook and hold Dawn at the same time."

"You can't cook without a baby; how are you going to cook with one?" Scott said, opening the fridge.

Olivia tried not to stare. He was a bit more dressed up tonight, wearing a pale-blue sweater that seemed to make his eyes the exact shade of the water in the Bahamas. His dark jeans weren't the usual worn-in ones, but these too fit him perfectly. And the warmth in his eyes—there was no judgment there. No awkwardness. So it was all her. She needed to get over her insecurities and just have a good time.

"Charlotte, do you mind if I whip something up?" Scott asked.

"Be my guest. I will totally help out," Charlotte said, standing.

"Nope. Not at all. I've got this. I know you're under the weather," Scott said, pulling a carton of cream out of the fridge and then heading to the pantry for tomato jars and a box of pasta.

Olivia tore her eyes from Scott, who was clearly at home in their kitchen, to Charlotte, who was sitting down beside Wyatt.

His hand was holding hers, and the other was resting on Dawn's back. Dawn was drooling on his shoulder, her eyelids not even flinching. Charlotte did look pale.

"Scott, why don't I help," she said, standing and heading over to the island. There. She was out of her comfort zone.

"Make sure he pours you a glass of wine first. You'll need it. He's a drill sergeant in the kitchen," Wyatt said, taking a sip of beer.

"Can I get you a glass of wine?" Scott asked, holding up the bottle that Wyatt always had on hand for her and Charlotte.

"That would be nice, thanks," she said, as he poured her a glass and handed it to her. His fingers brushed against hers, and it was like a current running down her spine, reminding her that she was indeed still very much alive.

"You're welcome. You don't have to help. I won't mind if you just want to sit down and chill out," he said, filling up a pot with water.

"Nope. Tell me what to do," she said, taking a sip of wine.

"Okay then, can you chop a few cloves of garlic while I dice the onions?"

"Sure. What are you making?"

"I thought I'd whip up some penne in a vodka sauce," he said, already dicing expertly.

"Show-off," Wyatt chortled.

They all laughed softly, careful not to wake Dawn.

"So how's Harry doing?' Scott asked as they worked side by side.

"Much better. I think Grandma said he's coming home tomorrow. I'm happy for them. We were so worried," she said.

Scott stirred the sauce that had started simmering. "That's good. Ruby deserves a lot of years with him."

"Definitely."

An hour later they were all seated around the kitchen table, Cat and Sam included. Dawn was slowly waking up, and she sat up with a start, her eyes wide and looking for Olivia. Wyatt immediately handed her over, and she seemed somewhat content to sit there for a moment.

"Okay, she's so cute. And those pajamas," Cat said, smiling at Dawn.

Dawn smiled back but then hid her face in Olivia's neck. The girls fussed over her, and soon Dawn was demanding some of the penne. Scott stood before Olivia could and filled up a plate of penne.

"Dad, omigosh, she's eighteen months, not eighteen with a plate that big," Cat said, laughing, and everyone joined her.

"Hey, wait till she tries my pasta. I can't have her leaving hungry," Scott said, sitting back down beside Olivia and placing the plate in front of her.

Dawn allowed Olivia to use a fork and feed her. Olivia wondered if it was because there was a crowd and her daughter was too shy to eat with her hands. Dawn's eyes grew wide as she tasted the pasta and then pointed for more.

Scott sat back with a satisfied grin. "Wyatt, I'd say that was a success. And as my mother would say, *mangia, mangia*."

As their laughter filled the kitchen, a warmth spread through Olivia. She had planned on an adult night, and now, with Dawn sitting on her lap, it was like it was meant to be. Everyone here had welcomed her as though she wasn't an inconvenience.

Olivia and Charlotte had always been an inconvenience when they were kids. But this—this was living. They filled up the table, and there was a mess everywhere. The giant bowl of pasta was almost done, and they were all full and happy and . . . real. They were family.

CHAPTER TEN

"You can't keep fussing over me, because I never actually had a heart attack, remember, Ruby?" Harry said, chuckling as she fluffed the pillow behind him. They were in his bedroom, and he was sitting up in bed.

"Nonsense. It was still a hospital stay, so you get to be fussed over," she said, stopping to give him a quick kiss.

When she pulled back, he held on to her wrist. "I know I left you in a bit of a lurch at the hospital."

"Oh, yes, that. I guess you had a good excuse," she said with a laugh.

"I hear it went well?"

She nodded. "You really have a great family. I think Anne was a little unsure, but hopefully she'll come around once she gets used to the idea and I get to know her better."

Harry let out a deep sigh. "She was always the one who was slightly more unsure. She was devastated when her mom died. I mean, we all were, of course, but she never really seemed to come out of it the way Matthew and Sarah have. Maybe it's because she's alone. But I'll talk to her too."

Ruby nodded. "Time can do amazing things."

"I wanted to talk to you about an idea I had. I know you want to be married on Christmas Eve at your house, and I think that's perfect, especially since it will be the anniversary of us first seeing each other again. But afterwards, for our honeymoon, what do you think if we go on a cruise? We'll have our privacy, because we don't have to hang around everyone on the ship all the time if we don't want. We'll see a bit of the world together. We can get a luxury suite with a balcony and a concierge. I think you deserve a little spoiling."

There was so much packed into that statement that she didn't even know where to begin. The honeymoon was something she'd thought about nonstop because she was nervous. Nervous about everything, but she couldn't deal with that now. The other thing was the money. It was a lovely gesture to have a suite and a—wow—concierge, but she didn't have that kind of money.

"Harry, that is a wonderful idea, but that sounds expensive. I mean, that could cost a lot, and I know this house is grand, but I don't have that kind of money."

He smiled. "I'm glad you don't mind. Ruby, money is not an issue for me. Of course I wouldn't come up with an idea like that and then expect you to help me pay. I have more than enough for both of us. If money is an issue for you, I hope you'd let me help you with your expenses."

She stared at him, not sure what to say. It was funny, because she'd been on her own since she was eighteen. She'd gone from *living a comfortable middle-class life under her parents' roof to being completely penniless, to being a housekeeper, to then inheriting this old house and running it as a bed-and-breakfast. And she hadn't done it alone—she'd had wonderful, strong women who'd helped her at every stage. But she'd never had a man's help. She would never have wanted it either. Harry had offered a few times over the years, but she had never let him help. But this was different now. They were getting married. It was okay to lean on him; it was okay to accept his help if she needed it. It didn't mean she was any less independent.*

She squeezed his hand. "I think I've said no to your offers one too many times, Harry. I'm all right, but it's comforting to know that if I'm not, you'll be there for me."

He leaned forward to kiss her. "Always, Ruby. Have you thought about where we're going to live after the wedding?"

Ruby held on to his hand. "I have. But it's a decision we need to make together. I would love it if you moved into the Christmas House with me. We don't have to run it as a bed-and-breakfast anymore, but I would love to keep the tradition of Christmas Eve dinner."

He smiled at her, his eyes twinkling. "I was hoping you'd ask me to move into that old house."

Her heart squeezed, overflowing with joy and relief. "Wonderful! I'm so excited. I think you'll love it, and living in Silver Springs will be a change of pace from the city."

"Agreed. Now I just need to break it to the kids that I'll be selling the house."

* * *

An hour later, after they'd all pitched in and tidied the kitchen, Sam and Cat stood in the doorway, arguing with their fathers about permission to go to a party. Dawn watched the exchange with avid interest. She was also polishing off a bowl of ice cream. Scott had handed them out to everyone, claiming dessert was necessary on Saturday nights.

"All right, let's just get the most important details. Whose party is this?"

Olivia watched as Cat and Sam exchanged eye rolls. "I told you, Dad, it's Jackson's party."

Scott gave Wyatt a look before turning to the girls. "I don't know Jackson. Do you know a Jackson, Wyatt?"

Wyatt shook his head. "Nope."

Cat threw her hands in the air. "He's a real person."

"I'd actually prefer it if he were fake," Scott said, and Wyatt laughed.

They grew serious again when Cat and Sam both whispered something, the word *immature* carrying across the room.

"Are there going to be parents there?"

Sam tapped a finger across her chin. "I don't think any of them are parents yet."

Wyatt's eyes narrowed. "So *not* the right answer for someone asking to go to a party."

Sam rolled her eyes. "I don't know; we can't ask."

"I can ask for you," Scott said mildly.

Cat inhaled sharply. "Uh, only if you want me to drop out of school and go into hiding."

"Then find out. And actually, when you get an invitation, that should be the first thing you ask."

Cat covered her face, muttering something about not believing this was her life.

"Are there going to be high schoolers?" Wyatt asked, taking a sip of beer.

Sam sighed theatrically and leaned against the counter. "Dad, that's worse than Scott's question. No offense, Scott," she said, shooting him a weak smile.

Scott's lips twitched. "None taken."

"Well, based on the total lack of information you've given me, I'm going to say no," Wyatt said, scooping some ice cream into a bowl.

"That goes for me too. Just for the record, your failure to provide any kind of detail is what made us say no on this one. So you might think of trying some of our suggestions next time," Scott said, grabbing the ice cream scoop Wyatt handed him and adding two scoops of strawberry to his bowl, not looking even remotely concerned at the gasps of outrage from the counter.

"If we actually asked those questions, we would have been uninvited," Sam said.

"This is so unfair. I don't even know how you guys expect us to ever have a life," Cat said, crossing her arms, her eyes flashing.

Scott wiped his mouth on a napkin. Neither he nor Wyatt seemed rushed or stressed at all. Olivia looked over at Charlotte, whose eyes were sparkling when she made eye contact with her. Clearly these types of conversations were a regular occurrence.

Olivia couldn't even imagine Dawn at that age. Right now, the endless messes and diapers and chaos seemed like a much easier phase to be in. Just the idea of Dawn glaring at her like Sam and Cat were glaring at their fathers was depressing. But

Scott and Wyatt seemed to be taking all this in stride. In some ways, they almost seemed to be enjoying themselves.

"You can have a life when you are able to give more details— or when you're an adult and you don't have to give me any details. Either way works for me. Actually, I'd prefer the adult part."

"You know what happens to overprotective parents, don't you, Dad?" Sam said.

Wyatt paused, spoon halfway to his mouth. "They get an award?"

Sam rolled her eyes as Cat shook her head. "No, they raise kids who end up breaking all the rules and sneaking off just to rebel."

Wyatt put down his spoon. "You know what happens to children and best friends of cops, don't you, Sam?"

Sam pursed her lips. Cat nudged her.

"Their cop parents and best friends get in a police cruiser. Then they drive around town while the best friend uses a mega-phone, yelling their names out the window of the moving vehicle so everyone hears."

Cat let out a strangled noise and looked at Scott. "This is so unfair. Would you guys even be saying this if we weren't girls?"

"Of course we would. Maybe the main concerns would be slightly different, but we'd be just as difficult and irritating. The main objective is to raise you without any traumatic events occurring. If we do that, then we've succeeded."

Sam looked back and forth between Wyatt and Scott. Cat shook her head. "Like, what, you two talked about this?"

Scott nodded. "Yeah, when you two avoided talking to us all of seventh grade. We had to strategize."

"This is just sad," Sam whispered to Cat.

Scott's lips twitched and Wyatt grinned.

"I still think you're way too overprotective just because we're girls. Mom wouldn't have done this."

Scott leaned back in his chair, taking his ice cream with him. "Mom was different. But Mom was also a realist. I want you to be able to go and do whatever you want to do, within reason. I want you to be able to walk down the street by yourself at midnight if you want to—but that's not the world we live in. It's not fair; I get it. But facts and stats are real, and they don't care about feelings. If you want to hate me for keeping you safe, then hate me. One day, hopefully, you'll see that we were right."

Wyatt raised his spoon. "Well said."

"You know there isn't some villain just ready and waiting to jump out of a bush, don't you?"

Something in Scott's demeanor changed, and what had been a jokey, lighthearted conversation became tense. "You don't know the world the way Wyatt and I do. That's it. End of discussion."

Cat threw her hands in the air, and both girls marched out of the room.

The four of them sat in silence until they heard the door to Sam's room slam shut. Scott and Wyatt looked at each other and then sank back in their seats.

"They're going to kill us," Scott said.

"I know. Thank God it's just one each," Wyatt said, before reaching for another helping of ice cream. Olivia caught an odd expression flash across Charlotte's eyes, but it was gone before she was sure.

Dawn started fussing, breaking the silence. "We should probably get going. Dawn is going to be way off her sleep schedule, and I'll pay for this during the night. I also have an early start tomorrow," Olivia said, rising and letting Dawn run to the door.

"I'm so glad you brought her over," Charlotte said as she helped Dawn get bundled up for the cold.

"Thanks for such a wonderful dinner." Olivia shot a smile at Wyatt and Scott.

Wyatt chuckled. "I can't take any credit."

Scott smiled. "I can. I'm glad you enjoyed it. Why don't I walk the two of you back?"

Olivia buttoned up her coat, very aware that Charlotte was watching this exchange closely while taking an inordinate amount of time bundling Dawn up. "Oh, thanks, but you don't have to do that. It's just down the street."

Charlotte stepped on her foot as she was getting up and Olivia gave her a look. What was she doing? Scott wanted to walk her home. They had just spent a fun evening all together, and she was refusing . . . what? To spend time alone with him.

"Well, you know if Scott doesn't walk you back, Wyatt will," Charlotte said, picking Dawn up and giving her a bunch of kisses on the cheek while she giggled.

Wyatt nodded. "Very true."

Olivia's heart raced as she looked up at Scott. "Okay, then, thanks. We'd love the company."

Scott grabbed his coat, and soon Dawn was buckled into her stroller and they were walking down the long driveway. A light dusting of snow had fallen, and it sparkled under the moonlight.

The crunching of snow beneath their boots was almost hypnotic, and Olivia knew there was something special about all of this.

"Dawn is already asleep," Scott said in a low voice once they'd reached the road.

Olivia peeked at her and smiled, bringing the cover of the stroller down a little farther. "It was such a late night. I'm surprised she managed so well."

"She was a champ. I wish Cat fell asleep like that still."

Olivia laughed. "I don't think Cat or Sam will be speaking to you or Wyatt for the rest of the night."

He smiled. "I know. I've learned not to take it personally. It's hard to separate the person she's growing into now from the one I remember. I still remember her at Dawn's age. Needing me for everything. The years go so fast. I know it's clichéd, but it's true."

Once they reached the porch at her grandmother's house, Scott lifted the stroller up the steps.

"Thanks. For what it's worth, I think you and Wyatt are doing a great job," Olivia said. "It's obvious how close you are. That's not easy. And it's not common anymore. Or maybe it never was. I don't know, I'm still figuring it all out. There's so much self-doubt."

"Thanks. And yeah, parenting is basically self-doubt and acting like you know everything and hoping you're getting it right."

"I think you're getting it right," she said, as they stopped in front of the door.

They stood on the porch in silence, the lights twinkling, the sky bursting with stars, and Olivia wanted to believe in the magic of this place, for it to touch her as it had when she was a child. At ten, she would have wished for her parents to be together forever and for them all to be happy. At twenty, she would have wished that the man she married to turn out to be like one of her teenage fantasies.

And now, closer to thirty than twenty, she wanted to wish that everything she sensed about Scott was true. She wanted to believe that starting over was easy or worth it. She wanted to trust her instincts again, but it was so hard. So hard to believe again.

It had been so long since she'd let herself believe in magic . . . in people. She'd grown up escaping the realities of her home life by pretending. She'd drowned herself in books, dolls, and dance. At one time in her life, when she was just a child, she'd known the kind of man a husband should be. She'd known in her heart; she'd known with her instincts. And somewhere along the way, desperation had demolished all those ideals and she'd forgotten what the little girl in her had always yearned for—love, stability, safety.

Olivia drew in a breath that was unlike any other she'd taken. She was sure it was the breath of the new version of her, the one who was finally on the right track.

Scott took a step closer to her, and she didn't move away. She wanted him closer.

She watched, wanting this moment to happen in slow motion so that she could relive it over and over again. Scott brought her hand to his lips and kissed it with a reverence, a gentleness, that was in complete contrast to the roughness of his stubble against her skin. The gesture, so completely restrained and proper, was the most romantic thing anyone had ever done for her.

It shouldn't have made her heart race and beat as if it hadn't been broken dozens of times by people who claimed to love her. It shouldn't have made her knees weak like she was a schoolgirl who'd never been kissed. It shouldn't have made her have faith in a man when she had promised herself she would never believe one again. But it did all of those things.

"What are you doing?" she whispered, because she didn't know what else to say and she couldn't quite bring herself to pull her hand away or step back or do anything that might yank her from the sweetness of this moment.

His blue eyes locked on hers. "I'm reminding you that there are good men out there. And I'm showing you that you can feel again, just like I can. And I'm hoping, from the tremor in your hand, that you'll let me take you out for dinner."

Well that, all of *that*, spoken in that deep, slightly gruff voice, managed to make some of the magic she'd wished for come to life. If the old Olivia had been standing there, she would have flung her arms around his neck and probably proposed to him. But this Olivia, no matter how taken she was with him, was still gun-shy.

"Scott . . . I, um, I'm coming off a few really tough years. I have this business that is going to require my full attention to make it work. I have a little girl that I already feel guilty about leaving for a few hours a day, who doesn't have a father around. I'm not sure that I have room in my life to take chances, but . . . I do want to go out with you. I want to watch Cat dance. So maybe . . . maybe we could just go as friends."

His jaw clenched for a moment and he took a step back, dropping her hand. The cold December air seemed to sink into her bones as she stood there, very aware that she'd just made a mistake.

"Sure, you call the shots. But for the record, I know we all have our pasts and our baggage. I know the temptation to drag that baggage into the present, to hold on to it and use it as a shield that will protect you from pain, but it can't. Because there's another kind of pain that will start, Liv, the kind that comes from being half-alive. I lost my best friend in the world, my lover, the mother of my child, and I turned from everything I ever believed in. I turned from my family, my friends, my own daughter, God. I was so damn angry and scared. I was scared to love my daughter the way I should because the pain was so huge, I couldn't breathe. I couldn't breathe for a year, it felt like, because every damn breath I was afraid Cat would be taken from me too. And then one day she told me that the day her mother died, she lost both of us. And that did me in.

"That was my wake-up call. I love Cat more than this entire life, and I think as a parent, you know exactly what I mean. And I know she's watching me and learning, and the last thing I want her to see is a man who's afraid to live out the years he has left to the fullest. I want her to be brave and strong and know that she can survive anything. I don't know exactly what you've been through, but I do know the pain that comes from not trusting the world anymore. And I think I know enough about people to know that you're worth waiting for, Olivia. So when you do think you're ready, I'll be waiting. In the meantime, I'd love to be your friend."

And with that, Scott had just relit the candle that the world, her father, her ex had extinguished. She stood still, afraid to breath and wake up from this delicious, heady space she was now in, and watched him walk away. He was tall and strong and more than capable. He was a loving father and a good friend. He was larger, fitter, stronger than her ex, and yet he didn't intimidate her. His strength was different. It was the kind that made her feel safe instead of scared.

He was the most beautiful man she'd ever met. And he was interested in her.

He walked down the driveway, and she watched him, unable to look away.

And then he was gone. Olivia stared at the large footprints on the porch and slowly stepped into them. She looked up at the stars in the sky and searched for the largest one.

And then she made a wish.

CHAPTER ELEVEN

Ruby heard Olivia getting herself ready at the door. She was just dying to talk to the girls together.

"Ruby, you do realize what's above, don't you?"

Ruby spun around, startled to see Harry standing there with a mischievous smile and a sparkle in his eye. She laughed, forgetting about Olivia for the moment as she looked up at the mistletoe hanging in the doorway to the kitchen. "Harry, you hung one of these in every doorway of the house."

He laughed, pulling her in for a kiss, and she forgot everything. She forgot that Olivia and Wendy were in the house. She forgot about how nervous she was about the next steps in her relationship with Harry. She forgot everything except how it felt to be in his arms and to have his lips on hers.

She forgot all of it until she heard Olivia gasp. Ruby quickly stepped back from Harry to see Olivia covering her eyes.

"Omigosh, I'm so sorry. I just forgot my keys in the kitchen," she said, ducking between them.

"Nothing to be sorry about, dear," Ruby choked out.

"Got them! You two carry on and pretend I was never here! Dawn is down for her nap, Grandma. Sorry, Harry," she said, wincing as she raced between them to the door.

Ruby was mortified, but Harry looked completely unruffled as he took her hand and they walked to the door, where Olivia was frantically trying to gather her things. "Don't worry about it, Olivia. I sort of set Ruby up with all these mistletoes everywhere."

Olivia gasped, her gaze darting from one room to the other. Then she laughed, smiling at Harry. "Harry, you are the perfect man for my grandmother. I'm so happy for you both," she said, the warmth in her smile making Ruby relax.

"Thank you, Olivia," Harry said, squeezing Ruby's hand as they watched her bolt out of the house.

Ruby sighed once her granddaughter was gone. "She's looking better by the day. I wonder if romance is in the air," she said, looking up at Harry.

His lips twitched and his eyes looked up. Ruby followed his gaze and burst out laughing as she spotted the mistletoe hanging there. She was still laughing when he lowered his head for another kiss.

"Just making up for lost time," he said, smiling against her lips.

* * *

The screen door skipped to a close as Olivia stepped out onto the porch of the Christmas House. She walked to her car quickly, carefully avoiding any icy patches. She had planned on an earlier start but hadn't quite managed it. It had been impossible to fall asleep the last two nights and not replay the porch, uh, conversation . . .

"And I think I know enough about people to know that you're worth waiting for, Olivia. So when you do think you're ready, I'll be waiting. In the meantime, I'd love to be your friend."

Really, if *swoon* were a regular word in her vocabulary, she would use it to describe that moment. She would never forget it. It would go down in her memories as one of the great ones.

Scott made her want to move forward, toward him, toward life again.

But what she'd just witnessed in her grandmother's house had been the sweetest thing ever. Harry was a romantic, and he was drawing her grandmother out of the protective shell she'd built around herself all these years. Could that happen to Olivia? She had never really thought she was that similar to her grandmother. Grandma Ruby had always been so wise, so composed, so strong. She'd been their rock. But now that Olivia knew more about her past, and about Harry's role in that past and all those feelings she'd had for so long, she was seeing a different side to her grandmother.

Maybe all that courage was also hiding someone who was so brokenhearted, so scarred from loved ones turning on her, that she was afraid to love again. Grandma Ruby had spent her lifetime alone.

As Olivia took the side roads as quickly as the weather would allow, her mind kept going back to the kiss she'd just witnessed between her grandmother and Harry. Not the *actual* kiss, but more what it meant. How it hadn't occurred to her before— because whenever she had brought up her concern that she and her daughter were an inconvenience, her grandmother and Harry had told her they loved having Olivia and Dawn around. While she believed them, she also believed they needed their own space. She didn't want to feel like she was always intruding. And what about when Dawn woke up in the middle of the night? Or all those toddler germs? She would hate it if she made either of them sick. No. She needed to find her own place with Dawn.

That, of course, presented a whole new set of problems—namely financial. But there was one idea that had just popped into her head, and she was going to ask Scott if it was feasible. She pulled into the parking lot and shrugged off the little dance her stomach did at the sight of Scott's truck.

Grabbing her purse, she hopped out of the car and dashed across the parking lot. She didn't stop to wonder if her racing heart had to do with the sprint to the studio or the anticipation of seeing Scott again. She opened the door and found him working on the small studio, lifting up the old floor.

"Hello," she called out as she crossed the empty lobby.

She was going to try to act as normal as possible. Her voice echoed and her breath caught in her throat as he stood up, turning in her direction. The smile he gave her was enough to make her momentarily forget that he worked for her and that she was never again going to trust a man and that they were going to stay friends.

"Hey, how are you, Olivia?"

She smiled as though she had her life totally together. "Good. Making good progress in here, it looks like?"

He shrugged, the motion drawing her eyes to his shoulders. He was wearing a T-shirt that revealed his athletic form and strong arms and shoulders. His jeans were frayed and worn in spots and might have been the best jeans she'd ever seen. "Not as fast as I'd like, now that one of my guys is down a few days with a cold. But we'll catch up."

"I wanted to run an idea by you. I haven't really thought it through, but I'm hoping it will work."

"Of course. What's up?"

"You know that old apartment on the third floor we were just going to use for extra storage?'

He nodded.

"What do you think about fixing it up enough to be usable as an apartment?"

She held her breath and waited.

"Like, to rent out?"

She shook her head. "No. For me. And Dawn, of course,"

He ran a hand over his jaw. "I don't know. I haven't really evaluated it. I mean, it's a possibility. Do you want to go have a look?"

"I was hoping you'd say that," she said, walking out the door and toward the stairwell.

"You didn't have to hope. I would hope you'd be comfortable enough to just tell me it was something you'd want to do," he said, as they took the flights of stairs up.

Embarrassment washed over her. He was right. What kind of spineless businessperson sat around wishing? "Something I have to work on," she said with a forced laugh.

"Nothing to be embarrassed about. There are worse things in the world than being too nice," he said, opening the door for her when they reached the third floor.

Her heart squeezed at the thoughtfulness of his comment. She turned on the light and found herself staring at a very minimalist, very dirty, very small apartment. Scott walked in, immediately testing taps and looking at pipes. She just sort of stood in the middle of the place, trying to imagine living there. It wasn't that it was *awful*. Or that it couldn't be fixed up. But it was more suited to one person. Not a person with a toddler.

She tried not to let her disappointment show, but even the ceilings weren't tall up here. The floor looked like a linoleum from the seventies, with several corners curled up at the edges and some patches missing. But there was something else about that floor that bothered her—aside from it being ugly. Something that made her not want to stare at it for too long.

The charm of the warehouse didn't exist up here—there wasn't any exposed brick or beams or pipes. The windows were small. The kitchen had dark-brown cupboards and a brown counter and a single sink. No dishwasher. There was a small stove and oven and a fridge that had missed the cool era and landed on the green of the seventies.

While Scott silently did his own inspection, she crossed the open area to the back of the apartment, where there were two doors. She pushed one door open with her finger, and it revealed a small bedroom. Then she poked her head into the bathroom. More green. A small sink, toilet, and shower. No tub for Dawn.

She slowly walked back to stand in the middle of the apartment, trying to figure out what it was she was feeling. It wasn't that she thought the apartment was horrible. She hadn't grown up in luxury. But there was this sort of underlying worry. Or self-doubt. The house she'd lived in with Will had been a dream home for the average family. This place was like taking so many steps back from that. Only one bedroom meant Dawn would have to sleep in Olivia's room, and there was barely enough space to fit a bed, let alone a bed and a crib and a dresser. There would be no place for Dawn to run around and play. She wouldn't be hosting any family gatherings here, that was for sure.

But the worst was the insecurity bubbling inside. She had just taken all the money from her divorce and invested in an old building, in a business, and she had no idea if it would work. What if this was the wrong path entirely? She could have taken that money and bought a small, cute house in Silver Springs and worked for her sister. She would have had money in the bank, and life would have been simple.

Who was she to start up a dance studio with no business background, no dance training for over five years, and now, no nest egg? What if she failed and Dawn hated her? She would have to move back into the Christmas House and be that kid who hadn't made it in life. Maybe she wasn't setting a good example for Dawn at all.

"Hey, I think this can work."

She spun around as she heard Scott's voice. He was standing in the doorway. She forced a smile. "Great. Can you get me some numbers on how much more you think it will cost to fix it up?"

"Sure. Tell me what you want to do up here."

She tore her gaze from his and let her eyes wander the room. She would have to buy blinds or something. She didn't know how to install those. Asking someone else to install them would cost money. She didn't even know how to use a drill. How ill prepared was she for life? Well, that was what YouTube was for, she guessed. Will hadn't known any of that stuff either, but they'd just hired people for everything.

Growing up, their dad had done those things, but he'd left when she was eight. She drew a shaky breath. *Get it together, Liv.* And what to do up here? Nothing. She couldn't afford anything. But it was embarrassing to admit that. What if people thought she was irresponsible, risking everything on a business that might tank within the year? "Um, I guess just the minimum in order for it to function. I can paint."

He nodded. If he was surprised, he didn't let on. "Sounds good. It won't be much to get it up and running at all. If you want help painting, I can give you a hand."

She crossed her arms over her chest, trying to brush aside the wave of vulnerability she felt. She didn't know what it was, why she couldn't shake this feeling. Her gaze rested on the linoleum, and suddenly she remembered why it looked so familiar. Out of nowhere she had this memory of her mother falling apart, drunk, on the kitchen floor. She hadn't really understood what drunk was, but Charlotte had. Charlotte had told Olivia to help drag their mother to the couch. Their mom had been crying and crying and saying something about not being able to do this on her own. That she hadn't wanted kids if she had to raise them by herself. Tears stung the back of her eyes and made her throat constrict painfully. She was a mother now, and it hurt even more to remember that time. It hurt more because it was so wrong. Because no matter how many times she failed at life, she would never fail Dawn, because Dawn would always be her priority. She would never blame Dawn for her own bad choices.

She wasn't her mother. She wasn't a quitter. She would be a single mom, an imperfect mom, but a mom filled with so much love for her little girl that it didn't matter where they lived. As long as Dawn knew she was first place in Olivia's life, that Olivia loved her more than anything in the world, she would be okay. Olivia would be okay. She forced a smile and looked up at Scott's concerned eyes. "Thank you, but I'll be okay."

"I know you will. But if you want my discount code at the paint store . . ."

"That sounds great," she said with a laugh as she followed him out the bedroom door.

"Okay, so just let me know your color choices, and I'll pick it up and leave it inside the apartment," he said, holding the front door open.

"Thank you, Scott. I really appreciate all that you're doing for me. Especially since so much of this is last-minute."

"Not a problem. That's just part of my job. People change their minds on things, or something structural that no one anticipated comes up. Damage control and redirecting happens all the time," he said as they walked down the three flights of stairs.

It occurred to her that there was no way she was going to haul a stroller up all these steps. She'd have to leave the stroller at the bottom, she supposed. Which meant she probably needed to pick up groceries and put them away when she didn't have Dawn. Or Dawn would have to be safely secured in her Pack 'n Play or something. Or napping. So much to figure out. It wasn't ideal, but it wasn't horrible. "How did you get started with your business?"

The walked back into the lobby of the building and stood in the middle of the open space.

"My dad was a contractor. He was a carpenter, actually. He loved it. He was always building something, even on the weekends. I followed him around and worked with him until he died. He had a great eye for detail. He was patient in a way I never was. I took some trade courses as well, but most of the important stuff I learned from him," he said.

"That sounds nice, having a family business. He must be proud, knowing you followed in his footsteps."

A shadow passed across his eyes. "He was."

She tore her gaze from his and the emotion she saw there. "I'm sorry."

"Thank you. It's been a couple years. It's strange, because even though I'm an adult, a parent, I still miss my own. I was close to both of them in different ways, and sometimes I catch myself almost picking up the phone to call them and ask them something. Same with my wife. It took a few years for it to sink in. I'd catch myself wanting to text her or take a picture to send her of Cat, and then all of a sudden maybe a year ago, I stopped. It finally clicked. I guess that's life."

Olivia stood still. He had already looked away, back at work. Maybe he regretted confiding in her. She should say something, like that she understood, but the love he'd had for his wife was something she had never experienced. The closeness he'd had with his parents was foreign to her as well. He had loved and he had lost, but he was still here. There wasn't a bone of defeat in his body, in the way he spoke or the way he carried himself.

Or maybe she could identify. Because she had loved her father like that once. With everything she'd had, but she'd been young when he left, the memories of that love intertwined with her feelings of betrayal and abandonment. He had been a rock for her and Charlotte. Their hero. In some ways what he had done had been more devastating than their mother's neglect, because he had been the one they relied on. They had never relied on their mother.

She needed to tell her dad that. He had come back into their lives last year, and typical pushover that she was, she'd been willing to accept what he'd told them without ever really telling him the toll his abandonment had taken on her.

Scott paused and glanced over his shoulder at her. "You okay? Did my depressing conversation ruin your morning?"

Say something, Olivia. Say something real. Heat washed over as she stared into his eyes, a sense of safety, of security, tugging memories from deep inside. They were all the memories she'd buried under desperate attempts at protecting herself and her family. They were all the memories she had buried by trying to find love and please others.

They were memories that would hurt her dad's feelings. And before they had been memories, relics of her past, they had been life, her life, moments that had crushed her and then molded her. Burying them had only made her more vulnerable because she had sought to soothe them rather than learn from them. She cleared her throat, her palms sweating as she stared at Scott.

"I used to hear my dad's footsteps, coming down the hall, for years after he left. I would wait in bed, thinking he was coming to give me a good-night kiss. And then I would remember that he wasn't. That he'd left us. Sometimes I would wake up in the morning and hear the clanking of pots or dishes in the kitchen and think he'd come home from working a night shift and was making us breakfast, only to realize it was Charlotte. After he left, I snuck his bottle of shaving cream and hid it under my mattress. I used to take it out at night, pour a little out, just so I could smell it. It smelled like safety and comfort. I told myself he was coming back. Even when Charlotte stopped believing, I kept waiting for him. When that bottle emptied, I cried for hours. I'm standing here, upset that this small place is all I have to offer Dawn, and that if I screw this all up, she will have nothing. But I'm trying to remind myself that as a kid, all I wanted was my parents, imperfect as they were, to just love me enough to keep me safe. But they couldn't. One walked away completely, and the other checked in and out like the revolving door of a hotel lobby. That floor, that stupid, ugly floor, was the floor in our apartment."

She stopped speaking abruptly, shocked that she'd just exposed memories she hadn't even gone through with her therapist, had never shared with Will. Everything was numb. The legs she was standing on, the palms that had been sweaty. It was all numb. Until she realized that she had tears rolling down her face and Scott was walking toward her.

When he slowly reached out to put his arms around her, everything that had been numb, dead, came back to life. And she let herself feel. The strong beating of his heart beneath her ear, the hard wall of his chest, of his back as she circled her arms around him, holding on to life. When had she stopped feeling? When had she stopped being Olivia?

She bunched his shirt in her fist, not ever wanting to let the moment go when she became herself again. Until she wanted more. Until she became aware of how good it felt to be held by

Scott. He was obviously a very attractive man. But he was more than that. So much more.

She became aware of how good he smelled: fresh, with maybe a hint of cedar and citrus. How strong he was. How his lips brushed the top of her head as though he knew her, as though they had done this a thousand times. And she wondered if this was how it was supposed to be, if this was how real relationships were. Will had never held her like this, not when they were dating, not even when she told him she was pregnant, never.

But she had never shared anything with Will either.

And yet here she was, holding on for dear life to a man she hadn't known long. As if he understood her. And a part of her was worried that if she let go, all the emotion coursing through her would vanish and she would go back to being the old, hollow version of herself.

Because she was starting to like this version—the one who actually acknowledged her feelings, even if they left her vulnerable again. And the other part of her worried that if she didn't let go, the other feelings, like suddenly being hyperaware of her body pressed tightly against Scott's and how good it felt, would be impossible to ignore.

So she did the only thing she could do—she took a step back.

* * *

"You know, for an old guy, you can still run really fast."

Shit. Scott almost tripped on the treadmill as Cat appeared in the doorway out of nowhere. He'd just been about to beat his personal best time. He quickly pressed the down arrow on the treadmill to a jogging pace before he flew off.

He'd been lost in thought. He hadn't been able to get his conversation with Olivia off his mind. He'd known a bit about their family, but hearing her open up to him was like being let into a secret space. There had been something in her face, in her voice, in the way she held on to him, that told him she didn't go there very often. He understood that. There were certain memories that had to be buried just so you could get through the day. The kind that derailed you if you thought about them constantly.

But she'd trusted him with something deeply personal. And then she'd trusted him to be the person she could hold on to.

"Why do you look so spacey?"

Cat's voice jarred him from his thoughts. He hadn't realized he'd drifted.

"I thought you were supposed to be studying for the entire night and I wasn't to bother you or interrupt you."

She shrugged. "I got bored and needed a break. Also, I was hoping you wouldn't mind quizzing me."

He nodded, slowing his pace even more until he was walking. "Sure, I just need like twenty to cool down and shower."

"No problem. I know old people need to take time to stretch after workouts."

He laughed. "I can outrun you any day, kid."

She crossed her arms, her eyes sparkling, reminding him so much of her mom. That pang hit him somewhere in the chest. He'd been thinking about Hillary a lot more than usual. He knew it was because of the feelings he was developing for Olivia—and the dread he had of telling her about the job he'd had before being a contractor. It brought up those old feelings of being a disappointment, of not being enough.

For a long time, he'd wished Hillary had died before he'd turned in his badge. Then he would have had only good memories. He wouldn't have that gray area. They had been high school sweethearts—they'd known early on they wanted the whole deal together. They had been inseparable. Cat had come along before they were married, before they had finished school, but they'd made it work. They had taken turns with her, and he'd helped Hillary as much as he could so she could have her career as well. Everything was fine until it wasn't. Until he needed to walk away from being a cop.

He didn't know what would have happened to their marriage if she'd lived. She'd made it so clear that she was disappointed in him.

He couldn't go back and change anything. He couldn't go back and see how that would have played out for them. But he could move on. Because the woman he was falling for had been disappointed in life too. She'd been hurt by the people she was closest to. And for a while, like that night on Ruby's porch, he hadn't thought he'd ever get through to her. But then the apartment had happened. And he'd witnessed a wall come down that must have been so damn thick and tall, because she'd looked as though she'd floored herself. And she'd let him in. She'd held on to him like she trusted him.

And that was something he'd never forget. Nor how perfect she'd felt in his arms.

"Hello, earth to Dad? Like, do you need some coffee or something?"

Hell. He shot his gaze to Cat, who was looking royally annoyed, which meant he'd probably drifted for all of thirty seconds. "Yeah?"

She rolled her eyes. "I said, do we have any snacks to make the studying any less painful?"

"What's your test in?"

"Science."

"There's nothing that can ease that pain. But how about hot chocolate? I also bought some of that holiday popcorn with the white-chocolate peppermint you like."

Her face lit up. "Perfect! Okay, meet you in the kitchen in twenty minutes," she said, running out of the room. He heard her barrel up the basement stairs and knew that twenty minutes was actually more like thirty.

Wiping the sweat off his face with his towel, he made his way out of their home gym and ran up the stairs to his bedroom. He grabbed some clean clothes and accidentally knocked over the box he kept his watches in. The interior panel had opened up as well, and he paused, knowing that if he pulled off the velvet-lined divider, he'd find his badge and Hillary's.

He snapped it shut. He didn't need to see anything. The memory had already surfaced; shit like that couldn't be contained in a little box.

He walked into his bathroom, locked the door, and stripped down. He stepped into the shower, angry with himself for still being so affected by something that had happened years ago with a woman who wasn't here anymore.

He'd gone to her, at the end of his rope. There had been nothing left in him. Hillary was dying at that point. Cat had been little. And work, that last case—it had been the end. He hadn't been sleeping, he hadn't processed what he'd witnessed, he wasn't moving on. He had turned into a different person, and it had scared the shit out of him. He had crossed a line, and work and his personal life had blended into a dangerous tangle.

"I can't do this, Hillary. I can't be here for you, I can't be the father Cat needs me to be, and still . . . be out there," he'd said, taking her hand, putting his head beside her on the bed.

"You have to. Just push through. Be strong, Scott. You'll get over it."

"I'm not getting over it. I don't have time to struggle. Cat needs me, more than ever. You don't know what it was like. That girl. Her parents."

"Detach. Compartmentalize, Scott. You made a big mistake; you took this way too much to heart. Let it go now."

He'd stood, feeling alone and betrayed by her unwillingness to even try to understand what he was telling her. It had taken everything for him to be vulnerable in front of her. And he'd instantly regretted it. She had never looked at him the same way after that. Her good-bye wasn't what it should have been.

"Dad! It's been like half an hour already!"

Cat's voice on the other side of the door jarred him from his memory. Maybe it was for the best.

"Yeah, I'll be right there," he said, turning off the faucet and reaching for his towel.

But the idea of sharing all of this again, with someone else he cared about, was actually far worse than eighth-grade science.

CHAPTER TWELVE

Ruby stood in Harry's kitchen, loading the dishwasher while coffee brewed. It was strange, being in the home he'd shared with his wife. This had been her kitchen. Around the large table, birthdays and holidays had been celebrated. Memories had been made. It was strange to think that if Ruby had accepted Harry's proposals, they could have shared a life here together.

She paused and admired the set of Christmas dishes, with their depiction of a winter village. Ruby and Harry's late wife had the same taste in china and a love for holiday tableware. She was happy that Harry had led such a good life, even though it hadn't been with her. The doorbell rang, and Ruby called out to Harry, who was in the basement packing some boxes. It was going to be an enormous undertaking, and Charlotte had suggested that they hire someone who specialized in downsizing to help.

She opened the door to find Anne standing there. "Oh, Anne, come in, sweetie. You know you don't have to ring the doorbell."

Anne lifted her chin. "Hello, Ruby. Well, I saw your car outside, so I thought it was best."

Ruby forced a smile, but everything in Anne's tone and posture told her that she was still having a hard time with all of this. But even more worrying was that the organizer was due to arrive at any moment and Harry still hadn't told his children that he was selling the house.

"Don't change anything you normally do on my account. Come on in."

Anne nodded and, after taking off her coat and shoes, followed Ruby into the kitchen.

"Harry, Anne is here," Ruby yelled down the stairs.

"Oh! That's a nice surprise. I'm on my way up," he said, and Ruby detected the strain in his voice.

The doorbell rang again, and Ruby stiffened. "I'll, um, go get that. I have fresh coffee, if you want to help yourself, Anne."

"Thanks," Anne replied, as Ruby left the kitchen.

Ruby tried to walk as slowly as possible to give Harry a head start at breaking the news to Anne. But she felt bad for making the poor woman wait in the cold on the porch. When she finally heard Harry's deep voice, she opened the door. "Hello. You must be Christine."

Christine smiled. "I am. Ruby?"

Ruby nodded and held the door open wider, struggling to hear how Harry was managing while also trying to be attentive. "Come on in out of the cold. We can meet with Harry in the kitchen."

"Wonderful. What a lovely home. I'll follow you, Ruby."

As they approached the kitchen, Anne's shrill cry stopped them. "How could you do this? How could you sell this house? This is our family home. This is Mom's house. What, all for that gold-digging tramp? She's after your money, Dad."

Ruby stood in the doorway, humiliation burning its way through her body. They hadn't spotted her yet, but Harry's face had become an ashen color, his jaw clenching. Christine put her hand on Ruby's shoulder.

"Anne, never speak like that about Ruby again. You don't know her. I know you don't want me to sell this house, I know it holds many memories, but I can't stay here and still move forward with my life. But all these memories will be with you no matter where we are. Me staying here won't bring Mom back, it won't bring your childhood back, it won't bring back the family we were. We have our hearts for that, Anne. All those memories—they will live on whether or not I'm in this house."

Ruby wiped her eyes, and Anne turned sharply to her. Her eyes narrowed on Ruby, Harry's touching speech clearly falling on ears not ready to listen.

"I don't care what my father says. I don't trust you, and I never will. I will never accept you as my father's wife."

"Anne," Harry bit out harshly.

Ruby moved aside quickly as Anne stormed down the hallway. She opened the door and slammed it with a thud that could rival Wendy's angry door slam. Harry looked at Ruby, his eyes filled with moisture. "I'm so sorry, Ruby. I should have told them all sooner. She is way out of line."

Ruby nodded, forcing a smile. "It's okay. She'll come around. Maybe we can arrange a time and both sit down and talk to her. She's feeling threatened, and I don't want that for her. This is her home, and I want her to be okay with all of this." She turned to the newcomer. "Harry, this is Christine."

A Christmas House Wedding

Harry grimaced. "I'm sorry for all the family drama and that you had to witness that."

Christine waved a hand. "Oh, Harry, I've seen it all. It's hard. Change is harder for some. Why don't we sit down, take a bit of a breather, and then get started?"

They walked into the kitchen and Ruby poured the coffees, but her mind was still on Anne. Her words had triggered those old feelings, and she wondered what Harry's parents would have said if they were still alive. She wondered how many times Harry had heard those words said about her. She forced a smile to her face and willed herself not to let old wounds ruin her present day.

* * *

Olivia walked down Main Street with a newfound skip in her step. The cedar roping smelled more intense; the wreaths were greener, the twinkling lights brighter. She glanced down at Dawn in her stroller and smiled. Her baby was happily lapping up all the decorations and lights while Olivia basked in the feeling of contentment. She was happy. Really happy for the first time in a long time. The weight of her marriage, of shame, of anger wasn't front and center. She felt more like herself than she ever had before.

She smiled as people passed, their arms and hands filled with packages and bags, everyone preoccupied with the December rush. She loved it. She hadn't looked forward to Decembers in a long, long time. She had almost finished up her Christmas shopping, and loaded bags dangled off the stroller handles and were tucked underneath. It was amazing to think that this time last year, she hadn't even had the energy for the twenty-minute walk to town from her grandmother's. Now she could walk into town with the stroller as well as wander the main street and go back without being winded.

She paused in front of the toy shop and took a deep breath as she stared at the window. She had so many great memories of visiting this toy shop with Charlotte and Grandma Ruby. It was one of those places that found unique things, not necessarily all the trendy things. The window display featured an electric fireplace, its mantel decorated with garland and lights and embroidered stockings. The Christmas tree beside it was filled with multicolored lights and bursting with toy soldiers. Underneath the tree was an old-fashioned train, whizzing around a circular track. "Dawn, look!" Olivia said, pointing to the display.

Dawn moved forward, gripping the edge of the handlebar on her stroller. "Go, Dawn, go."

Olivia laughed, turning the stroller so they could go in. "Okay, sweetie. You're going to love this."

"Olivia!"

She froze, recognizing her dad's voice. *Ugh.* She wanted to just have a fun time and enjoy the Christmas atmosphere. She didn't want to see her dad. He was walking toward them quickly, a big smile on his face. He greeted Dawn first, making her laugh with some funny faces, before standing up again to say hi to Olivia.

Ever since her conversation with Scott about the apartment, she hadn't been able to stop thinking about her dad and the old memories she'd repressed. It was strange, because Charlotte was four years older than her and remembered so much more than her. She wondered if that was why Charlotte had a harder time letting go of the past and trusting her parents again.

Her dad's gray hair was windblown, but the sparkle in his eyes was something she remembered. And it made her uncomfortable. Because it reminded her that there had been good times. It would have been easier if there hadn't been, if he'd been awful before he left them. In some ways she wished she remembered more of those good times like Charlotte did. But he'd broken Charlotte's heart, because he'd been her hero. As for Olivia, she'd come out of that house not trusting her parents at all, only Charlotte and Grandma Ruby.

"I'm so glad I ran into you girls. Do you have time for a coffee?"

Olivia hesitated and looked down at Dawn, who kept looking back at the window display. Someone opened the door to the toy shop, and Dawn pointed. "Go, Dawn, go."

Olivia and her dad shared a laugh. "She's dying to get in there."

Her dad gestured to the store. "Then how about we go in and then grab a coffee."

Olivia looked away from the hope in his eyes, feeling torn. She had just wanted this to be a fun time with Dawn with no family drama. She didn't want to wander around a toy store and, instead of looking at toys for Dawn, have to share what should be a happy time with memories she didn't want to think about.

"Coffee with a toddler after she's already been sitting for half an hour won't be relaxing. Maybe we'll just go in the toy store, because there's no way we can skip that without full-on tears."

He nodded and opened the door for them. The sound of "Rudolph the Red-Nosed Reindeer" greeted them as they entered the bustling shop. The aisles were crowded, and Olivia maneuvered the stroller in the direction Dawn was pointing. The smell of hot apple cider filled the air, and Olivia spotted a little refreshment station, complete with sugar cookies decorated with sprinkles. Exactly how she remembered it. When they were kids, Grandma Ruby would talk to the store owner while she and Charlotte took in all the displays.

She rounded the corner, her breath catching at the dollhouse display. Dawn squealed, and Oliva's heart squeezed as they made their way over. She was in her own world, engulfed in her own memories, when her dad spoke.

"So how have you been? How's the reno going?"

It was an innocent question and the appropriate kind of small talk she would normally be happy to engage in. Surfacy and pleasant was usually where she liked to keep things. But it was getting harder. Maybe her talk with Scott had happened for a reason—maybe this was the next step in reclaiming her life. In being bold enough to vocalize her issues.

They stopped in front of the dollhouse, which had been decorated for Christmas. Artificial snow covered the rooftops and the electric fireplaces were on, miniature Christmas trees in each room. Dawn sat captivated, watching.

Olivia stared at the house, all at once at one with the child she used to be. Except she was an adult now, with a child she loved more than the entire world and an ex-husband who couldn't care less about his daughter. She had been holding on to the past in everything she did. She was afraid of a future with people who really could come through for her. Like Scott.

He'd said he'd wait for her, however long it took.

No man had ever waited for her. Not the man beside her, not the man who'd married her.

"It looks like Dawn has inherited your love of dollhouses," her dad said, his voice filled with warmth.

Olivia stared at the house, at all the little people inside. In that house, there were freshly baked cookies and hot chocolate. All the beds were made. There weren't any liquor bottles inside. The people around the tree were happy and grateful and . . .

"Dad . . . I . . . I used to wait for you."

She continued staring at the house, not wanting to see his face, knowing she was hurting him. "White Christmas" came on, the melody floating around them. People stepped around them, the occasional shopping bag banging into her, but she couldn't move.

"Sweetheart, I'm sorry. I know I will never make up for the trust I betrayed or for the years I missed. I can't ever make that decision right. I regret what I did every single day. It's the first thing I think of every morning when I wake up and the last thing I think of when I go to sleep at night."

Emotion swelled in her chest when his eyes filled with tears and his voice broke. She knew all this. This was his part in their family story. He had worked hard last year, trying to rebuild his relationship with her and Charlotte, and they had all gotten to a certain point that she wasn't sure she wanted to go past.

It was a murky place, a little too thick to ever come out of too quickly, and that made it feel safe, even though it wasn't ideal. Trudging through the sludge required work she wasn't sure she was willing to do, because in the end, she didn't really trust that he would be there on the other side, waiting for her. When her parents had been together, her entire existence had been filled with this heaviness. After he left, the only person in her family of four she had been able to rely on was Charlotte. As she slowly turned now to look up at her dad, at the lines on his face, at the tears in his eyes, she knew he was sincere. She could feel it.

But her instinct was to run and hide in the activities she was going to fill her day with. She just wanted to be a mom to her daughter. She just wanted to enjoy the season. She wanted to hear Dawn's bubbly laughter right front and center, not in the background while her mind wandered to her past.

She clutched the handles on the stroller and forced herself to be present. Then she could go on her way. "Dad, I know you're hurting. I know you've suffered and you feel guilty. I appreciate that you're trying. I'm not going to keep you out of our lives . . . but I also don't trust you. I don't know that I will ever fully trust you.

"I married a man who checked out of our marriage, and now I'm the only parent Dawn has. I need to be here fully for her. I need to protect her from people who won't or can't put her first. I don't know that you won't just walk away from us again if things start getting too hard with Mom or life. I don't want Dawn to experience the hurt that comes with knowing that someone she loves walked away and is living a life that doesn't include her anymore. Just like her dad is doing. Maybe that's unfair, but I can't seem to separate myself from the things that have happened to me.

"So yes, let's spend time together. But I will be proceeding with caution."

He shoved his hands in the pockets of his wool coat and looked down for a moment. She held her breath, her body trembling, maybe a reaction to actually having had the nerve to speak the truth. It hadn't been easy, and she hated causing someone else pain, but she'd had to. She had to protect her daughter. It wasn't just about her anymore.

Her dad finally raised his head. "I can understand where you're coming from, Olivia. Thank you for your honesty. I'd still love to grab that coffee, if that's okay with you. Maybe after I buy Dawn a couple of presents."

Olivia nodded, taking a deep breath and letting some of the heaviness lift from her.

CHAPTER THIRTEEN

Ruby closed her book when she heard the front door open and close softly. A moment later Olivia appeared in the doorway, her face drawn despite the smile she gave her.

"Hi, Grandma. I think I'm just going to run up to bed. I'm exhausted."

Ruby felt a pang in her chest as she took in her granddaughter's expression. Even though Olivia was grown up, with a child of her own, Ruby could still see the frightened little girl on her front porch the day Wendy had dropped them off. Charlotte had been stoic and Olivia had been despondent. Ruby had worried about the two of them constantly, about how they were coping with the instability in their lives. She could still picture Olivia playing with all those dolls, long after most girls her age had given them up. Ruby understood that those dolls had given Olivia the escape and security she needed. But now that her own real-life family hadn't turned out like the world of make-believe she'd created,

Ruby wondered if she would ever believe in happily-ever-afters again.

"How about you sit with me for a few minutes, dear?"

Olivia offered a tired smile but sat down on the couch. "Sure, Grandma. How was your day?"

"It was good. I helped Harry pack up some more of his house, and that was a little emotional but to be expected. I watched Dawn, and that was wonderful as ever. She's such a smart one."

Olivia beamed at the mention of her daughter. "I know, she's very clever. I'm so grateful for all the time you're spending with her, Grandma. As soon as the studio is a little safer to be in, I'll bring her with me. I know you're busy with Harry and the wedding."

"Don't worry about it. I'm enjoying my time with her. And how is the studio going?"

"Really well. Scott is moving so fast. He's already done more in a few weeks than the other contractor has done in a month. I'm actually starting to believe we might be up and running for the beginning of January."

"Good. I don't doubt it."

"I've also decided I'm going to live at the studio. There's a small apartment on the third floor, and Scott's going to be able to fix it up. I want to give you and Harry some space."

Ruby's stomach dropped. "This house is the size of a small hotel. We don't need more space. We would love to have you and Dawn here. Harry adores you both."

Olivia tucked a strand of hair behind one ear, and Ruby noticed the dark circles under her eyes.

"You've always been so supportive and encouraging, Grandma. I really appreciate your offer, but I wouldn't feel right. You and

Harry are starting a new chapter of your lives together. It should be just the two of you."

Ruby frowned. "I don't like the idea of you living in a giant empty warehouse, Olivia."

Olivia waved a hand. "We're not. It's the apartment above, and it's nice and cozy."

"Regardless, it's in the middle of nowhere, between two towns. I don't like it, Olivia."

Olivia stood, giving her that forced smile again. "We'll be just fine. I have a security system installed. Now I really need to get to bed—I'm so wiped."

Ruby nodded, the worry still sitting on her chest as Olivia leaned down to give her a quick hug. "Don't think I'm going to just drop this, Olivia."

Olivia smiled at her before she left the room. "I know, Grandma."

Ruby listened to her footsteps as she walked up the stairs. Staring into the fire, she thought about what Olivia had said about her and Harry starting a new life. When she had first come here, she'd been alone and scared. She'd been pregnant. The daunting reality that she would soon be a single mother, in a time where that wasn't common, weighed her every step. She'd been a different person. Harry had been different too. She had lived a life here, a real life. She had built a life. She had dreamt a life for herself. She'd always felt she was a little like both of her granddaughters. Charlotte had her pragmatism, and Olivia had a heart that could dream. But Olivia also wore the worry of a parent who didn't know if they could make it—Ruby understood that.

She took a deep breath, letting her gaze wander the enormous parlor room, remembering the woman who had generously taken *her in. Taken her in and given her a future, given her love without judgment. And hope.*

That was what Olivia needed now. She needed hope for a future.

This place was beginning to feel like Ruby's past. But Harry was Ruby's future. She didn't know, all of a sudden, if they should be starting their new life together in a place that was solely hers. Just as he was packing up his house, his lifetime of memories, maybe it was time for her to consider doing the same.

Maybe it was time to say good-bye to the Christmas House.

* * *

Olivia placed her hands on either side of the small of her back and stretched, groaning out loud. Who knew painting could be so difficult? No wonder there were so many painting companies out there. This was grueling work. And she wasn't very good at it either. But as she stared at her accomplishments, her chest swelled slightly. Not bad. Not bad at all. All she had left was the bedroom.

The two coats of paint she'd applied in a neutral taupe color had transformed the place. She was thinking that some weekend after they'd moved in, when they were settled, she'd tackle the kitchen cabinets too. Fresh paint would make them look brand-new.

The pinging of her phone sounded above the Christmas music softly playing. She assumed it was Charlotte. Their Hallmark movie night—along with some wedding planning—was scheduled for when Wyatt and Sam would be away the weekend after next.

When she picked up her phone, her stomach clenched. It was a message from Will. She hadn't heard from him since . . .

well, since she'd left. All other communication had been through their lawyers. She stood there, not knowing if she should read the text. Would it derail everything for her? She had to get this apartment finished. She was in a good place. She was stronger. Would reading his message just set her back and send her down the hole of self-pity?

But if she didn't read it, would she be thinking about it all night? Nausea swam through her at the terrifying thought of this being about Dawn. What if he'd actually realized he wanted to act like a father and wanted custody? One of the hardest things she'd had to grapple with at the end of her marriage was that she was married to a man who would be a crap father. When he'd shown no interest in either of them, she'd taken it as a blessing. Sure, her conscience had pricked her because she knew what it was like to grow up without a father, to be rejected by a father, but she took solace in the fact that Dawn would be too young to love him and then lose him. But what if Will had changed his mind? Charlotte didn't trust him at all. But he had rights. And he had the money to pursue those rights legally if he chose. But a legal battle would sink her financially.

She slowly swiped to read his full message, nausea gripping her.

Hi.

Hi? That was it? He hadn't spoken to her in over a year, and that was his text? She was about to toss her phone on the counter in disgust when the three dots appeared. Great. Now she even had to anticipate what he was writing and wait. She held her phone, her back sweaty, as she stared at the screen.

How are you?

Ugh. What was this? She didn't want to answer. She was still staring at the screen when those stupid dots started blinking again. After everything, he was texting her like some long-lost friend?

I miss you.

Okay, what? That wasn't what she had been expecting to hear. She continued to stare at the screen, letting his words sink in. He missed her. He had never told her he missed her. How far those words would have gone at one time in her life, when she'd been willing to accept crumbs or a kind word here and there. Well, she wasn't that woman anymore.

She turned her phone over. She would not let him get into her head. She was still trying to get his stupid voice out of her head some days. But what had made him want to reach out? Maybe he was drunk and had no one with him. Maybe he was completely desperate. That was kind of a satisfying thought—that he was sitting in a drunken stupor of regret for everything he'd lost.

She took a deep breath, noticing how dark it was already. Glancing at her watch, she was surprised to see that it was already seven. Grandma Ruby was looking after Dawn tonight, so Olivia could start on the main bedroom. She paused when she heard a sound downstairs. Scott wasn't supposed to come by tonight, so she knew it wasn't him. It struck her how eerie it felt, knowing she was the only person in this giant empty warehouse. But at least there were now cameras and lights. The alarm wasn't on, but the doors were locked.

When she didn't hear the noise again, she breathed a sigh of relief. It was probably the old vents or pipes or something like that.

Slam.

Olivia sucked in a breath as a cold sweat broke out over her body. Until she heard Scott's deep voice. "Olivia?"

She breathed a sigh of relief, her body trembling. The sound of his footsteps was reassuring, and a moment later he was walking through the door. If she hadn't already decided she wasn't going to fall for him, she might have flung herself in his arms. He was standing there with a bottle of wine and a pizza box. And he looked better than both. "Hey, I thought you could use help painting, or at least dinner," he said, walking in and placing the items on the counter.

Her heart skipped a few beats as she walked toward him. "Are you serious?"

He gave her a quizzical look. "Of course I am. Actually, I have something else to bring in here. Hold on."

As soon as he ducked out of the room, she peered at her reflection in the window and tried to fix her hair. That was silly, of course. It didn't matter what her hair looked like, because Scott was a friend. A friend who'd wait around until she was ready to be more than friends. A friend whose body was still imprinted in her memory.

She resumed fixing her hair until she heard him approaching.

Her mouth dropped open when Scott appeared in the doorway with a Christmas tree.

"Omigosh, what did you do?"

He poked his head around the tree and gave her a grin that lit up everything inside her, that made her not care that Will had just texted her, that made her wish she wasn't so jaded and Scott could be everything she wanted him to be.

"You can't have a new place in December and not have a tree. Where do you want it?"

"Uh, um, how about in that corner?" she said, pointing to the far corner.

"Sounds good. I've got a tree strand, too, so this should be set up in a couple minutes," he said, hauling it in as though it was no big deal.

"I can't believe you did this," she said, following him.

He balanced the tree. "It's really not that big a deal. Here, can you hold it while I get the stand set up?"

"Sure," she said, quickly grabbing the tree as he put the stand in place.

He worked on setting the tree in the base and then sat on the ground. "I'm just going to tighten everything up. Just maybe stand there in case it comes crashing down," he said with a slight laugh as his head disappeared under the tree.

She didn't know what was happening to her, but as Scott lay on the ground, she couldn't look away, and she was thankful he couldn't see her. But his T-shirt had ridden up, exposing an expanse of taut abs and a smattering of hair . . .

"Liv?"

She almost died. "Huh? Yes? Sorry, did you say something?"

"Yeah, I said, is the tree straight?"

Heat flooded her cheeks. What was wrong with her? She quickly moved away from the tree and looked at it. "It's perfect."

"Great," he said, sliding out and then standing, brushing his hands on the front of his jeans. They were standing close together, and she hoped he couldn't read any guilt in her eyes.

"Um, so I was thinking you should just add the cost of the tree and stand onto my bill."

"Are you kidding me?" he said, walking to the kitchen. "Please tell me you don't think I'm so much of a cheap-ass that I'd go and buy a tree without asking you and then expect you to pick up the bill."

She swallowed a nervous laugh. "No, I didn't think that. I just feel guilty."

"Well, don't." He eyed the space. "You've done a great job in here. Especially for someone who's never painted."

She smiled. "Thanks. I have to say I'm feeling a little proud of myself," she said with a laugh.

"You should be. So, do you want some pizza now while it's still hot? We can always have the wine while we paint," he said, opening the box to reveal a fully loaded pizza.

"Are you sure you want to give up your night? You can always leave this and go," she said, as he pulled out some paper plates and cups.

He gave her a look. "So, first, I bring you this tree, and you try and pay me for it. Now you think I'm just going to leave you here with wine and pizza? What kind of jerk would drop this off and then leave?"

She took the plate of pizza he offered. "Was that a rhetorical question?"

He stilled, the corner of his mouth still slightly upturned, but a harder glint came into his eyes. "It should be."

She nodded and looked away from that knowing gaze. "Do you want to sit on the . . . ground? This pizza smells delicious."

"Yeah. Hope you like it." They sat down next to each other, their backs against the wall and facing the Christmas tree.

They ate in silence for a few moments. "Wow. This is delicious."

"I'm glad you like it. So, do you need help installing those blinds?" he asked, having somehow already inhaled two slices of pizza while she was still finishing her first.

She nodded, blotting her mouth with a napkin. "Yes. Well, no. I was kind of hoping to do it myself. I know Wyatt offered, but I don't want to bother him."

"Do you want me to show you how?"

That would be embarrassing. She already felt her face heating up. "I'm a real novice. Like, I wouldn't know the first thing about installing them."

Totally true. She barely had the patience for reading instructions. Charlotte was much better at following instructions, and Olivia imagined her sister color-coding instruction manuals.

"I taught Cat how to use power tools last year, and she was a pro in no time. Finish up your pizza and we can get them hung. Not to freak you out or anything, but I could see into this apartment crystal clear from the parking lot," he said, crossing the room and then picking up one of the boxes containing the simple white blinds she'd purchased.

She grimaced. "Okay, that's freaky. I didn't think the windows were big enough to get a clear view from down there."

She took a few sips of wine as he opened the box and began setting up the contents as though he were getting ready to put together a Lego town. "Yeah, they are. Do you have enough for the whole apartment?"

She nodded. "Yes. The two windows in here and the one in the bedroom."

"Okay. I'll grab my tools in the truck and be right back."

"Are you sure you want to be spending your free time helping me with this?"

He flashed her a smile before leaving. She let out a long breath once she heard his footsteps on the stairs. She hadn't planned on this. Or on making a fool of herself with power tools.

There was something about Scott that went beyond the good looks and muscles and charm that drew her in. But she didn't quite know what it was. Yes, he was a devoted father, and that was a major . . . well, it was something she admired and loved—liked about him. There was something else, though. An undercurrent she picked up on now and again. Nothing that set off alarm bells per se, but something that told her there was more to him than just smiles and charm.

Glancing down at her half-finished glass of wine, she decided she needed to slow down and start painting the bedroom or she'd be too relaxed and sleepy to do anything. She picked up the can of paint and was about to pry open the lid when she noticed water dripping down the wall. She inhaled sharply and ran over to the window. The sill was drenched, as were the trim, wall, and floor, where water was pooling. When had this happened?

She ran out into the main room when she heard Scott come back into the apartment.

"What's wrong?" he said sharply.

"Water is coming in from the window in the bedroom," she said.

He frowned and strode across the room. She stood on the sidelines as she watched him assess the window. She heard a few curse words under his breath. "Can you get some of the painting tarps?"

"How bad is it?" she asked, dreading his answer.

He cringed. "It's not great. I think this didn't just happen . . . oh, hell," he said, his voice trailing off as he looked up.

She followed his gaze and gasped at the sight of water dripping out of the old light fixture. "Oh no," she whispered.

Scott was already leaving the room. "I've got to shut power down to the room. Just get as many tarps as possible, and I'll be right back. I'll bring a flashlight from my truck."

What a disaster. She ran around the apartment, gathering all the tarps and then rushing back into the bedroom to place them under the window and under the dripping light fixture. She pulled out her phone and turned the flashlight on as soon as the lights went out. Ladder. He would need the ladder. She quickly retrieved it in the main room and then positioned it under the light.

Seconds later she heard Scott running up the stairs, bringing with him a stronger beam of light.

"Hey. Oh, great, you got the ladder. Thanks. Can you hold this and aim it up at the light for me?" he said, already climbing the ladder.

"Sure," she said, doing as he asked.

He took apart the fixture, handing the pieces to her and working in silence. He swore when the last piece of the light came off and more water poured out of the ceiling. "I think there's a leak on the roof. That snowfall the other day was probably sitting there, and then today when it warmed up, it created this mess. I'm going to make a call," he said, climbing down the ladder and walking out of the room.

Olivia stood there, feeling completely useless and guilty because Scott was now spending his night doing damage control. It was even worse than having him help with the painting. But there was nothing she could do to help. She listened to the foreboding drip of water as it clanked against the metal step of the ladder until Scott's deep voice became impossible to ignore.

"Hey, Rick, I thought you guys finished this roof."

She nervously chewed her lower lip.

"So you were paid in full and left the roof unfinished. It's Saturday night, and now this is my problem to deal with? I don't think so. Get your sorry ass down here tomorrow morning and fix it properly. I swear, Rick, I'll tell everyone we know about this shitty job and you won't work for all of next year. And if there's any damage, Olivia is also going to bill you for that. What? Huh? Yeah, fine, but then you're driving them next Tuesday. See ya."

Olivia stood completely still, wishing she could just hide under one of the tarps. What was even happening? So the roofer had scammed her? How humiliating. And then Scott . . . he sounded so angry.

And that triggered a memory she really didn't feel like processing right now. And if it hadn't been pitch-black and there hadn't been a water catastrophe, she would have made a beeline to her abandoned wineglass. But that would look way too obvious right now. Like, taking her phone flashlight and tiptoeing over to where the wine was would look desperate. Pathetic.

Olivia, stop being a damn moron and clean up the kitchen. And for God's sake, go put on some makeup and look like you give a shit.

Olivia couldn't breathe as the memory surfaced. She'd been standing in the kitchen, feeling like hell because of morning sickness that lasted all day. Even showering had been an accomplishment at that point in her pregnancy. Will had just informed her that his boss was going to drop by for drinks. But she'd been so sick that doing anything other than sleeping had felt like too monumental a task.

She was glad it was dark and Scott was still in the other room. She had the sudden urge to run. She didn't know where to. She wanted out of this room, out of this apartment, out of this building. No, she wanted out of her skin.

She didn't want to talk, to . . .

It was the anxiety coming back. She forced herself to take a deep breath.

Just one, Liv. Take one deep breath.

Close your eyes.

Take another breath.

You're okay. Will isn't in your life anymore.

She rolled her shoulders and slowly opened her eyes.

She had controlled her anxiety. She had controlled it. Not the other way around. Wow. Long time coming. But a massive step in the right direction.

Unlike the next step she took when she heard Scott approaching—she walked into the ladder and knocked the paint over. Scott caught the ladder, and they both landed on the floor with a thud. She prayed that the old floor might just swallow her up and shoot her out into the basement by herself.

She could feel cold paint on her ankle. "Omigosh, Scott, I'm so sorry. I'm such a moron. First the roof, then this. What a mess. You go home, I'll deal with all of this, and—"

"Hey, hey," he said, taking her shoulders gently before she could stand. She became very aware of how they'd landed on the ground. She was sort of sitting between his legs, close enough that if she wanted to lean forward and put her head on his shoulder, she could. But she didn't want to do that, because she wanted him to leave so she could be by herself with her embarrassment.

She didn't say anything, but she didn't get up and run either.

"What's going on?" Now he sounded nothing like the man she'd just heard on the phone. But it shouldn't bother her how he'd sounded. If he wanted to be angry, he could be. Because they weren't involved and they never would be. They couldn't be. No matter how good he looked in jeans and T-shirts.

She frantically thought of something to say that wasn't too close to the truth. "Nothing. You just sounded really angry."

Even though the only light in the room was from the glow of the moon, the surprise on his face was obvious. "What? With Rick?"

She gave a nod.

"That's the way I talk to Rick when he does something stupid. We're good friends. Went to high school together. He was always an idiot. Sometimes I pick his daughter up for ballet, and he does the same for me and Wy. That's the way we speak to each other all the time."

This could have been funny. This *should* have been funny. But the relief she felt was confusing. She was happy she'd just witnessed guy-speak and not some kind of uncontrollable anger. But she was happier than she should be for someone who wanted nothing to do with Scott.

"Oh. I guess, sorry. Anyway, I should clean up this mess and clean off this paint before it dries."

"Hey, wait."

The softness in his voice seemed to touch every part of her that had been closed off. The gentleness, the patience in his voice, in the feel of his warm hand on her wrist, lingered around her heart so that she couldn't be so quick to dismiss him. She made the mistake of meeting his gaze, because when she did, she forgot everything except the way he made her feel.

She didn't say anything, and he slowly pulled his hand off hers, and the disappointment that washed over her was almost unbearable. But then he lifted his hand and slowly raised it to cup one side of her face. She wasn't quite sure if she sighed audibly. His hand was rough, large, warm, and so gentle. His thumb slowly grazed her cheekbone, his gaze on hers, his eyes glittering with something she really, really, liked. Something that made her stomach swirl with excitement, something that made her heart wish this could be real.

"What did he do to you, Liv?"

Her mouth dropped open, and instead of wanting to run, she wanted to curl into him and the shelter he was offering.

"I . . . it's not . . . it's not what you're thinking. He never . . . he never physically hurt me."

His jaw clenched. "There are lots of ways to hurt people. Things that stay inside and come out when you least expect them to."

She could look away and just shut down, but all of a sudden, she didn't want to. She didn't want to keep hiding. What she wanted to do was put her hand on him as well. Maybe on his knee. But instead, she spoke.

"When you were yelling at your . . . friend, it triggered a memory, and I froze. It's strange, because I never realized how abusive my relationship was until I reached a breaking point. It's like I ignored it for so long, I justified his behavior for so long, and then all of a sudden when Dawn was involved . . . that was it for me. I had to leave. But I never counted on the scars that stayed long after I left."

"I think when we love people, we tend to make excuses for them. You were married. He was supposed to be the person you could trust over anyone in the world. He should have been your best friend. Your partner in life. The father of your baby. He abused his role."

"I beat myself up so many times for ever falling for him. For not seeing right through him. I was so young and naïve, and he honestly swept me off my feet. Looking back, I can't believe I fell for all of it."

"How did you meet him?"

"In Toronto. At the coffee shop next to the dance studio I worked at. We had seen each other a few times. He was always dressed up—suit and tie—and just so sophisticated. He's eight years older than me, and . . . he was everything I never had growing up. He had money and stability and confidence. He said all the right things . . . took me out to restaurants and the theater . . . all these places I didn't even know existed. It was like a different life. There were signs, though. Signs of control I should have picked up on. I was working my way through dance school, and he always dismissed it. After we got married, he kept coming up with reasons I should scale back my hours, and before I knew it, I was working like one day a week. I gave up everything. And then when he thought I wasn't good enough anymore . . . he treated me like garbage."

"He took advantage of you. How old were you?"

She closed her eyes briefly. "So young. Nineteen."

"You . . . you are lovely, Olivia. Beautiful. I thought so. The moment I first met you. I knew you'd been through a lot. You were off-limits. And I get it if you want to stay friends. I can do that. I can be your friend. But more than anything, right now, I'd love to kiss you."

She didn't think she would ever be able to breathe normally again. His voice was rough, and deep, and scraped deliciously through her body. *I'd love to kiss you.*

Instead of answering, she leaned toward him. He placed both hands on either side of her face, looking deep into her eyes, and connected with her in a way she'd never connected with anyone. And then he lowered his mouth and proceeded to kiss her like she'd never been kissed before.

She hadn't known it was possible to feel this way. His mouth was gentle at first, and when she brought her arms up to the nape of his neck, everything changed. His kiss became one that made her unable to deny her feelings any longer. Soon she was wrapped against him, and all she could think about was Scott. The feel of his mouth, the feel of his strong body holding hers, and the realization that she had never been held like this.

She held on to him, to this moment, and imprinted it in her mind.

When he finally pulled back, he kept one hand on the side of her neck, his thumb lightly brushing against her skin. Like he couldn't stop touching her. Like he saw something in her that was special. And she saw the same in him, in his eyes. It was that thing she'd been running from when she first met him— a depth, a passion, a warmth that terrified her. He was real. Scott was real, and he loved people. He'd loved his parents, his wife, his daughter. He didn't leave when life got tough.

"I think you're amazing, Olivia."

"I think the same about you. I'm sorry it took me so long to trust you."

He leaned forward to kiss her again, like he couldn't get enough of her. "Do you and Dawn want to come over for lunch tomorrow with me and Cat?"

A warmth spread over her. A thrill. This could be her life. A year ago she'd walked away from a prison sentence. A year ago she'd decided she would rather try for an imperfect life with her daughter, because at least it wasn't abusive. But in the process, she was finding herself again. And somehow she had found Scott.

"I'd love that."

CHAPTER FOURTEEN

"*Grace will lead you home.*"

Ruby closed her eyes and remembered those words, spoken to her when she was afraid and alone, as she stared at the picture of Olivia and Charlotte that sat on her hall table. This was their home. They were a new chapter, the next chapter. Both girls had loved this home as much as she had—appreciating all its old quirks and drafty windows. This home meant hope for them as well. And now, maybe it could be even more.

The doorbell rang, and she took a deep breath before heading toward the front door. She was expecting Harry, and he was always punctual. She knew this was something she should discuss with him before speaking with the rest of the family. Olivia and Dawn had just left for Scott's house, so she knew they would have the privacy needed for this conversation.

She knew she was doing the right thing, but that didn't mean it wouldn't bring repercussions. He was leaving his home for her; it was only fair that she do the same. But this wasn't going to be easy, even if it was the right thing to do.

The Christmas House was a part of her past. It held her broken heart, her healed heart. It held the memories of dear friends and moments. How could she ever let go of the past if she was living in it every day?

She wanted to start her life with Harry in a new place.

She opened the door and found Harry standing there, reminding her of last year, when he'd stood on her porch. It had always been him. It had always been him reaching out to her. Maybe leaving the Christmas House would be her chance to do something for him.

Now all she had to do was convince him she was really ready to say good-bye to this old house, her old friends, to start this new life with Harry.

* * *

"Dad, I'm totally happy for you. And don't worry, this time I won't do anything stupid," Cat said, setting the table in the kitchen. Olivia and Dawn were going to be here soon, and Cat was helping him get ready.

He opened the oven and placed the homemade pizza inside. "Thanks. Just be yourself. Olivia already loves you."

Cat walked past him and patted him on the shoulder. "Now we just need her to love you," she said, grabbing some glasses from the cupboard.

He coughed. "*We* don't need to do anything. You don't need to worry about our relationship. This is just adult stuff."

She frowned, pausing as she laid out the glasses. "Sure. Whatever you say. But you know, Sam and I were thinking.

If you, like, married Olivia, then Sam and I would be kind of related, wouldn't we?"

Scott held up a hand. "Whoa, that is way too premature, Cat. Olivia is really cautious about relationships. And we are barely dating. Marriage is something serious. Like, it takes a long time to know if you can make it work for the long term. You can't just jump headfirst."

Cat nodded with the wisdom of an adult. And then she opened her mouth and spoke with the maturity of a teenager. "Right. All of that. Plus, poor Olivia married that loser who wants nothing to do with his kid? Jerk. You're not like that at all. Sam and I were saying that, for an older person, you'd be considered a good catch."

Scott reminded himself not to have personal conversations with his daughter too often. "I'm glad. Hopefully I'll find someone before my eyesight is completely gone."

Cat rolled her eyes. "So what are we going to do? Like, you'll impress with your homemade pizza and stuff, but after that, what?"

He cringed. "I don't know. Dawn is in that stage where she won't want to sit still for too long."

Cat nodded. "True. Maybe we can go outside and play in the snow or something."

Scott prepped the coffeepot. "That's not a bad idea. Maybe Olivia can join in on the snow fight competition we have."

"Dad, we don't want to scare her off. You get nasty when you're competing."

He turned around and leaned against the counter. "This coming from the person who planned an advance attack on her father using contraband buckets of snow?"

She threw her head back and laughed. "It was so worth it. Okay, fine, maybe Olivia would like it."

The doorbell rang, and Scott drew a deep breath. He'd never had a date with his daughter around. Or a toddler. But part of it felt right, because their kids were their worlds. And he also thought maybe it would help take some of the pressure off Olivia if it wasn't one-on-one.

He and Cat walked to the door and opened it together. Olivia was standing there with Dawn, who was crying as though the world were coming to an end. He quickly held open the door.

"Omigosh, I'm so sorry, guys. She's really upset because we couldn't find her favorite stuffed animal, and I just didn't have the time to keep looking for him," Olivia said as Dawn screamed.

"Hey, hey, hey, Dawn. Maybe I can help you," Scott said, holding out his arms. To his surprise and delight, Olivia took his word for it and let him pick her up.

She stared at him. "Molly," she said with a hiccup.

"Molly's your stuffy?"

She nodded, her blue eyes welling up with tears again and almost breaking his heart. "Maybe we can find another friend. Do you want to go look?"

"Yeah, Dawn. I have a whole box of stuffed animals. Do you want to come with me and I'll show you?" Cat said, stepping in.

Dawn gave her a wobbly smile and nodded. He put her down, and Olivia stepped in and took off her little red coat.

"Okay, you are too cute in this little dress," Cat said.

The dress was a velvet-type material with tiny Rudolphs printed all over it. Her white tights and black patent shoes reminded Scott of all the little clothes Cat had worn when she was that age. Cat held out her hand, and Dawn grabbed on to it eagerly. They walked out of the room slowly, Cat telling her all about her favorite stuffed animals.

He turned to Olivia. The warmth in her eyes was unmistakable. "Hi. I don't think I said hi." He took a step closer to her and took her hand.

"That's okay. We were all in crisis management mode," she said with a smile.

"Are you hungry? I've got lunch," he said, walking to the kitchen. The timer went off just as they entered.

"It smells amazing in here," she said.

He grabbed the oven mitts and pulled the pizza out of the oven. "Thanks. My mom's recipe. Homemade pizza," he said, placing the pan on the counter.

"Oh wow. That looks so good," she said.

"I hope you like it. I'll wait a couple minutes, then slice it and call the girls."

There was something about that. Something that sounded so right. Like this could be their life. Which was ridiculous for him to even contemplate. He didn't think like that. About anyone. It was strange, because he'd always felt more domestic than Hillary. At first, he'd thought it was because he'd learned to cook from his mom, but later it came out in different ways. It had always been him who caved and did something for Cat when Hillary was too busy. It had always been him who added something else to his plate if it meant doing what was right for Cat.

And, in the end, none of it had mattered, because she'd thrown it all back in his face.

"I hear so much giggling from upstairs," Olivia said. "Looks like you and Cat saved the day for Dawn."

Both girls appeared in the doorway, Dawn with a giant smile on her face, holding an armful of stuffed animals.

"Wow, Dawn, did you take all of Cat's stuffies?" Olivia said, crouching down to see.

Dawn nodded and held each of them up.

"Cat, this is so sweet of you. But we won't take all of these. Dawn will just pick one, and then we'll be sure to replace it," Olivia said.

"Oh, no, really, I don't need them anymore. Seriously, Olivia," Cat said.

Scott watched the exchange as he cut the pizza.

"Dawn, honey, why don't you pick one to take home?"

Scott already knew what was going to happen. *Been there, done that.*

Dawn frowned and shook her head. "No, Mama."

Olivia's face turned red, but her voice remained calm. "Dawn, we can't take all of these."

Dawn hugged them to her chest tighter. "Mine."

Scott tried not to laugh at the adorable picture Dawn made. "Olivia, really, if Cat says it's okay, then it's okay. Dawn is probably saving us an hour's worth of cleanup anyway."

Olivia groaned and stood. "I feel so bad, Cat," she said, putting her arm on Cat's shoulder.

Cat smiled. "Seriously, totally fine. I didn't even realize I had so many of those in the back of my closet."

"Then it's settled. And I hope everyone's hungry, because pizza is served," he said, placing the large cutting board with the sliced pizza on the table.

They sat around the table and enjoyed a lively lunch. When they were finished, he and Olivia cleaned up the kitchen while Dawn played on the ground with her new toys and Cat sat at the table messaging Sam. Snow was slowly falling outside and coffee was brewing. It was domestic bliss, something he hadn't experienced in forever. It was different, of course, but it was right in its own way.

Cat looked up from her phone. "I think it's time we got out and played in the snow."

Dawn looked up at Cat, her eyes round with excitement. "Snow!"

"How about I take Dawn outside while you have your coffees? Dawn, do you want to make a snowman with me?" Cat said, holding Dawn's hand.

Dawn sucked in a big gulp of air and nodded.

"That's so sweet, Cat," Olivia said, walking over to the entrance. "I have Dawn's snowsuit and boots in the diaper bag. I had a feeling playing outside might be an option today."

"Cat is the expert snowman builder in the family," Scott said, joining them in the entrance. In a few minutes the girls were both ready to brave the cold. Olivia had wrapped Dawn up so well she could barely walk.

"Omigosh, you're the cutest, Dawn," Cat said as Dawn looked up at her. Her eyes were barely visible under a Hello Kitty hat that covered her ears. Dawn reached up to take Cat's hand, and hell if that didn't just choke him up a little.

Scott opened the door for them, the blast of cold air rushing inside. He closed it behind them. He hadn't stopped smiling all morning. Everything in his world finally felt right. The four of them here made him want it to be like this every day. He reached out for Olivia's hand. "Want to spy from the front window?"

She smiled. "Definitely. Cat is so sweet and patient with Dawn," she said as they stood with their coffees, watching.

Cat was still holding Dawn's hand as she guided her onto the snow-covered front yard. Dawn almost toppled over a few times, but Cat managed to steady her. The towering pines swayed, and every now and then, a mist of snow fell from the branches. Scott had fallen in love with this property and the amount of space there was for Cat to play. But he'd never dreamed of this . . . of someone like Olivia and her daughter with them.

"She is. She's always loved babies. She took that babysitting course with Sam this summer and loved it."

"Right. Good to remember," she said with a laugh.

He put his arm around her, and she curled up against him, her arm wrapping around his waist as they watched the girls slowly start the process of rolling the snow into a boulder. "I'm a sucker for a snowman in the front yard. Last year I had to practically bribe Cat to make one with me."

Olivia pulled back to look at him, her eyes wide. "Are you kidding me? Wow. You never cease to surprise me. What other secrets are you hiding?" she said with a laugh, turning back to look out the window.

He stiffened, his cup of coffee halfway to his mouth. He had to tell her. The longer he waited, the worse it would look. Cat was flailing both arms and Dawn was jumping up and down, staring at them. He couldn't do it now. Not with everyone here.

"I think we're being summoned."

"Okay, I'm actually really excited about this. One of my favorite memories of Christmas at my grandmother's is the snowmen we'd build. I'm up for it if you are," she said, turning and looking up at him, excitement lighting her face.

He leaned down to kiss her. "I'll build a better snowman than you."

She punched him lightly in the stomach and then ran to get her coat on. "You wish. You'll regret the day you entered a competition with me, Scott Martin."

He laughed, liking this competitive side of her, then proceeded to get dressed faster than her so that he'd have a head start. "What a show-off," she said as he opened the door.

Guilt pricked at his conscience, so he waited on the porch for her. She joined him a minute later, and instead of thanking him, she flung his hat off his head and chucked it in the boxwood. Her shriek of laughter made him laugh, as did the sound of his daughter cheering Olivia on.

For the next hour, Olivia and Cat teamed up against him and Dawn. And Dawn, he realized, was as much of a badass as her mother. Just as he'd finish rolling a boulder, she'd decided she should sit on it. And as it crumpled under her weight, she'd scrunch up her nose and smile sweetly at him. Then he wouldn't be able to help himself, because she was pretty much the sweetest, so he'd pick her up, give her a hug, and remind her not to do that again. They would repeat this cycle for the next five boulders he rolled until his traitor daughter yelled that they were finished.

He picked Dawn up to walk over to look. Olivia and Cat were standing on either side of an acceptable-looking snowman. "I don't know, Dawn. I don't think this snowman will win any awards, do you?"

She pointed to the snowman. "Go. Dawn. Go."

He whispered in her ear that she should do to this snowman exactly what she had done to theirs. She nodded and then ran straight into their snowman, and he watched with unabashed glee as it crashed to the ground and Dawn sat happily in the ruins of the champion snowman, clapping her hands.

"Dad! This means war!"

He tensed. He knew what that meant. Cat might think she wasn't sporty, but she could whip a snowball better than any pitcher he'd seen.

"Fine, Cat. Three against one, and none of you stand a chance," he said, before taking off and hiding behind one of the spruce trees.

He smiled as he heard Olivia say he was so arrogant.

His only option for survival was to make as much ammo as possible while Cat strategized and filled Olivia in on their snow-ball fight obsession. Luckily, Cat spoke loudly. He chuckled as he heard Olivia patiently trying to tell Dawn not to break all their snowballs. They were doomed.

He had less than two minutes, he predicted. He worked hard and fast. Crouching down, he managed to roll and make a pile of twenty snowballs. He'd crammed a couple in the front pockets of his jacket and picked up two more, ready to aim, when he heard footsteps behind him.

He turned, ready to pummel Cat with them, when he stopped.

It was Olivia.

His hesitation cost him three snowballs in the face.

"What are you doing?" she yelled, half laughing.

He swiped at the icy snow on his face. He raised his arm, pulling it back . . . and then stopped.

Snow fell around them, and she was standing there, the most beautiful smile on her face, her bright-blue eyes alive and sparkling, her cheeks rosy and flushed from the cold, and he realized he'd never seen her like this.

She wasn't carrying the weight of the world on her shoulders. He wanted to think that maybe he'd had a hand in that. Because the other image he had of her was her staring at him with distrust in her eyes after she'd heard him ripping into Rick. Then she had told him a bit about her asshole husband, and it had made sense. And he couldn't do it. He couldn't throw a snowball at her.

"What are you doing? You realize you're finished, right? Your daughter is planning an epic ambush the second I chase you around that tree," she said, walking toward him.

He cleared his throat. "I, uh, I can't do it."

She frowned, standing in front of him now. "What? Why not?"

He shrugged and thought it best to walk away.

She tripped him.

He face-planted in the snow.

And then all he heard was her unbridled laughter.

She'd freaking tripped him. He flipped over and stared up at her. She was laughing over him, clutching her sides, taking huge gulps of cold air. And he couldn't help but laugh.

He sat up and plotted his next move. Cat yelled out that she was going in with Dawn for hot chocolate because all her ammo was destroyed, which gave him a great idea.

"Here, the least I can do is help you out, since I'm the champion," Olivia said, still smiling ear to ear and holding out her hand.

Excellent. He grinned, reaching for her hand, and the second hers closed around his, he yanked her down. He caught her as she screamed and fell on him.

"Your kindness will be your downfall," he said, laughing as he kissed her.

She kissed him back, and soon the laughter was gone and he was filled with the need to be alone with her, to have more of this side of her. She kissed him back with the same urgency.

"Dad! We ran out of marshmallows!" Cat's cry of outrage from the porch cut through one of the best moments of his life.

Olivia sighed against his mouth. "Why didn't you buy marshmallows?"

He laughed as he and Olivia scrambled to sit up.

"If your offer still stands to go to dinner together, I think I'll take it," she said, as they trudged through the snow.

He grabbed her hand. "Offers never expire for you. Tomorrow night?"

She nodded.

"For the record, I think I'm the one that won today."

CHAPTER FIFTEEN

"Mary, what are you doing?"

Mary looked up from her phone. "I'm checking in with Scott. I feel like he's been avoiding me lately, and I want to make sure everything is okay."

Ruby finished tying the red ribbon on one of the gifts they were wrapping. They had set themselves up in the kitchen and were surrounded by tape and ribbons and dozens of unwrapped presents. Harry was due to arrive in an hour, and she really wanted to make sure all his gifts were wrapped first.

A week had passed since she'd planned on telling Harry about selling the Christmas House. She had chickened out. But she had tossed and turned all week, the weight of it on her shoulders. "He's fine. He's been busy with Olivia and Dawn. They're actually going on a date tonight . . . Mary, put your phone down and put your finger here," Ruby said, gesturing with her chin to the ribbon.

Mary placed her finger on the right spot. "What? At what point in time were you planning on telling me this, Ruby? The wedding? And by that, I mean theirs."

Ruby finished tying the knot and looked at Mary. "They are not getting married. Don't be putting unnecessary pressure on them."

Mary waved a hand and picked up her hot chocolate. By this point she had done way more gabbing than wrapping. "Must I remind you, Ruby, that I'm the one responsible for last year's great match?"

Ruby laughed and cut a large piece of vintage-looking wrapping paper. "You remind me all the time. But as I remind you, I had a hand in Charlotte and Wyatt's marriage too. But life's not that simple. Olivia is so cautious. It's different. She has Dawn to worry about. She's carrying around so much guilt over her divorce, I don't see her jumping into a new relationship."

"Hmm . . . true. I wonder if I can put in a good word about Scott. About what a wonderful man he is. Of course, he does need to come clean about everything or she'll be mad."

Ruby looked up sharply. "What does that mean—come clean?"

Mary's face turned red, and suddenly she was all about wrapping gifts. Ribbons and paper were flying, and she couldn't string two words together.

"Um, Mary, how long have we known each other? Do you really think I wouldn't notice you avoiding me?'

Mary put down the scissors with a thud. "You're right, Ruby. It's just not my secret to tell."

Ruby's heart raced. "Secret?"

* * *

A Christmas House Wedding

"Okay, so the flowers have been ordered. Red and white roses are basically going to be everywhere. Lots of fresh boxwood for the railing on the staircase," Charlotte said, reading off her color-coded list.

They were sitting in the great room of her house, and the coffee table was filled with white-chocolate- and peppermint-drizzled popcorn, hot chocolate, and sugar cookies. Hallmark movies were playing in the background, the fireplace was lit, and the Christmas tree was glowing. It had been the perfect day of just sister time. They had spent the day together wrapping Christmas presents and had picked up lunch in town. The plan was that Scott would pick Olivia up here and bring her back here so she and Charlotte could have their holiday sleepover.

Charlotte sighed with a smile on her face. "Okay, well, let's hurry up. Have you ordered the cake?"

Olivia nodded. "Yup. All taken care of. Oh, hey, do you have any idea what Grandma is wearing? I've heard no talk of any dress."

Charlotte tapped her pen to her chin. "I'll see what I can find out."

"I'm so happy we spent the day together. I love this house, Char. I know it was Wyatt and Sam's before you moved in, but I can totally see your touches everywhere."

Charlotte smiled, taking a sip of the hot chocolate. "Thanks. I love it too. Kind of my dream house, really. And Sam loves decorating, which makes it even more fun. Okay, let's hurry through this list, because I know you have to get ready for your date with Scott."

A jolt of panic hit Olivia. The good kind of panic. The kind that almost made her want to squeal like a kid. "I know, okay. Like five minutes and then I'm getting ready."

"I mean, I don't want to be an *I told you so* kind of person. But I told you so!" Charlotte said triumphantly. Her pens slipped off her planner and fell to the floor.

Olivia laughed. "Fine, I'll let you gloat."

"I plan on staying awake so I can get all of the details," Charlotte said, grabbing a handful of popcorn.

Olivia shifted in her seat, tucking her leg underneath. "Char, there's something I didn't mention. It's not a big deal, but when I was shopping in town last week, I ran into Dad."

Charlotte's mouth opened slightly, and Olivia could read the surprise in her eyes. "How did that go?"

Olivia shrugged. "Okay, I guess. He came to the toy shop with us. And then a part of me got really upset. I'm not sure where it came from, but lately all these old memories have been surfacing. I told him how I used to wait for him to come home."

Charlotte broke her gaze and looked down. "Yeah . . . Dad's . . . a tough one. In some ways I'm more mad at him because . . . he was great when he lived with us. I didn't see it coming, you know? Mom was the obvious train wreck, and we knew we couldn't trust her or count on her. But Dad . . . he was the best."

Tears stung the back of Olivia's eyes. "I know. And it's hard, because I know he feels bad. And he's easy to talk to and sweet and just as I remember him."

Charlotte nodded, grabbing a blanket. She was looking really pale, and Olivia realized this was not the right conversation for tonight.

"Well, to further my tales of men from the past, Will texted me."

Charlotte choked on her popcorn. "What?"

Olivia nodded. "Yeah. It was dumb. Just like 'I miss you' and stuff like that."

Charlotte looked as though she were ready to catapult off her chair. "What did you say?"

Olivia shrugged. "Nothing. Not a thing. Scott came in, and I was . . . distracted. But I did think about it again, and I think I'm most disgusted by the fact that he never even asked about Dawn. Like, talk about nail in the coffin. I mean, the nails were already there, believe me, but he didn't even ask for a picture, nothing. She's his baby. And if there's one thing I've learned, watching Wyatt and now Scott with their daughters, it's how a dad should be. A parent should be. I miss Dawn if I don't see her for a few hours. I have no idea how he can have a child he hasn't seen in a year and not care."

"I'm sorry, Liv. That is awful. You deserve so much more. So does Dawn. And you're right, Wyatt and Scott have taught me a lot. And it's painful, because it's a reminder of what we didn't have either. They would go to hell and back for their kids. Even this weekend—Wyatt is chaperoning that class trip. They do things without hesitation. I know maybe it's not fair of me to say, but I'm glad you left him. I think you're sparing Dawn the pain of what we went through."

"That's what I think too. I'm glad you have my back, and I'm so glad we're living in the same town again and can talk like this," Olivia said, fighting the emotion bubbling in her chest.

"Me too. Okay, but on to exciting and positive things— what are you wearing and where are you going? And shouldn't you be getting ready yet?" Charlotte asked, scrambling to tidy things up once she looked at her watch.

"I brought two different dresses, and I have no idea where we're going," Olivia said.

"Okay, if you need help deciding which one, I'm here. Why don't you get ready? The shower in the guest room is all stocked with everything you need. Ask if I missed something or you need anything."

Olivia stood, starting to feel a flurry of nerves and excitement mix together. "All right. I'm going. I'll come out with the first dress and get your opinion."

Charlotte gave a little squeal. "Okay, go! I'll clean this mess up."

*   *   *

An hour later, Olivia stared at herself in the full-length mirror hanging inside the closet door in the guest room at Charlotte and Wyatt's house. She looked . . . good. Maybe great. But it felt weird thinking that. She hadn't given herself permission to like the way she looked because she'd been so caught up in trying to look like the old version of herself. But the before version had never been good enough either.

But this new version of her was also lovely. Sure, fifteen of the fifty pounds of baby weight had stuck around, but she wasn't so sure she minded anymore. Her curves were a little curvier, and she kind of liked the way she looked. She ate healthy, she worked out, and she was actually fitter than she'd been prior to Dawn because she was dancing for the joy of it rather than to maintain a certain dress size.

She smoothed the velvet fabric of the sheath dress she was wearing and had to admit it fit like it was made for her. She'd borrowed the strappy black patent heels from Charlotte after the two of them had decided on this dress, and she liked the way they seemed to elongate her legs. Tugging at the bodice, she attempted to hide some of the cleavage she was so used to being embarrassed by, but when it refused to cooperate, she reminded herself that she didn't have to pretend to be something she wasn't anymore. If Scott didn't find her attractive, then . . . then she'd be crushed. But she'd walk away. She would never try to fit someone else's mold again.

The doorbell rang, and Olivia gasped. He was here. Where was her sister? Charlotte was supposed to come in for the final look. Actually, Charlotte had said she'd come in while she was doing her hair but never had. She must have gotten caught up in something, or maybe Wyatt had called.

Olivia glanced in the mirror one more time and took a deep breath before walking over to open the door. She paused as she placed her hand on the doorknob. Could she do this? Could she really do this? What if she really fell for Scott? Was she prepared to enter another relationship?

Will had been her only relationship. She'd been young and he'd taken advantage of her naïveté, of her desperation for a home and a family. How did she know what it took to be in a real relationship? She and Scott both had kids—at entirely different stages. That day at his house had been one of the best days of her life. But it had been foreign. She and Dawn had fit in there like they were meant to be there. How was that possible? How could it be that easy?

When she realized she'd been standing there for a few moments, she forced all those worries aside. They were just going on a date. She was still in control. She could press pause at any time.

She opened the door, and Scott was standing there, and she had been fooling herself. The moment his eyes met hers, she knew. She knew this was more than just dating some guy.

His gaze flickered over her, and when he raised his eyes to meet hers, there was not a doubt in her mind that he liked the way she looked, just as she was. And she liked what she saw too. He was all dressed up in a pale-blue button-down shirt that hugged his wide shoulders and narrow waist. His navy pants were tailored and highlighted his athletic body. His wool coat was dressy and completed the look. Good grief, he'd even shaved and combed his hair.

He cleared his throat. "You look beautiful, Olivia. You are beautiful."

Those simple words shouldn't have brought tears to her eyes, but they did. Not because he'd complimented her or thought she was beautiful, but because of the emotion behind them. The affection clinging to his deep voice. He was a man who wasn't so superficial as to assign a label of beauty based on size. It went beyond that.

She was about to tell him she thought the same about him when she heard Charlotte yell her name. It wasn't a normal yell; it was one that gave Olivia goose bumps. It wasn't just her, because Scott immediately joined her.

Her heart stopped when she saw Charlotte at the top of the stairs, her face an eerie shade of white with unmistakable streaks of tears. Instead of walking, she slowly sank to the ground. Scott pounded up the stairs.

A Christmas House Wedding

"What's wrong?" he said, crouching on the step below her. Olivia sat beside her, shaking in panic as Charlotte leaned heavily against the wall.

"Char, what's wrong?"

Charlotte drew her legs up. "I think . . . I need to go to the hospital," she said, her voice a thin whisper now. "I . . . I'm pregnant, and I'm bleeding."

Olivia's stomach dropped.

Scott took her wrist, and Olivia watched as he took her pulse and then looked in her eyes as though he knew what to look for. Olivia had no idea how he knew any of this and watched as he took over. "Are you cramping?"

Charlotte nodded. Scott sprang into action and lifted her up. "I'm okay, I'll walk . . . what are you doing?" she whispered.

"Going to the hospital," he said, marching down the stairs.

Olivia raced after them.

"Grab her coat and purse. We'll take my truck," he said, and she grabbed all their things and locked the door. Moments later they were on the road, Scott deftly navigating the back roads to the hospital.

"Does Wyatt know you're pregnant, Char?" Olivia asked gently, leaning forward from the back seat to place her hand on Charlotte's shoulder.

"No . . . I wanted to tell him in person when he came home tomorrow night. I wanted him to be the first to know. I had a hunch, but . . . I . . . I was too scared and in denial. I just found out yesterday for sure." Her voice broke on a sob, and Olivia squeezed her shoulder. Charlotte never broke down.

"It's going to be okay," Olivia whispered.

"I can call him now—you can tell him," Scott said, handing her his cell phone.

Charlotte shook her head and huddled down into the seat even more. "I can't . . . I . . . he'll be so worried, and he's three hours away."

"Charlotte," Scott said in a gentle voice, reaching out to take her hand. "Let him know. He can decide what he's going to do, but if it were me, I would want to know. I would be devastated to think my wife went through all this without me there."

Charlotte drew a shaky breath. "Of course. Yes, you're right. I'm not thinking clearly . . . ow . . ." she said, moaning and holding her abdomen.

"Char, it's going to be okay. Just hang in there. Here, hold my hand," Olivia said, reaching forward and clasping Charlotte's hand. A shiver stole through her at the feel of her sister's clammy hand.

"We're almost there," Scott said.

Charlotte suddenly lurched forward. "It hurts so badly," she said, her voice a tiny cry.

Wyatt's voice filled the car. "Scott, why are you calling me? Aren't you supposed to be on a date with—"

"Wy, you're on speaker. There's an emergency. I'm on my way to the ER with Charlotte and Liv. Charlotte's pregnant. Cramping and bleeding and—"

"Charlotte, I'm on my way. It's going to be okay; I love you," Wyatt said, the panic and determination in his voice bringing tears to Olivia's eyes.

"Love you," Charlotte said weakly.

The line went dead, and it took them a few more minutes to reach the hospital. As soon as they pulled up to the ER doors, Scott was out first, and he had Charlotte in his arms and inside in less than a minute while Olivia trailed behind with all their belongings. A young nurse ran out to meet them, pushing a wheelchair. Scott was ready and placed Charlotte in it. They both jogged behind the nurse, telling her every detail they knew, and soon they were standing in the empty hallway, the doors the staff had whisked Charlotte through closed in front of them.

It had all happened so fast.

Now Charlotte was gone, and Olivia couldn't go with her.

She covered her face, praying everything would be okay, that Wyatt would get here soon.

Olivia turned to Scott, and before she could say a word, he pulled her to him.

CHAPTER SIXTEEN

"Ruby, tell me what's going on. Unless it's that you're having second thoughts?"

Ruby stared into Harry's worried eyes and decided she was being immature by not telling how she really felt. They were enjoying dessert and coffee by the fire. Dawn was sleeping, and Olivia was over at Charlotte's for a girls' night and her date with Scott, which made Ruby so happy. It felt like things were finally settling down for her girls.

Now she had to come clean with Harry. She reached over and took his hand in hers. "I've been holding back. The truth is that I'm just not used to sharing my ideas, I guess. And I'm sorry, Harry. After what's happened with Anne and seeing you pack up your house, it's made me think that maybe it's time to sell the Christmas House. As much as your family home is your past, this old place is mine too."

His eyes misted over, and he squeezed her hand. "I don't want you to sell this place. It's part of who you are. You don't have to give up who you are to marry me, Ruby. That's the last thing I want."

She paused, his words sinking in. Was that what she was unintentionally doing? "It just feels like this is my home, my business, and you had no part in it. You're giving up so much by moving here, and what am I giving up?"

"Don't you think you've given up enough in life, Ruby? God, I'm not going to be a man who comes in and takes more from you. Let's retire here together. My kids aren't that far; we can use the bedrooms to host them on the weekends. Let's start a new chapter. Didn't you say Mrs. Pemberton's dream was to see that dining room filled? Well, between my family and yours, it will definitely be filled."

Ruby leaned forward to kiss Harry, something she realized she rarely initiated. She had so much growth ahead of her. But as he kissed her back, she loved him even more, for understanding what this place meant to her. It took her a moment to realize her phone was ringing.

She pulled away from him and glanced at the display. A trickle of worry hit her when she saw Olivia's picture come up. "Hello?"

"Grandma, don't panic, Charlotte will be fine. But I wanted you to know that we're at the hospital. Charlotte's pregnant, Grandma!"

Ruby shut her eyes. Goose bumps and emotion traveled through her. Harry placed his hand on her knee, and she covered it with her free one. "Why is she there, Olivia?"

"She was bleeding, and Scott and I brought her in. Wyatt is on his way back from his trip and is with her now. The doctor thinks she'll be fine and the baby will be fine. She wanted me to tell you, but don't feel you have to come."

Harry was already standing, knowing Ruby would want to go. "Is it all right if we get Dawn bundled up and bring her? I really must see Charlotte."

"Of course, Grandma. We're still in the ER, but I'll text you if they move her to a room before you get here."

"Okay, see you soon."

Ruby stood on shaky limbs. Her Charlotte. She had known something was off with her. She walked toward Harry, who was getting their coats at the front door.

"I can't believe it, Harry. I know Olivia said she'll be fine, but I really must see for myself. Wow, my Charlotte. I just . . . I can't believe it. Pregnant. I'm so happy. So happy. This is everything."

"What? Charlotte's pregnant?"

Ruby's stomach dropped at the sound of Wendy's voice.

* * *

Wyatt burst through the corridor doors, looking as though he'd just lost his entire world. His eyes were panicked, his face steely. "Where is she?"

Olivia pointed to the room they were sitting in front of, not even bothering to fill him in, because she knew he needed to see for himself that Charlotte was okay. Scott squeezed her hand, and she turned to him. Sitting here with him the last three hours had been an emotional roller coaster. She had gone from panicked for her sister to relieved when the doctor had come out to inform them that the bleeding had stopped, the baby was fine, and Charlotte was sleeping. "Poor Wyatt; he looks as though he's just been through hell," she said softly.

"Because he has. I can't imagine the drive he just had. Charlotte and Sam are his whole world, as they should be. And then to be so far away when it happened . . . hell, I'm sure that took a couple years off his life," Scott said with a rueful laugh.

Olivia absorbed everything he was saying, the certainty with which he said it. Scott's wife had been cherished and dearly loved. Just as her sister was dearly loved. There hadn't been an ounce of anything but anguish in her brother-in-law's eyes as he'd run down the hallway.

It was strange, because she and Charlotte had grown up together and had approached their lives in completely different ways. While Charlotte had closed herself off from love and relationships, Olivia had sought them out. She had wrongly believed she needed a man, a spouse, to give her the life she always wanted. But she'd been willing to risk her own self-worth for the picture-perfect family. She'd thought it was simple, like following a recipe: find a man, get married, buy a house, have a baby . . . live happily ever after. But she'd never understood that love wasn't easy, that it couldn't be faked. That real love had the power to break the strongest person right down to their core.

Wyatt's face, his eyes, in the one minute she had with him as he ran down the hallway, held more emotion in it than she'd ever seen from any of the men in her life. And he'd been with her sister for barely a year. And Scott . . . he understood exactly what Wyatt was going through.

But Olivia had gone through a horrible and long labor by herself. It had taken that—being left in the delivery room, with her legs in the air, pushing her baby into the world, watching the disgusted expression on her ob-gyn's and nurse's faces as her husband left to answer texts—for her to finally realize that this wasn't love. And when she'd finally held Dawn in her arms, a mix of pain and exhaustion and grief threatening to overwhelm her and steal the joy of the blessing in her arms, she'd let it all go.

All her ideals and silly daydreams. And she'd clung to the reality of the miracle she held and vowed she would never let her little girl down.

Wyatt came out of the room half an hour later, looking a little better. "She's good. Thank God, she's good. The baby's good."

Relief surged through Olivia as his words sank in, and she couldn't even bring herself to move. She stood silently, watching as her brother-in-law leaned against the wall and covered his face, letting out a ragged breath that sounded like a sob. But Scott went to Wyatt while she stood still, a foreigner among all of them. Among all this love they had, this secret world they'd experienced. Scott put his hand on Wyatt's shoulder for a moment before Wyatt nodded. He took his hands off his face and looked at Olivia.

"She wants to see you, Liv."

Olivia nodded, realizing just then that her hands were tightly clenched together. "Thanks. I won't be long."

He nodded, and she shot them a wobbly smile before she walked into the hospital room. Tears stung her eyes at the sight of her sister in the bed, the sound of machines and the sight of the IV bringing her right back to one of the most conflicting days she'd ever experienced. Dawn's birth had been the best and worst day of her life, and she hated that. She hated that a horrible memory was tied to the day of her daughter's birth, and she didn't know if she'd ever forgive herself for that. She would work on it, though, because she knew, deep down, that it wasn't her fault. She blinked, brushing those thoughts aside as she approached Charlotte.

"Hey, how are you feeling?"

Charlotte gave her a shaky smile, her own eyes glistening with tears. "Really, really thankful. I'm so sorry—I must have scared you and Scott. I was going to tell you, Liv. I only just found out, and honestly, I think I knew, but I was in denial. Wyatt and I hadn't planned this at all. We only just got married this summer, and . . ."

"Hey, hey," Olivia said, interrupting her. She sat in the chair beside the bed and took her sister's free hand. "You don't have to apologize. I get it. You wanted to tell Wyatt first. Of course, I get that. I'm just so happy you're okay and the baby's okay. And now I get to say congratulations! You're going to be an amazing mom," she said, not bothering to control the tears that dripped from her eyes.

Charlotte was crying too as she squeezed her hand. "This is it, Liv. We made it. You have Dawn, and I'm going to have a baby, and they will have cousins. Our kids will get to play together. They'll have a real family."

Olivia nodded through her tears. "Yes, yes, they will. And sleepovers. And every holiday. And birthday parties. And Christmas together."

Charlotte let out a small laugh. "All my Pottery Barn dishes are out of storage."

Olivia's chest ached, knowing what those dishes symbolized, knowing what her own had symbolized. They were about creating their own lives, their own families. For Charlotte, it was a happy ending. For Olivia, not so much yet. "I sold all of my Williams Sonoma ones, and I'm glad I did. The next time I buy dishes . . . well, my life will be very different . . . I just want you to know that I will always be grateful to you, Char. I wouldn't be here without you."

"Same goes for me," Charlotte said, handing her a tissue before blowing her own nose.

"Not true, but thanks," Olivia said with a laugh.

"Don't ever say that. You've always been my best friend. You've always been a part of my heart, Liv."

Olivia choked back a sob as she stared into her sister's eyes. She had so many regrets from the past few years with Will, separated from her family. From Charlotte. If she could go back, she would. But it was a fine line, because she'd never regret Dawn.

"I love you. I love Wyatt. I'm so happy for you both. Are you staying overnight?"

Charlotte nodded. "Just to be safe. Does Grandma know?"

"I called her. I assumed you'd want her to know. I don't think Mom is home."

"I really can't deal with Mom right now," Charlotte said, rubbing her temples.

Olivia squeezed her hand. "Okay, listen, I don't want to get you stressed out about this. I'm going to go, because I have a feeling Wyatt's going to be sitting here beside you until they let you go home. Love you," she said, standing.

Charlotte squeezed her hand again. "Love you too. And say thank you to Scott, okay? I don't know how he was so level-headed and quick-thinking."

Olivia nodded. That thought had occurred to her too. It seemed like it could be more than just quick thinking. But it didn't seem like him to keep something from her.

"Will do. Just rest up, okay?"

* * *

"Thank you. Char told me what you did, how fast you got here," Wyatt said, his voice raspy and heavy with emotion.

Scott leaned against the wall beside him. "You know you never need to thank me for anything. I'm just glad she's okay. And the fact that you called it in, that we were en route, made things move really fast here. And the baby. Hell, Wy, you're going to be a dad again. Congratulations."

Wyatt let out a rough laugh, leaning his head against the wall. But there was no mistaking the smile that transformed his otherwise haggard-looking face. "Yeah, I swear that was the biggest surprise. I, uh, I don't think there is any possible way I could be happier than I am right now. It's impossible to think it can get even better than this."

Scott rubbed at his chest, the ache there deep. "You deserve it. Charlotte, Sam, this new baby, all of it."

Wyatt shot him a look. "So do you. You were here with Olivia tonight. Have you told her?"

Scott ran his hands through his hair, tugging a little to release some of the tension in his fingers. "No. I have to, I know, but hell, this isn't shit I've talked about in detail."

"I get it."

"I don't know, Wy. I don't know that you can get it. You're here, still standing, still with a badge. I left."

The words didn't come easily, and they never had. He and Wyatt never spoke about this. There was an understanding there, and he trusted Wyatt with his life, but it was hard. It was a wound that would never heal. And he'd never told him about those last days, those last conversations with his wife.

"You did what you had to for your family. For Cat. You put them first. You knew the signs and you got out when you could, before things got bad. That's something you should be proud of, and I swear to you, man, I would do the same in a heartbeat. Don't think I wouldn't. Don't think I judge you. I would do anything for Sam. I've waited a lifetime for Charlotte. And this new baby, this new chance. I'd give it all up in a heartbeat if it meant being there for them, giving them the best of me, not the worst."

Scott took a deep breath, some of the weight lifting. "Thank you. I just don't know that Olivia will see it like that. Hell, I don't want to be grouped into her father's category."

Wyatt nodded. "I get that. But you're not. You knew what was happening and you listened to the signs. You did put your family first, Scott."

"Thanks. Do you need me to pick up Sam for you or is there anything you need?"

Wyatt shook his head. "Thanks, but I didn't want to ruin her class trip. Cat is there for her too. I told her there was a work emergency. I hated lying, but I didn't want her worried. I'll call her later and let her know everything's fine, and Charlotte and I can tell her about the baby together."

The door opened and Olivia came out, her eyes rimmed with red, but the smile on her face made him want to believe that second chances were possible for both of them as well.

"You can go back in, Wyatt. And, um, congratulations," she said, reaching out to him. Wyatt hugged her for a moment.

"Thanks, Liv. Thanks to both of you. And, uh, go ahead and get some rest. I'm sure we'll see you both tomorrow," he said.

"Where is she?"

Olivia inhaled sharply at the sound of her mother's shrill cry. The three of them turned to find her mother, father, Harry, and her grandmother, who was pushing Dawn in a stroller, running toward them. Olivia winced as she turned to Wyatt.

"I didn't think everyone would be here."

"Don't worry about it," Wyatt said, already shifting over so he was standing in front of Charlotte's door.

"Wyatt, let me in," her mother said, making an attempt to sidestep him.

Wyatt was a wall. He held up his hand. "I'm sorry, Wendy. She's allowed one visitor. She already saw Olivia. I can see if she's up for one more, but that's it."

"I'm her mother."

Wyatt's jaw clenched, and Olivia could tell he was trying to hold on to what he really wanted to say. Heck, what she wanted to say. "I know. But she has high blood pressure, so the last thing she needs right now is to get agitated."

Her mother inhaled sharply. "Are you implying that a visit from me will raise her blood pressure?"

Everyone looked away except Wyatt. "Wendy, I'll be right back. I'll go ask Charlotte if she's up for a visit."

"Thank you so much for bringing Dawn," Olivia said, joining her grandmother and trying to distract her mother.

"Of course. Harry and I bundled her up well, and, sweetie that she is, she fell back asleep in the car," Grandma Ruby said, then whispered, "I didn't say anything; your mother overheard."

Olivia gave her a quick hug. "I thought something like that. Don't worry, Grandma."

Wyatt came back out a moment later, and everyone was silent as they waited for him to speak.

"Grandma Ruby, you can go in."

CHAPTER SEVENTEEN

Ruby opened the door to Charlotte's room, distancing herself from Wendy's cry of outrage and focusing on her granddaughter. "Oh my, Charlotte, how are you, honey?"

Charlotte smiled at her and held out her hand. "Hi, Grandma, I'm totally fine. I didn't want to worry you, but I would have hated for you to think I didn't want to tell you about something so big."

Ruby gave her a kiss on the cheek and settled into the seat beside the bed. "I'm glad you let Olivia call. I had a hunch something was up with you these last couple weeks. A baby! Congratulations."

Charlotte smiled at her. She looked tired and worn out, but the happiness in her eyes was clear as day. "Thank you, Grandma. I think I was almost in denial, and I'm not sure why. Well, no, I guess maybe I was nervous on a subconscious level because we weren't exactly planning on a baby right now."

"Oh, Charlotte. That man outside would go to the moon and back for you. Heck, he even stood up to your mother," Ruby said with a laugh.

Charlotte winced. "Poor Wyatt. I'll worry about Mom tomorrow, I guess."

Ruby patted her hand. "I'll deal with your mother. You are to worry about nothing. Let the doctors and nurses and Wyatt take care of you. Rest. That's your job. You rest until you're allowed to resume normal activities."

"Sure, I will. I can plan your wedding from bed," she said with a smile.

Ruby tilted her head. "Charlotte, you are not to worry about my wedding. Everything is practically done anyway. I'm going to tell Olivia not to let you do anything."

Charlotte rolled her eyes. "Color-coding lists is actually therapeutic for me."

Ruby chuckled as she stood and leaned over to give Charlotte a kiss on the forehead. "Rest. I must leave, because Wyatt warned that you need your rest. He's a good man, Charlotte. Don't hold things back from him, dear. I know it's hard. I know it goes against your instincts because of . . . well, because of what you've been through. But you have to push through that. He's your husband. You have to trust him with everything," she said, mentally making a note to take her own advice.

Charlotte's eyes welled up with tears. For a second Ruby caught a glimpse of that serious, stoic little girl with the tragic blue eyes who'd arrived on her doorstep all those years ago. Charlotte had carried the world on her shoulders from a young age.

"Grandma, thank you for everything. You've always been there for me. I don't think I would have ever had the courage to have a relationship with Wyatt if it hadn't been for you."

Charlotte's image blurred as Ruby choked back her own tears. "You would have found your way to him, Charlotte. I know it. Now trust yourself and trust him too."

Charlotte nodded, pulling the covers up a little higher and closing her eyes.

Ruby took a deep breath and left the room with a lighter heart.

*   *   *

"I just don't get it. I'm her mother," Wendy said.

Scott made eye contact with Olivia, who was buttoning up her coat, her face red.

"Wendy, Charlotte had to make a choice. It doesn't have to be a personal snub," Wyatt said, glancing at his watch.

"She's my child, Wyatt. Of course it's personal."

Mac put his hand on Wendy's shoulder. "She could only choose one person. I think it's probably fair that she chose Ruby."

Wendy shrugged his hand off her shoulder. "Not now, Mac. I don't need to hear excuses. Fine, well, Wyatt, you can tell Charlotte congratulations, and if she would like to see us, we will be here right away."

Wyatt gave her a nod. "Will do, Wendy. It really isn't personal. I don't think Charlotte wants you to feel badly."

Mac extended his hand, and Wyatt shook it. "Tell her we understand. And congratulations, Wyatt. I really am happy for you both, and if you need anything, just call."

Victoria James

"Appreciate it. I'll be sure to pass the message to Charlotte."

"Good night, everyone," Mac said, placing his hand on the small of Wendy's back and giving her a slight push.

"Good night," Wendy repeated, and the two of them walked down the hallway.

There was an audible release of tension once they were out of earshot. Ruby came out of Charlotte's room, and Harry met her. "How is she?"

Ruby smiled, but she looked tired. "She's good. Very good. Wyatt, congratulations again. You can go in. We'll leave now. Let us know if you need anything."

Wyatt reached out and gave her a kiss on the cheek and shook Harry's hand. "Will do. Thank you both."

Harry and Ruby came over to say good-bye to him and Olivia. "We'll get going and bring Dawn home with us."

"Are you sure you're up for it? It's been an exhausting night. I don't mind taking her," Olivia said.

"No, no. You two were supposed to be on a date. At least you can take a long drive back, just the two of you," Ruby said, reaching out to give Olivia a hug.

"I'll help with Dawn," Harry said, giving Olivia a hug as well before shaking Scott's hand.

"Okay, thank you both so much. I hope Dawn stays asleep for you," Olivia said, pulling down the stroller cover.

They exchanged good-byes, and Ruby and Harry waved as they walked down the corridor.

After saying good-bye to Wyatt, Scott and Olivia headed out, hand in hand. He was relieved by the blast of cold air that hit them as they went outside.

226

He looked at Olivia, at the emotion in her eyes, and knew he had to tell her the truth. If he was ever really going to move forward, if he was ever going to earn her trust, it would have to be done. He had never been one to lie or hide things, and he knew that if whatever this was with Olivia was going to become something real, sooner was better than later.

He felt that there was something different between them, like a wall had come down. In her, yes, but in him as well. Olivia brought out a side of him he hadn't expected. She brought out a protective instinct that was different than the one he had for Cat, but there nonetheless. And it wasn't because she wasn't capable, because she definitely was. It was more on the emotional side of things. He knew how deep her hurt went.

"Ready to go home?"

She nodded, giving him a smile. "Definitely." They walked to the car, snowflakes starting to fall around them. Down the quiet rows of the parking lot, his eyes on the doors ahead, his mind on the future, ready to let go of his past. The December air was cold and damp and the sky filled with stars.

"You okay?" he asked as they reached his truck.

"Yes. Exhausted. I think the adrenaline's worn off. I could sleep for days," she said with a laugh as he held open her door and she got into the passenger seat.

"I bet. Do you want to go back to Charlotte and Wyatt's or your grandmother's?" he asked, before hopping into the driver's seat.

"I guess my grandmother's. Just in case Wyatt needs to come home and pick something up. I don't want to invade his space."

Minutes later he glanced over at Olivia, who was staring out her window as they drove in silence. "There's something I wanted to tell you. Something I've been meaning to tell you, just waiting for the right time," he said.

She turned sharply to him. "Sure. Do you want to come in for a drink?"

The thought of Ruby—or worse, Wendy—overhearing their conversation wasn't appealing. But it was late, and there was nothing open in their small town. He pulled into the driveway, the twinkling lights from Ruby's famous display almost making him think this might be the perfect spot. "Maybe we can sit on the porch."

She looked over at him, her smile not so easy now. "Um, okay. Sure."

They walked up the porch steps, and she huddled farther into her coat as they sat on the first steps. "What's up?"

He turned to face her, taking a moment to search for the right words. But the longer he took, the more doubt crept into her eyes, which was exactly what he didn't want.

"I haven't been completely honest about my past. It's not something I really share. Not many know. Wyatt. Aunt Mary, of course, and Cat."

She stiffened, and he knew she must be bracing for the worst. "Okay . . ."

"I was a homicide detective."

Her mouth dropped open. "What? When?'

He wanted to reach across the step and pull her hand into his, to be able to offer—physically—the comfort his words couldn't give her right now. He knew that was two counts against him:

the secret and the career. Two counts for a woman who'd already been given way too many reasons not to trust people. "I left years ago."

Her brows furrowed. "Why?"

"A few different reasons. But there was a case I was working on. That I solved and . . . could not move on from. I . . ." He ran a hand over his jaw and forced the details back into his mind to give her context. But they were things he'd trained himself not to think about. "You may have even heard about this one. It made headlines in the city. It was a brutal case. A ten-year-old girl had been kidnapped. Broad daylight. Nice neighborhood. Walking home from school one day. There was no trace. It shook up the entire community. We had no leads. Until some jogger found pieces of a human body washed up on the shore of Lake Ontario."

He stopped talking when she gasped. But he couldn't stop for long, because he needed to get out the most important parts and be done with this. "We had our lead with the traces of DNA on the body. . . . we found him . . . I can't . . . there's no need to go into details. I lived and breathed this case. I was a different person. I didn't sleep. I didn't laugh. I wasn't there for my wife, for Cat. I can barely even remember myself those days or picture myself at home. But I couldn't rest. But what he did to her . . . how she suffered . . . it was on all our minds when we found him. But I struggled with arresting him. I wanted to kill him.

"Cat was so little at the time, and it was hard to separate my . . . instincts, my feelings as a father, from those of a detective. I mean, we all wanted this guy to pay. We knew our evidence was airtight. He'd go away for life. But that wasn't enough. The idea that he'd spend the rest of his life in a first-world prison, when he was literally the epitome of evil and had tortured a child and her parents would never recover from this, made me sick. But I did it. I played by the book, but after . . . I wasn't . . . I wasn't right. I spoke to Hillary about it—she was a cop, but she didn't get it. I went to counseling. I took a leave of absence. And then . . . then Hillary was diagnosed with cancer, and, uh, my world literally fell apart in front of my face."

When he least expected it, from the woman he least expected to ever reach out on her own, a hand wrapped around his. Olivia's. And it had an effect he would never have anticipated; *she* had an effect he never would have thought possible.

She hadn't judged him.

She was taking his word for it.

And she made him want all those things again. She made him want more than today, more than a night, more than a fling. She made him want to lean into that softness, that warmth that promised a soft place to fall, a shelter from a life that had stripped him of his trust. And he wanted to be that for her.

"I'm sorry," she whispered, her voice shaky.

He swallowed hard and looked down at her hand on his, resolving to finish the rest of this, the parts he'd never told anyone, including Wyatt. Because he knew there was no going forward without the truth.

"Hillary never got over me leaving. She was tough as nails, but she'd never worked a case like that. And she judged me for it, I know.

"There was this divide that formed between us that last year that was never there before. Or maybe nothing had ever happened between us to expose it. One of the issues I was fighting was my paranoia over Cat's safety. I had new locks installed on her bedroom windows. Alarm contacts on them. Then some nights I would sneak in and sleep on her floor. I wasn't sleeping more than a couple hours a night and would have to take care of her, take Hillary to her treatments, and life started piling up. I knew I wanted out. I wasn't living anymore. I was trying to keep everyone alive around me, but I was going to break. I continued with the therapy but turned in my badge.

"Hillary and I had a major fight when I did, and she told me she didn't think she'd ever get over it. She was disappointed in me. We were never the same. I loved her. I was there for her. And saying good-bye at the end was hell. It was hell for all of us. For the family we'd built. For Cat. I felt like I was saying good-bye to the woman I'd loved forever and also to our marriage, because I don't know that it would have survived even if she had.

"And I spiraled into a really dark place for a while. My parents stepped in to help with Cat. Wyatt moved back here. I continued with the therapy and got my shit together after a year of not knowing what the hell I was going to do. I started my business, I learned how to be a single father, and I accepted my decisions. Wyatt helped with that. He didn't judge me like Hillary did, and he got it. I have a hard time talking about this. I don't share this. But you aren't just some woman I'm dating. And you have your own history that probably doesn't help my case."

He finally turned to her. She was staring at him, her blue eyes filled with tears and raw emotion.

"You put your family first. You put Cat first. You knew what you could handle. You took the harder road by admitting it and getting out before there was nothing left for you to give. You shouldn't be ashamed of that. You should be proud of that. Cat is very blessed to have you as a dad. To have all of you here."

Something inside him changed as he processed her words. Those blue eyes were looking up at him with understanding and compassion and . . . something else. The something he didn't want to ignore anymore. The something that pulled at his heart-strings and made him want to be who she needed him to be. He slowly raised his hands to frame the sides of her face, catching the sigh that escaped her mouth as her lips parted. Snow tumbled out of the sky around them, and for a minute, the magic of this place, the Christmas House, the magic of the woman in front of him, made him believe all things were possible. And as he lowered his head to kiss Olivia, as he had wanted to do every time he'd seen her since he'd first met her, he was able to put his past to bed and finally be fully present.

And soon his hands were tangled in her hair and she was wrapped up in his arms, and he didn't think anyone had ever felt so right. He kissed her, lost in her, memorizing every little sound, every taste, until all the porch lights turned on like they were onstage. It was like they were sixteen. Olivia was holding on to his forearms, and he wasn't quite ready to let go and face whoever was out there either.

"Talk about timing," he finally said, glancing over his shoulder to see Olivia's mother standing at the door.

Her mother's voice slipped out of the house. "Olivia, is that you? Just checking up on you to make sure everything is okay."

Olivia rolled her eyes, and for a second, he felt like a teenager. "I'm fine, Mom. I'll be in a minute."

"All right."

Olivia looked up at him, her lips full and almost smiling. "That kind of parental involvement might have been beneficial fifteen years ago. At almost thirty, it's a little irritating."

He laughed. He was inordinately pleased that she hadn't taken her hands off him. "Very true."

"Thank you for sharing what you did. It makes a lot of sense and answers a lot of questions I had about you. Things I'd noticed. Scott . . . I meant what I said. I wish my dad had recognized the signs before he reached his breaking point. I will never get back those years that were lost. The ripple effect of his leaving was devastating. You're . . . you're a good man."

He leaned down to kiss her one last time before walking her to the door. She was a woman who'd been hurt by the two men in her life she'd trusted. He didn't take any of this lightly.

But he knew she was also his second chance, and he would never take for granted that she was trusting him with her heart.

CHAPTER EIGHTEEN

"Ruby, I owe you an apology."

Ruby stared at Anne, seated across from her in the parlor room. When Harry's daughter had shown up on the porch unannounced, Ruby had braced herself for more derision. But Anne's face was pale, and her eyes were filled with sadness. "Oh, Anne, it's okay."

Anne shook her head, wrapping her hands around the cup of coffee. "It's not okay. I'm embarrassed and wish I could take back what I said to you. I . . . I've always been the loner in the family, and if I'm being completely honest, I think I was jealous. I was jealous that my dad could move on and find someone, and . . . I guess what I'm trying to say is that my reaction had more to do with me than it did with you, and I'm sorry."

Ruby let out a long sigh. "That's a lot to be dealing with. The fact that you can identify all that in yourself is commendable. A lot of people aren't that self-aware. I know it's hard to admit all that. It's easier to just be angry sometimes than admit the truth.

But please know I'm not holding a grudge, and I haven't judged you at all."

Anne closed her eyes for a moment and smiled. "Thank you, Ruby. I really am happy for you and my dad. I know you're not just some woman he met. I haven't seen him this happy . . . well, I don't even know how long it's been. You're both really good for each other."

Ruby smoothed the fabric of her dress as she searched for the right words. "Thank you. I think so too. I, um, I've been alone for most of my adult life. For all of it, really. What happened with Richard sort of scarred me, and I wanted nothing to do with men, honestly. I was determined to find my own way in the world, I made good friends, I raised Wendy. I didn't think I needed more. Until your dad came to the door last Christmas. He was worth waiting for. It's never too late."

Anne leaned forward, her eyes serious. "I've always been so shy and insecure and just didn't want to risk everything for a chance at love. But honestly, seeing you and my dad together makes me regret my choices. I'm alone, and I'm too old to start a family."

"Like I said, Anne, it's never too late."

Anne smiled. "Thank you. And thank you for accepting my apology. Now, at least, things will be perfect for the wedding tomorrow."

They both stopped when they heard a noise in the hallway. "It's just me and Dawn. We're getting ready to meet Scott for some Christmas shopping," Olivia said, poking her head in the doorway. Dawn was tugging on Olivia's hand, all dressed in her bright-red coat and jeans rolled up at the cuffs to reveal red flannel that matched her boots.

Ruby laughed. "You'd better get going. By the looks of things, Dawn is very excited."

"She is. We'd better run or we'll be late. Nice seeing you again, Anne," Olivia *said with a smile before she and Dawn left.*

Ruby's chest swelled at the brightness around Olivia. She was going to have to update Mary. But so far, it was looking as though this Christmas was going to be the best one yet. Even Anne had come around. Nothing could go wrong now.

* * *

"I can't believe tomorrow is Christmas Eve and my grandmother is getting married, my sister is having a baby, and I . . ." Olivia stopped speaking abruptly, her face hotter than the hot chocolate in her hand.

Scott paused on the sidewalk, a look that was somehow earnest and mischievous sparkling in his eyes. She clutched the handlebar of Dawn's stroller and opened her mouth, prepared to make up an excuse that would be completely wimpy. But something stopped her. Maybe it had a little to do with some of the conversation she'd overheard between her grandmother and Anne. She was happy for her grandmother that Anne was coming around, but something about the way Anne spoke of her regrets had resonated with her. She understood that. Being too afraid. And she didn't want that anymore. She didn't want to regret not trying.

She didn't know if it was the magic of this town, of the snow that tumbled gently, dusting everything with a little hint of magic, or if it was the picture-perfect downtown, or if it was the man beside her. The one who had already spent more time with her daughter than Dawn's own father. The man who'd made her feel safe enough to open up to. The one who encouraged her dreams. The one who held her and didn't make her feel weak for needing him. The one who was staring at her like he really, really cared about what she was about to say.

Her palms were suddenly sweaty inside her gloves as she opened her mouth, ditched the filter she'd been using for the last few years, and blurted out what she really thought: "I wish I'd met you first. I mean, I know we can't go back and see the future or unravel the thread too much, or the people we love wouldn't be in it. And of course, I don't ever want to wish for a world without Dawn. Because that's not what I meant at all, and I know you were very much in love with Hillary—and thanks for telling me about all that, by the way—but—"

"Olivia?"

She drew in a gulp of air, mortified by the verbal tornado she was responsible for unleashing, and looked up at him. "Yes?"

"Me too."

"What?"

Somehow, even though shoppers bustled by them, she was holding on to a baby stroller, and they were standing in the middle of the sidewalk, Scott made her feel like the three of them were the only people on earth. He nodded and took a step closer to her, raised his hands and cupped each side of her face, and kissed her. Like he didn't care who saw or how many people they were irritating by blocking their path. And the moment he kissed her, she didn't care about any of those things either. She didn't remember anything until she heard a forceful little voice and felt a tug on the stroller.

"Go, Dawn, Go."

Scott smiled and pulled back. "I think we'd better go."

Olivia laughed and poked her head over the top of the stroller to see Dawn pointing at the toy store. "Okay, sweetie. We'll go into the toy store."

Dawn pumped her legs. "Go!"

"Do you think she's going to last in the stroller, or can I pick her up?" Scott asked as they made their way down the sidewalk.

Olivia's heart squeezed at the question. "I think she'd love that. But I have to warn you, I'm not sure she'll want to be held for long."

He grinned. "Of course not. Don't worry, Cat was ridiculously fast in stores, and there was never a damaged display on my watch."

Olivia laughed and watched as he deftly unclipped the stroller straps and picked Dawn up. Her daughter was beaming as they made their way into the shop. Olivia trailed them with the stroller and wasn't surprised at all when Dawn made a beeline for the dollhouse. Scott crouched down beside Dawn as she stood in front of the house. "How did I know you were going to come here, Dawn?"

Scott stood beside Olivia as Dawn picked up some of the people and furniture. Luckily, all the figures and furniture were wooden, so Olivia didn't have to worry about anything breaking. "Just be gentle with everything, okay?"

Dawn nodded and continued to play, her back to them.

"That's a pretty great house. All wood. Solid," Scott said, running his hand over the roof.

"I know. I used to be obsessed with dolls and all of that, wishing for the perfect house and family. I was actually thinking I might surprise Dawn with this," she said, lowering her voice.

He frowned. "There's a sold sign on the back, Liv."

Her heart sank. "I should have bought it when I was here with my dad."

He put his arm around her, the gesture feeling natural and right. "Maybe we can see if we can get one at another toy store? We could drive into the city."

She looked up at him and smiled. "Thank you, but we don't have time to be running to Toronto the day before Christmas Eve. It's not a big deal. It was an extra gift. Maybe a nostalgic one. I don't know. But I already bought a ton of gifts for Dawn."

Dawn swung around, as many dolls and pieces of furniture as she could hold in her little hands piled against her chest. Pieces fell to the ground as she looked up at them. "Mine."

Olivia was torn between laughing and crying. Dawn's big blue eyes were glittering with determination, her full cheeks red, almost the same color as her coat. "Mama, mine," she repeated.

"Oh, sweetie, it's almost Christmas. Santa will be bringing you so many presents. We have to put all this back, okay?"

Dawn shook her head, and Scott made a choked noise. When she looked over at him in desperation, he crouched down in front of Dawn. "I've got this, Olivia. Cat was a little shoplifter until she was three."

Olivia stifled her objection and watched with avid interest as Scott tried to negotiate with her clever and precocious daughter. "Mommy is right, Dawn. What if Santa doesn't come at all if he thinks you already have all these toys? You can't buy presents now, sweetheart. Tomorrow night, Santa will be coming down the chimney with gifts."

Dawn's head tilted, and she studied Scott's face, her brow furrowed. Scott shot Olivia a smug grin, clearly thinking victory was his. Dawn clutched the toys to her chest. "Mine."

"This is going to end badly," Olivia whispered, already dreading the scene that was about to unfold. Today she was going to be the parent hauling out the screaming toddler in the packed toy store.

Scott rubbed the back of his neck, still crouched down in front of Olivia. "How about this. If you put all those pieces back nicely in the dollhouse, I will buy you any one of those Christmas stuffies," he said, pointing to the bin overflowing with brightly colored stuffed animals.

Dawn's eyes widened, and she looked at the stuffies.

"Scott, you don't have to do that," Olivia whispered.

He held up a hand. "This is a pivotal moment in the negotiation, Liv. Trust me."

Dawn looked back and forth from the stuffies to Scott, making no attempt to release her armload of toys. Scott reached over and picked up a stuffed polar bear dressed in a Christmas sweater and Santa hat. "Wow, he's so soft and cute."

Dawn quickly shoved the figures into the dollhouse and grabbed the stuffy from Scott and hugged it. "Fank you."

Scott ruffled her hair before standing up. "You're very welcome." Then he turned to Olivia and gave her a smug grin. "A little parenting tip from a pro. Negotiation always works if it's some kind of trade."

Dawn appeared in front of them, holding two more stuffies. "Mine."

Olivia burst out laughing. "She conned you, Scott."

Scott was laughing as he reached down to pick up Dawn and her three stuffies. "That's okay. I think I'm the one who got the better end of the deal."

As if Dawn understood what he meant, she reached out and circled her arms around his neck and held on, a polar bear, reindeer, and unicorn dangling over his shoulders, her eyes sparkling as Olivia followed them up to the cash. Her throat constricted as she watched Dawn and Scott together, as though they had always been this way. And she wished that this was the way it always was. That now they'd be on their way to pick up Cat and then the four of them would have a lively and fun dinner together. That they could so easily become a family. But that was almost too good to be true, too amazing to wish for. Dawn's biological father didn't want her, and yet this man had already shown her daughter so much affection and kindness . . .

CHAPTER NINETEEN

"Wendy, promise me you will be nice," Ruby said, taking her pale-pink suit out of the closet. It didn't help that her hands were shaking as she hung it on the back of the door.

It was her wedding day. Hers. And here she was, standing in Mrs. Pemberton's grand bedroom. Ruby had first walked into this room as a pregnant and scared teenager. And somehow she'd found a way to raise her daughter and help raise her granddaughters. And now it was her turn, her turn to fulfill her dreams.

Wendy let out a loud sigh as she glanced over at Ruby's suit. "I really am trying not to be insulted. What is it you think I'm going to do? Pull someone's chair out from under them as they go to sit down?"

Ruby joined her at the mirror and picked up her hairbrush as she searched for the right words. "Of course not. But it's the more subtle things—the drive-by almost insults—that I'm more concerned about," she said.

Wendy started pacing the room, and Ruby regretted bringing anything up. "That is just so not fair. I don't know why everyone always assumes the worst about me. I'm so happy for you and Harry. Really, Mom. I'm so glad he came to the door last Christmas. I want to see you married and living what's left of your life to the fullest."

Ruby put her brush down and tried to relax her shoulders. "Wendy, I have no intention of going anywhere soon. I'm not ninety-five. But I do appreciate the sentiment. I think you'll really like Harry's children when you get to know them better. Especially Anne."

"I'm sure I will. It's exciting to think there are all these cousins we barely know. But the biggest question is, why the heck did you buy a suit when I told you that was boring?"

Ruby crossed her arms. "I don't know. I have regrets. But I can't think about that. I don't want to have to think about the dress I really wanted but waited too long to get. I won't have to wonder about how it's going to feel to actually be married. Married, Wendy."

Wendy walked over to her, and for a second, Ruby let the years and the arguments and the disappointments slip away. Wendy must have been on the same wavelength, because she suddenly threw her arms around her. Ruby didn't think they'd hugged like this in years.

"I'm really happy for you, Mom."

Ruby hugged her back, emotion catching her chest. "I love you too, Wendy. Thank you."

When she pulled back, she found Mary standing in the doorway to the bedroom, holding a garment bag. But it was the tone of her voice, the look in her eyes, that told Ruby she was holding on to an even bigger secret.

"Ruby, you might want to sit down for this. Wendy, you too," Mary said.

"I think I'm too nervous to sit," Ruby said with a small laugh.

Wendy crossed her arms and stood beside her. "Me too, Mary. What's up?"

Mary looked over each shoulder and then held up the bag. Ruby's heart raced as she watched Mary slowly unzip the bag and pull out the dress. The burgundy dress from the window. Both she and Wendy gasped while Mary laughed and dangled the dress on the hanger.

"Happy wedding day and Merry Christmas to my best friend in the world!"

Mary charged at Ruby and they hugged, laughing and crying at the same time. "How did you do this?" Ruby finally asked when she could speak.

Mary shoved the dress at her. "Nothing you need to know about. Now I think you should hurry up and try this on just in case there are any minor alterations we need to make."

Ruby touched the beading, tracing it with her finger, as Wendy held up the dress. "This is gorgeous. I think it's going to look great on you, Mom."

The gasps from the doorway made Ruby look up. Charlotte and Olivia were standing there. "That is stunning, Grandma," Olivia said.

"It is. Please tell me that's what you're going to wear," Charlotte said as they walked over.

"Let's hope it fits," Ruby said, sizing it up again.

"It has to," Mary said.

"You don't think it's too much, do you?"

A Christmas House Wedding

"Too much, for a wedding at Christmas, for a wedding that was over fifty years in the making? Are you serious?" Wendy asked.

Ruby smiled sheepishly. "Well, when you put it like that . . ."

*   *   *

Olivia was almost skipping down the hallway when the doorbell rang. This was a Christmas Eve she would never forget. Everything was finally falling into place for her. She almost didn't recognize herself. Last Christmas Eve, her already disastrous life had taken a turn for the worse when she'd found a surprise standing on the other side of the door. It had almost torn apart the relationship she and Charlotte had rebuilt. But this Christmas . . . nothing could shake this happiness.

And now her grandmother and Harry were about to get married. She wondered if this was a last-minute guest. Her grandmother knew so many people. The house was bursting with guests already, all of their closest friends.

She swung open the front door, a smile on her face, ready to greet whatever lovely soul was on the other side, only to find herself staring at the man she never wanted to see again. The man who'd given her the most beautiful daughter; the man who'd taken away all her self-worth. Will was standing there, in his suit and tie and pristine white shirt, without a wrinkle or bad angle. His dark hair slicked back. His face clean-shaven. She lifted her chin to meet his gaze but found herself struggling to hold on to her self-esteem. It had been there. Just a minute ago. It had been there when she'd been laughing with everyone in the dining room. When she'd built her business this year. When she'd moved into her apartment. When Scott had kissed her.

And now . . . now she had trouble making eye contact with Will. Words and memories flooded her mind, and she clutched the doorknob, forcing herself to focus on the moment. "What are you doing here?"

His face softened. "I came . . . I came to say merry Christmas, I miss you, I love you, and I'm sorry."

I miss you, I love you, and I'm sorry.

Was this a joke? Olivia stared at Will and tried to process her emotions and his words. A part of her wanted to slam the door in his face while the other wanted to yell at him. But then she heard Dawn's giggle from the dining room, and she was reminded that no matter how badly she wanted to push this man off a cliff, he was Dawn's father. Granted, in his proclamation, he hadn't mentioned a thing about their daughter . . . but still.

He held the door open wider. "Can we talk? In private?"

Olivia glanced over her shoulder and then back at him. "You have five minutes. On the porch. If one of my family members sees you, it'll be less."

"Fair enough," he said, emotion filling his voice.

Olivia crossed her arms over her chest and shivered as the cold air hit her when she stepped outside.

"Here, you must be freezing," he said, taking off his coat and attempting to put it on her shoulders.

She held up her hand, her heart pounding in her chest. The idea of accepting anything from him, or him touching her, made her queasy. "I'm fine. There have been many times where I've been freezing, both in this last year and during the years we were married, and you didn't care to help. What's going on? Why are you really here?"

He winced. "I'm sorry. I'm sorry I did that to you. I've spent the last six months in therapy, Liv, and I realize how wrong I was. I treated you horribly. I also realized that letting you go was the biggest mistake of my life."

It was like she was listening to a different man. The Will she had been married to never would have gone to therapy, because that would have meant admitting that something about him or his life wasn't perfect. And admitting that he'd treated her horribly . . . she didn't know how she felt about that. But there was still so much wrong with what he was saying. She tucked a strand of hair behind her ear as the wind carried it away. This was the man who'd made her ashamed to go out in public, to look in the mirror, to look in his eyes. Even now, the words he'd used taunted her, made her almost too embarrassed to meet his stare—and it was for that reason that she forced herself to.

"What did you do to me? How did you treat me horribly?"

He frowned. "You know what I did."

She shrugged, trying not to let her nerves show, or the trembling that was starting deep inside. "Well, you didn't know then, so how do I know you know now? Why don't you name some of the things?"

He swallowed audibly. "I wasn't a supportive partner."

She tapped a finger on her chin, trying to look as though her confidence on the outside matched what she was feeling inside. "That sounds like something you read on the back of a marriage counseling brochure. I'd like some examples."

He cleared his throat. "I should have been around more."

Olivia spotted the curtains in the living room moving, but she didn't have time to be distracted or worry that they were being spied on—mainly because they probably were. "Oh, like you mean for Dawn's birth? Which brings me to another point—not once since you've been standing here in this new version of yourself have you even asked about our daughter. Not once in this last year have you even so much as asked for a picture."

His face turned red. "I didn't think you'd give me one. I don't deserve to even ask. But yes, I would love to see her. And yes, for her birth, I should have been there for her and you."

She stared at him, this version of him, but all she saw was the man who'd walked out on her, who'd humiliated her over and over again, who'd taken advantage of her when she was at her most vulnerable. She had been a child in so many ways when she'd met Will. There were so many signs she'd ignored because she'd wanted to believe the best in him. But his best wasn't good enough.

"What were you doing?"

"Liv . . ."

She blinked away the moisture in her eyes, because she refused to ever cry in front of this man again. But the emotion was there, swooping back in like the bitter winter wind. "No. I want you to say it."

"I was involved in another relationship."

"Because I was fat and ugly."

He made a sound and kicked his foot against the porch floor. "No, no. I never meant any of that. I'm sorry if you misinterpreted what I meant."

She inhaled sharply. "So it was my fault? I misunderstood what you meant? All the scathing remarks about how I looked? That was just me not fully understanding what you really meant?"

He took a step closer to her. "You were always a beautiful woman, Olivia. I just . . . work was demanding, and my own upbringing . . . I didn't have the right role models. I didn't know how to make a marriage work. I regret so much. I know I don't have a right to ask, but I want another chance. To prove that I've changed. That I can make you happy."

He had never made her happy. She realized that now. She had told herself she was happy. But she had been happy about the idea of marriage. About the idea of stability and having a home life like she'd never had growing up. She had been so naïve that she'd thought that if she did the things her mother had never done, her family would work.

She'd thought if she was taking care of their home, cleaning and cooking and being a supportive spouse, it would work. But the missing ingredient from her recipe for a great marriage was a deep love. It wasn't about a fresh-baked pie or a clean floor or fresh flowers on the dinner table; it was all about love. She didn't love Will.

"That's not enough anymore. Maybe right after Dawn was born, that would have worked. I would have tried again, but now . . . now that I've rebuilt my life, this is too little and too late. There is so much wrong, and I have so many doubts about you. Again, you barely even mentioned our daughter. That breaks my heart but also reaffirms that I did the right thing for her. It took me until now to get over my upbringing with parents who couldn't make their children a priority. Dawn is everything to me. If she's not happy, I'm not happy. No man will ever come first. I almost messed up badly, but I realized it and I'm trying to correct it. I almost raised Dawn in a home filled with so much anger. She would have heard you. She would have grown up hearing you call me names. She would have watched me desperately trying to please you and look good for you only to have you show me with your actions just how worthless I was in your eyes. How worthless I felt. I will *never* do that to her."

He took a step closer to her, his jaw clenched. "I'm sorry. I'm so sorry. Liv, I want another chance to prove to you that I love you. That I love Dawn."

She took a step back. "I don't believe you."

"Then spend time with me. Don't you think we owe it to Dawn? Can you really look at her one day and tell her that when her father came to try again, you rejected him without a chance? One more chance, Liv."

"You're trying to manipulate me. So that this is my fault. Her parents are divorced and it's my fault? You cheated on me. Repeatedly. Unabashedly. While I was in labor. That's kind of a deal breaker, Will. For me and a lot of other people. Hopefully."

"What about for better or for worse?"

She threw her hands in the air. "Where is this coming from? Why now? Where were you the first time you hurt me? Or all last year? Or how about when I filed for full custody and you didn't even ask for visitation? What changed? Why would I believe any of this?"

The curtains in the parlor room moved again, and Olivia tried not to get distracted. Figures her family would be spying. "I told you. I went to therapy."

She crossed her arms. "Why?"

"I didn't know what I lost until it was too late."

She stared into his eyes, instinctively searching for something. She realized she was searching for signs of another man; she was looking for signs of Scott, and found none. None of the warmth, none of the fire . . . none of the recognition. Scott recognized her, the real her, the one she had forgotten. This man—the man she had married, the father of her daughter—this man didn't know her at all. And she didn't trust his motives. People didn't just change, not who they were at their core.

"I don't trust you, Will. I won't ever be able to trust you again."

His lips thinned, and he started looking a little more like the man she remembered, the one who lost his patience when she dared question him. The one who, instead of answering her questions directly, would turn the tables on her and make it an insult so humiliating she would shrink away like a scared animal.

"I'm doing all the work here."

She nodded slowly, feeling somewhat proud she hadn't fallen for a word of his claims. At least she had grown up this last year. It was scary to think that at one time she would have fallen for all of that.

"This isn't work. This is nothing. Not after what you've done. I have a feeling I know what's happened—your mother. Your mother remembered that you had a child and now you're divorced and have no relationship with your child. She's probably embarrassed. Maybe some of her friends even remember that you have a child. It looks bad, doesn't it? It's probably even more embarrassing than having a fat, ugly, bitchy cow of a wife, isn't it?"

"I told you I'm sorry. What's happened to you? You're not the same woman I was married to."

That made her chest ache. She wasn't the same. But she was sad for that woman he'd been married to. She had thought so little of herself. She wanted to go back and tell the Olivia from before that she could do so much better, that being married wasn't worth sacrificing her self-worth. "I'm not the same. I will never be that woman you were married to again."

He placed his hands in the pockets of his wool coat. "There's someone else, isn't there?"

Her face turned red, and she had no idea why. It wasn't like she was doing something wrong. They were divorced. But she wasn't going to hide as though she were guilty of infidelity. Like he'd been.

"Yes, there is."

He took a step closer to her, and she could see the ticking of his jaw. "So, what, Dawn just gets a new daddy?"

"That's none of your business. You have no rights to Dawn anymore, and if you cared at all, you would have been her dad."

"I'm going to tell you something, Olivia; this won't last. You think I'm responsible for the way we turned out? Just take a good look at yourself. You're so innocent? You are immature and selfish and whiny. A total victim. It takes two to tango, sweetheart."

"That's a joke," she said, but something inside her felt slightly on guard. Like maybe he was right. She had been young when they married. She'd had no idea how to be in a real relationship. She'd come from pure dysfunction; who was she to attempt marriage?

"Sure. Everything started out great—you were happy. You were living the good life—provided by me. I was working, bringing in all the money, the cars, the nice house. Exactly how did you contribute? Your part-time dance instructor job? Joke. Everything was great then, wasn't it? But then you turned nasty and bitter and had a problem with everything I did. You think I'm the only guy who would have a problem coming home to a nasty wife who nagged him over everything? Then you wanted a baby, so we had a baby. But instead of being happy to be pregnant, you went around whining about how sick you felt. Instead of taking care of yourself, you just sat around and ate food all day and got fat. What kind of man would put up with that?

"You don't think this is going to happen all over again? You're a spoiled brat. You couldn't make it in the real world if you tried. Look at you, living at your grandmother's. Always running to your grandmother."

He reached out and grabbed her wrist. Not the way Scott had that night. Scott's rough hand had touched her as though she were the most precious person in the world; a caress, a stroke of affection. Will grabbed her wrist like he owned her.

"I can give you back your life, Olivia."

She lifted her chin, making sure he saw her clear eyes, void of any tears. She refused to blink, to back down from him ever again. This Olivia stepped closer to him.

"You? Give me back my life? I have a life. One that doesn't include you. You walked out on my life. Right when I was in the middle of labor. I will never forget that."

"That pregnancy was going on forever. Again, total drama queen. You'd been ready to pop for weeks."

Red. There was red everywhere. Not the Santa suit red but the rage kind of red. "Pop? *Pop?* I wasn't giving birth to a balloon animal. Nothing *popped* out of me. My stomach didn't *pop* a child out like a piñata pops out a bunch of candy. And let go of my *wrist*," she yelled finally, yanking.

He held on tighter. "You're my wife."

She had warned him. She lifted her foot and slammed one of her gorgeous heels, the ones she'd bought with Charlotte, into his shoe, and he let out a roar and released her wrist.

The door swung open and Scott burst through and had Will pinned against the wall in seconds. The rest of her family—and Harry's family—all piled out of the house and onto the porch.

But her eyes were on Scott and on Will's bulging eyes. She didn't hear what Scott was saying to him. She held her breath until Wyatt stepped in and clamped down on Scott's shoulder. Scott finally released Will.

Will stumbled back, his face red, his eyes scanning the crowd. Grandma Ruby stepped forward. She was holding Dawn.

"William, never come here again," she said in a voice shaking with rage.

Olivia stood there, on the sidelines, her heart breaking as Will didn't even pause to look at Dawn. He walked away from all of them, the disdain for them clear in his eyes, in his posture. She was shaking, right down to her toes.

Will had arrived here, a blatant reminder of a past she was responsible for creating.

And then she looked around, at the crowd of people peering out the parlor room windows, at her family on the porch, at her grandmother and Harry. She had ruined their wedding. This was their big day.

Scott reached out and clasped her hand. "It's going to be okay. Everyone inside; we've got a wedding to attend!"

But she knew, as she and Scott trailed the crowd, that it wasn't that simple. She could feel it in the tension emanating from his body. She could feel it in herself.

Right now, this moment, was all about her grandmother, but tonight she needed to tell Scott that she couldn't move forward.

CHAPTER TWENTY

Ruby felt as though she floated down the aisle. Her granddaughters had set rows of chairs on each side of the parlor room. They were gold Chiavari chairs, and all the ones on the aisles had bouquets of red roses hanging from them. The aisle in the center was marked with a red runner, and the altar was at the big bay window. Where Harry was waiting for her.

She walked down the aisle alone, her choosing, because it felt right. Because when Harry had asked her to marry him that first time, so long ago, she'd been alone. And the women who'd helped her were gone now. Everyone from that era was gone, everyone except her and Harry. And she wanted to come to him independent and free.

She had thought it would feel strange to have everyone stand and watch her walk down the aisle, but all she saw was Harry. She saw him as he was outside that day, when she'd been pregnant with Wendy, taking down the laundry. She saw him as he was last year on the porch, trying one last time with her. And she saw him now, as the man she was finally going to marry.

They exchanged their vows with love and respect, and soon she was dancing with him in the other parlor room as everyone watched.

Tomorrow she would worry about Olivia and Scott.

But tonight, she was finally Harry's, and he was hers.

*   *   *

Scott already knew.

He'd felt Olivia's retreat immediately after Will left. He saw it in her eyes. They had joined in the celebrations, they had played along as though everything were fine, but now, out on the porch as the last of the guests left, she asked to speak to him.

Her long, navy dress swayed in the wind, and he put his coat around her shoulders. And the minute he did, she raised tear-filled eyes to his.

His gut turned over. "What's wrong?"

"Will coming here has brought up a lot of issues for me, Scott," she whispered, moving away from him to sit on the first step. The sky was filled with stars, and the moon lit the blanket of snow in front of them.

"I can imagine it would. But you don't have to go through everything alone. I'm here. I can go through it with you," he said, even though he knew it was a lost cause. Because of Will. Because she was threatened by Will, and in turn, Scott was a threat.

"I know that," she said with a sniffle. She still had her profile to him, and it took everything he had to just sit there and wait for her to tell him. "Scott . . . you and Cat are very important to me, but I don't know if I can be the person you want or need me to be. For you or for Cat."

Okay, that wasn't what he'd been expecting. In some ways it was much worse. "You are *exactly* who I need you to be. I need you to be Olivia. The woman who had the courage to leave her douchebag husband so that she and her daughter could have a better life. The woman who bought a warehouse and is turning it into a business. The woman who threw three snowballs in my face. That's who I need. That's who Cat needs."

She covered her face for a moment. "Scott, I don't know if that's me either. What if . . . what if I disappoint you? What if my business goes bankrupt? What if I fail as a wife and as a mom? And I barely know what I'm doing with Dawn, let alone Cat, who is a teenager."

"Hey, don't you think you're getting a little ahead of yourself with all these problems? You could never disappoint me. I'm not looking for perfection in the way you're thinking. You *are* perfection. In every way. You make me happy. When you smile, I smile. You gave my life meaning again, and you made me want something serious when I never wanted serious again. You accepted me and my flaws. And so what if you're business goes under? What, I just stop loving you? I just walk away? Come on, Olivia. And being a parent to a teenager—every parent of a teenager feels like they're failing at least five times a day. Being a parent in general makes you doubt everything. And that's what makes a good parent. Because if you don't doubt, you never get better. Parenting doesn't mean perfection. It means loving enough to do better. I don't doubt you are a great parent."

She let out a small laugh at that one but still didn't look him in the eyes. "I can't . . . trust myself. Some of the things Will brought up are true. I did marry him for the wrong reasons. I should have known better. What if I'm running to you because I'm insecure? What if this was all about me being selfish and wanting someone to depend on because I'm alone? I don't think I can deal with a long-term relationship right now."

He stood, her words cutting him. He was angry. He was angry with her and with himself. He should have known. That night, when she had said he wasn't her type, he should have known she wasn't ready. He had gotten ahead of himself. He had fallen for her.

But he was also angry for another reason, and if he'd had a few more minutes with that asshole, he would at least have had an outlet for his anger.

"I'm sorry, Scott," she whispered in a hoarse voice.

"So am I. I can't make you do something you don't want to do. So . . . uh, I'll finish the reno as planned, and then we don't have to see each other every day. That will make things easier for both of us. And then it'll be your business. I'm going to get Cat and head home."

"Scott," she whispered, standing.

But it hurt to look in her eyes, because she was hurting too. "Yeah?"

"I'm sorry."

CHAPTER TWENTY-ONE

"Olivia, don't let him go because you're afraid or you think you're unworthy of his love. A lifetime will go by. Look at me. Really, look at me. I know you and Charlotte think I'm wise and that I've got it all together, but it took me over fifty years to get here. And you know what? I'm still afraid. I'm still afraid Harry will wake up one day and realize I'm not good enough for him. So what does that tell you? It should tell you that we have to work hard to push away those thoughts and live. I let Harry go. Twice. He proposed to me twice. He went on to start a life with someone else, because I told him to. Because I didn't want to be a burden. I missed out on decades of loving that man because I didn't think, deep down, that I was good enough for him. And then he walked back into my life last Christmas, and I was finally wise enough to love him back.

"Now, I'm not saying to jump in headfirst with Scott if you're not sure how you feel about him. But, dear, if you know deep in

your heart that he's the man for you, then go and get him. Be brave. Claim the love of your life before life slips by you."

"Grandma, Will brought up a lot of things that have made me second-guess everything. I was immature and didn't know much. How could I have a relationship that was healthy?"

"Olivia, he is trying to play mind games with you to guilt you into going back to him."

Olivia shook her head. "Grandma, I barely have my life together. I'm starting a dance studio that may be a total bomb. I may have thrown all my money down the toilet. I have risked Dawn's security by opening a business when I barely know what I'm doing. I'm going to live in a one-bedroom apartment above a warehouse. That's what I'm able to provide for her."

Her grandmother shook her head. "You should be proud of that. And you should be determined to make it work. Taking risks is a part of life. Would the woman who showed up on my doorstep last Christmas even try and open a business on her own?"

Olivia drew a shaky breath and looked down. "No . . . but, what if it fails? Then what? I move back here? How pathetic! What will Scott think of me?"

"That you tried and it didn't work."

"I have to bring something to that relationship. I can't be this deadbeat who's going to be dependent on him. I've done that before, and look where it got me."

"Do you really think you're the first person who's started a business? And stop talking about it failing before it even starts! Would you love Scott any less if all of a sudden his business started doing poorly?"

Olivia ran her hands through her hair. "It's not the same. He's had another career before his business too. And there's no way his business would go under; he has more jobs than he can even handle. And then what if things start changing? What if I start letting myself go again, like I did with Will? What if he's not attracted to me anymore if I look the way—"

"You're going to stop this right now. Let me tell you something, I may not be the expert on love because of all the relationships I never had, but in some ways, that's given me a lot of perspective. I met Harry when I was a teenager. My skin was perfect, my hair was long and full and shiny. My body was fit and healthy and in shape. When I met him, he was the most handsome man I'd ever seen. And then we were gone from each other for decades. When he showed up on my doorstep last Christmas, he was still the most handsome man I'd ever met. With his wrinkles, with his gray hair, with his aging body. Wyatt and Scott don't compare to Harry—Harry is still in a league of his own. Because I love him. Because I see him and I see perfection. He is my soul mate—bald, overweight, or unable to walk, whatever it is, he is still the most beautiful man I've ever met. That's love, Olivia. That is not what you had with Will."

Olivia covered her face for a moment. "How did you get so wise?"

Her grandmother laughed. "It took me a long time to get here. But I want you to really think about this. Not about your parents' relationship. Not about your marriage. I want you to think about Wyatt and Charlotte. Do you think Wyatt would ever speak to Charlotte the way Will spoke to you?"

Olivia swallowed and shook her head.

"Do you think Wyatt would ever criticize her appearance and humiliate her?"

Olivia shook her head.

"And what about Scott? Would you love him any less if he put on weight and lost his hair? Would you make fun of him and speak down to him?"

Olivia felt sick to her stomach just thinking about it. "Of course not," she finally managed to say.

"Then stop hiding from your life because you're afraid every man out there is like Will. He was part of your youth. He was part of you growing up from the house you were raised in, and he is not a part of your future. The man who is part of your future is the one who's working all through the holidays to try and fix up an apartment for you and your daughter. The one who looks at you the way Harry looks at me and the way Wyatt looks at Charlotte."

Olivia stood and walked over to her grandmother and hugged her. "I don't know what I would do without you, Grandma. You are so right. I need to find Scott and fix this. Instead of trusting him, I hurt him because I was so afraid."

Her grandmother hugged her back and then placed her hands on her shoulders. "All I ever wanted was to see you girls happy. Let go of the old, Olivia. Seal up those wounds and start fresh. He needs to know how much you love him. You will figure out the rest together."

* * *

Olivia followed Wyatt and Charlotte into the airport. Dawn was looking from her stroller, her head going each way as she watched the throngs of people moving alongside them. There was still a feel of Christmas in the air, of the holidays and the festivities.

Too bad she didn't feel any of it.

She had lost at love again. She didn't know how to fix this. It wasn't as simple as telling Scott she loved him. It required being able to take the next steps with him, and she wasn't sure she could do that. Somewhere along the way, she had stopped trusting her instincts. Seeing Will again on Christmas Eve had reminded her of just how poor her instincts could be.

What if she did it again? And what if this time, Dawn got hurt? Because hurt was coming for Dawn. Her sweet girl was too young to understand now, but one day she would be old enough to understand that her father wanted nothing to do with her.

They spotted Harry and Grandma Ruby over by the check-in desk for their airline.

"Wow, that generation did fashion way better," Wyatt said.

Charlotte nodded. "I know. They look like they should be on the cover of a magazine."

Olivia agreed. Harry had on one of his handsome wool coats with a white collar showing under a navy cashmere sweater and dark wool pants. Her grandmother had on a red coat and navy pants with a matching navy sweater. Her hair was done, her makeup impeccable, and she sported ruby earrings Olivia was pretty sure were new.

They spotted Harry's family, and soon they all crowded around the newlyweds. Olivia was pretty sure they were irritating to the rest of the passengers. They were all loud and laughing, and it was the way family should be.

Except Scott and Cat were missing, and Olivia knew it. And she felt guilty about it.

Olivia's parents approached, and she braced herself when her mother stood on one side of her and her father on the other. "We like Scott, Olivia."

What? Olivia turned to her mother. "Pardon?"

Her mother nodded. "We like him. He's a good person. Like Wyatt. I mean, as much as Wyatt can bother me with his whole 'I'm the protector of Charlotte' shtick," she said, waving her hands as she spoke. "It's nice. It's what he should be doing."

Olivia was speechless. And kind of uncomfortable.

"What your mother is trying to say—"

"I know what I'm saying, and I said it. I wasn't trying to say—"

"You went off script, Wendy; that wasn't what you were supposed to say at all. What we wanted to say is that we know your childhood wasn't ideal. Your mother and I had our own issues, and you and Charlotte were the ones who suffered for it. We don't want you going through life afraid to love people because of what happened. If you love Scott and you want to be with Scott, then you should be. You should tell him you love him."

Olivia took a shaky breath as her dad put his arm around her. How she'd wanted that arm so many times as a little girl! But it was okay. That little girl had grown up. And this woman knew she was strong enough to start over again. She could take everything that had happened to her and use it to move forward from and learn from. She could teach Dawn one day. And Cat. And she could have a family again, a different one, a whole one.

She just had to have the courage to try.

As she stood there amid this crowd of extended family, she waved along with the rest of them to Harry and her grandmother. Her gaze was fixed on Grandma Ruby, remembering all the things she had been through. And now she was starting over. It was never too late.

*　*　*

Scott stood in the middle of his kitchen and stared out into the backyard.

More snow. Dawn had barely broken, and he could see a deer in the distance. Normally, this view would make him happy. But as he sipped his coffee and leaned against the island, he just felt the gutting sense of loss. He wanted to tell Olivia she was making a mistake. He wanted to punch her ex in the face and was disappointed he hadn't had the opportunity. He wanted to tell Olivia he loved her one more time. But he couldn't push. He knew that would only scare her away.

He heard a loud yawn in the doorway and turned to see Cat standing there. Her hair was half standing up, her eyes were red and squinty, and she was frowning.

"Dad, we need to deal with this Olivia situation."

He wished he could laugh. Because it was laughable to think he'd be getting dating advice from a thirteen-year-old who still secretly slept with her stuffies. "I appreciate the sentiment, but this isn't your mess to deal with, and I'm not sure there's anything I can do."

"Okay, first things first, I need a coffee," she said, walking across the kitchen, her feet shuffling against the hardwood.

He watched with fascination as she poured herself a cup, took out a carton of chocolate milk and added a few splashes, then dumped in three spoonfuls of sugar. Then she took a sip, made a face, added another spoonful of sugar, and sipped again. "Not bad."

"Uh, since when do you drink coffee?" he asked, half-amused, half-concerned.

She shrugged, sitting at one of the counter stools. "I save it for mornings when there are major problems that need solving. Like this one. So, you should know that I texted Olivia."

He choked on his coffee. "What?"

She nodded. "Yeah, I was trying to do a parent-trap type of situation, but Olivia kind of knew what I was up to. It was impressive."

He stared at her, not knowing what to say. "Pardon?" was all he could muster.

She took a sip of her coffee, looking closer to twenty than thirteen. Had it not been for the copious amounts of sugar and the chocolate milk she took in her coffee, there would be no indication she was still a kid.

"Yeah, Sam helped me. It was a really solid plan too. We were going to have you guys meet up under the clock tower at midnight on New Year's like Wyatt and Charlotte. But I guess, since Olivia remembered that whole thing, she knew that was what I was planning."

"What, uh, what did Olivia say?"

"Well, she was totally cool about it. You know how nice she is. Sam and I really tried to make the texts sound like something you would say, and since you're old, we were trying to think like older people. But then I couldn't remember if you used to have . . . you know, what are they called? Oh, right . . .

videocassettes to watch movies on as a kid, but then we remembered that Olivia is younger than you so she might just know about DVDs. Anyway, the whole thing was kind of a wreck."

Scott blinked, not even knowing who his daughter was anymore and how the hell he was ever going to show his face again. It was so absurd he wasn't even angry. "What, uh, why were you even talking about videos?"

"Oh, I was like asking if she wanted to come over and watch some old videos of you playing baseball. You know, when you were younger."

Dear God, no. He needed to know everything to understand fully how bad this train wreck was. "And, uh, where does midnight under the clock tower come in?"

"Right. So then I said that if she didn't want to do that, you could meet under the clock tower and that you love her, blah, blah, blah."

He didn't know if he wanted to know about the *blah, blah, blah.* She sipped her coffee, and he decided against knowing. "And what exactly did she say?"

Cat pulled out her phone. "She said . . . *Oh Cat, sweetie, is this you? I don't think your dad would say all these things. But you and I can still hang out, okay? Let me know when you want to get together. Love, Liv xo.*"

He cleared his throat from the lump of emotion there, especially when Cat's eyes filled with tears and she looked thirteen again.

"Hey, I really appreciate you doing this, trying, but it's not up to you to fix my personal life."

"I know, but she's my personal life too, and when she was in our lives, you were so happy. You'd hum under your breath.

You shaved more. You didn't wear the ratty T-shirts with the holes in them. And then when her loser ex-husband showed up, everything changed. I don't get it. She's not with him, but she's not with you either."

He took a deep breath, her words reminding him again of how whatever he did impacted Cat. "It's complicated. I think she's scared of making another mistake. I think she's scared of being hurt. And scared of how all of this will impact Dawn. I feel pretty crappy, honestly. But I have to respect where she's coming from, Cat. It's also what makes her a good parent—she's looking out for her little girl. She needs to make sure she can handle whatever comes her way, and I get that. I made the same decision once, when you were little. I don't regret it. I put you first, and that will always be the right decision, even if it meant I lost out on something else. You are my number-one priority, and Dawn is Olivia's, and that's the way it should be."

Cat stood and walked over to him and surprised him by throwing her arms around him. He hugged her back, one of those great big hugs that reminded him he was still important to her, even if she pretended he wasn't half the time.

"I love you, Dad."

"I love you too," he said as she pulled back. He was relieved that at least she seemed okay with how things were.

"I think you need to make another pot of coffee. We need to fix the Olivia situation."

CHAPTER TWENTY-TWO

Olivia pulled open the door to her studio, her stomach churning. She juggled a heavy box and managed to get in without having it crash to the ground. Scott's truck was in the otherwise empty parking lot, and she really didn't want to see him. Not true; she wanted to see him, but the way they were a week ago, not now. She didn't know what to say to him. She wished she could take back too much of what she'd said. She wanted to be with him but didn't know how to make it work. The thought of being dependent on someone else terrified her. She needed time. And she needed him.

But as she walked through the empty studio, she didn't see Scott anywhere. Was he avoiding her? That didn't seem like something he would do, but it was a possibility, and she wouldn't even blame him.

She took the steps to her apartment as fast as she could with the heavy box and cursed the three flights of stairs it took her to reach the top. Putting the box down with a thud outside the door, she pushed it open and flicked on the lights.

Her stomach dropped, and she clutched the doorframe. Scott was standing in the middle of the room with an expression she couldn't quite read. But as she tore her gaze from his, she realized why everything looked so different—the linoleum was gone. That awful linoleum with all those memories. He'd replaced it with dark, wide-planked hardwood floors. And the kitchen cabinets had all been painted white, with new hardware. The countertop had been changed to a fresh white, and there was a new faucet as well.

She blinked back tears as she slowly turned back to him. "What did you do?" she managed to choke out.

He shrugged, a corner of his mouth tilting upward. "I've been thinking a lot about what you said that night. While I don't agree with some of it, I understand all of it. And I don't want to be that guy that forces you into something you're not ready for. I'm not out to take away your independence. I want you to have it all. But I also love you. And I want you to be able to trust me and that I have your best interests at heart and I always will. Part of being in a healthy relationship is being able to trust each other. Will betrayed that. Your father betrayed that. But I can promise you that I won't. I want to be there to support your dreams, to help you when you flounder or are unsure. And I want you to do the same for me. Cat and I love you and Dawn. We want to be in your lives however you'll have us."

She already had tears streaming down her face before she ran to him. But when he caught her and held on to her like he'd never let go, as so many others had, she knew it was time to trust him completely. She pulled back slightly so that she could look into his eyes and he could see the sincerity in hers when she spoke. "I love you too. And I love Cat. And I love the four of us together. I shouldn't have reacted to Will the way I did. I put up all those walls again because I was so scared of being hurt. Because you have the power to hurt me more than Will ever did. Because you're you. You're a good man. With a good heart, and you've got all of my heart. And I don't know how I would ever recover if you broke it."

His eyes gleamed with emotion, and he framed her face with his hands. "I will never break your heart. You've got me. Forever, if you'll have me."

She closed her eyes as he leaned down to kiss her. She kissed him with a new freedom, with the confidence of who she was now, and who she could be with him. Scott was all the things she'd ever wanted in a partner, and she would never let fear drive her away from the people she loved. When she pulled back, she couldn't let go of him. "I can't believe you did this for me," she said, tearing her eyes from his to look around.

"I'm glad you like it. I can't take all the credit. Cat helped. She painted all the cabinets. She said it was to make up for pretending to be me."

Olivia laughed through her tears. "Omigosh, she is so your kid. She's a total sweetheart, and honestly, it crushed me to have to call her out on impersonating you. She has such a good heart, and she loves her dad so much. I totally got where she was coming from."

"So you'll come over and watch old VHS recordings of me playing baseball?"

Olivia burst out laughing. "It was pretty funny. But yes, I'll watch all your old movies."

He reached out to kiss her again, and as she stepped into him, she realized that he did this often. He would reach for her. Her hand, her wrist. An arm around her shoulder. A hug. A kiss. She had never been shown that kind of affection before. It felt good. It felt like a warm blanket on a blustery winter's night. She had never known how much she needed it or how important it was until she'd experienced it.

"Okay, there's one more thing," he said.

She tilted her head, trusting him completely as he jogged out of the room. He emerged from the bedroom a minute later, dragging . . . a giant dollhouse. A big, gorgeous, wooden dollhouse . . . that looked like his home. "Scott," she whispered as she walked forward slowly.

"Do you like it?"

She was speechless as she ran her hand over the smooth rooftop and then peered into the open back. She gasped, tears filling her eyes as she looked in all the rooms. There were four bedrooms. And four people standing together. A man with light-brown hair, a woman with dark-brown hair, a shorter woman . . . and a child. She covered her face because she didn't know what to do with all the emotion coursing through her. All the emotions she'd learned to hide along the way. "All of this . . . all my dreams, right here in this house," she managed to choke out before she threw her arms around his neck.

He held her close. "I was hoping you would feel that way. Again, no pressure. That house and those people will be there, waiting for you and Dawn, whenever you're ready. In the mean-time, Dawn gets her dollhouse."

She pulled back to look at him, into his eyes. "I love you, Scott. I hope that you know, through all of this, I loved you. I just needed to find a way to make this work."

"I think I have a way. You move in here, as planned. It's a fresh start for you and Dawn. No old ugly floor to remind you of the past, because I don't think it's good to have our pasts staring us in the face all day when we're trying to move forward. So, you open your business. I will be beside you every step of the way to support you. You get in a routine with work and Dawn. The four of us proceed as we have been. No pressure. I told you before we ever dated that I would wait for you, and I mean it. If you are in my life and we love each other, that's all I need until you're ready for more."

She reached out to put her hands around his waist, to put her head on his shoulder. "My entire life, I've been searching for home. My own home. In my home, there were parents who loved each other deeply, there were kids, there was laughter. I've been searching for this, and when I thought I had it, only to realize that it was just a dream, that it wasn't real, I gave up thinking it existed. At least not for me. I thought I had to be perfect, to be a certain way, to be deserving of that. And then I met you. And I was so scared of the feelings you brought out in me until I real-ized those were all the right feelings, even if they were scary. And slowly, I started dreaming again. What it would be like to start over again. With you. And you showed me what real love is, what it means, that it's not based on perfection. That I don't have to be perfect to be perfect for you.

"Everything you're saying is exactly what I needed to hear. I don't know how you do that, actually. And I just want you to know that my first instinct is to throw caution to the wind. It's to jump in and forget slow and steady. But I promised myself I wouldn't do that. If I know that you are my finish line and you'll be standing there, then yes. Let's do this."

He lowered his head to kiss her. "I will always be there for you. You and Dawn are worth waiting for. I love you, Olivia."

ACKNOWLEDGMENTS

To all the talented and dedicated people at Crooked Lane and Alcove Press: Thank you for believing in this book and me! I'm so excited to be working with you. You have all been such a dream to work with and I look forward to our next book together.

To Faith Black Ross: Thank you for believing in my stories and for being such a joy to work with! You are such a talent and I'm so blessed to work with you. Your edits and feedback are always inspiring and motivating. I can't wait to work with you on our next adventure!

To Melissa Rechter: Thank you for keeping everything running smoothly and for being such a bright spot in my inbox!

To Madeline Rathle: Thank you for your marketing attention and ideas and for being so approachable.

To Rebecca Nelson: Thank you for your attention to detail and all your hard work.

Acknowledgments

To Louise Fury: Thank you for always being so enthusiastic about my ideas and being a true champion of my books.

To my Readers and Bloggers: Thank you for joining me as we travel to new small towns together! I hope this book brings you the joy of the season and leaves you with hope and happiness. All of your emails and reviews mean so much to me. I'm thrilled to be back at The Christmas House again with you!